I0665939

A Weary World Rejoices

A Mosaic
Christmas Anthology VI

STACY MONSON * ELEANOR BERTIN
JOHNNIE ALEXANDER
ANGELA D. MEYER * SARA DAVISON

The Christmas Kiss © 2024 Stacy Monson
Unremarkable Sue © 2024 Eleanor Bertin
Love Christmas © 2024 Johnnie Alexander
Gifting Christmas © 2024 Angela D. Meyer
The Back Door Christmas Tour Company © 2024 Sara Davison

ISBN: 979-8-9893942-2-7

Scripture quotations marked (NIV) are taken from the Holy Bible,New International Version®, NIV®. Copyright © 1973, 1978, 1984, 2011 byBiblica, Inc.™ Used by permission of Zondervan. All rights reserved worldwide. www.zondervan.comThe "NIV" and "New International Version" are trademarks registered in the United States Patent and Trademark Office by Biblica, Inc.™

Scripture quotations marked (NIrV) are taken from the Holy Bible, New International Reader's Version®, NIrV® Copyright © 1995, 1996,1998, 2014 by Biblica, Inc.™ Used by permission of Zondervan. All rights reserved worldwide. www.zondervan.comThe "NIrV" and "New International Reader's Version" are trademarks registered in the United States Patent and Trademark Office by Biblica, Inc.™

This anthology contains works of fiction. Any reference to historical or contemporary figures, places, or events, whether fictional or actual, is a fictional representation. Any resemblance to actual persons living or dead is entirely coincidental.

All rights reserved. No part of this book may be used or reproduced in any manner whatsoever without written permission from the author except in the case of brief quotations embodied in critical articles or reviews.

eBook editions are licensed for your personal enjoyment only. eBooks may not be re-sold, copied or given away to other people. If you would like to share an eBook edition, please purchase an additional copy for each person you share it with.

Published by The Mosaic Collection
Minneapolis, Minnesota
mosaiccollectionbooks.com

Cover design by Indie Publishing Services
Original generated AI Image Credit: Christmas snow globe decor by Mynn Shariff

A Christmas anthology from The Mosiac Collection
Our mission is to change hearts with the gospel through fiction.

Welcome To The Mosaic Collection

We are sisters, a beautiful mosaic united by the love of God through the blood of Christ.

Several times a year, The Mosaic Collection releases faith-based novels and anthologies in a variety of genres. This year we are celebrating five years since the release of our first book, *When Mountains Sing* by Stacy Monson in 2019. Our stories range from romance and suspense to literary and women's fiction.

Join our Mosaic reader family and discover soul-affirming stories of truth and hope at www.mosaiccollectionbooks.com

Join our Reader Community, too!

Find us at www.facebook.com/groups/TheMosaicCollection

Books In The Mosaic Collection

ELEANOR BERTIN

Lifelines (The Ties that Bind #1)

Unbound (The Ties that Bind #2)

Tethered (The Ties that Bind #3)

Flame of Mercy (Burning Bright #1)

Flicker of Trust (Burning Bright #2)

SARA DAVISON

Lost Down Deep (The Rose Tattoo Trilogy #1)

Written in Ink (The Rose Tattoo Trilogy #2)

Every Star in the Sky (two sparrows for a penny #1)

Every Flower of the Field (two sparrows for a penny #2)

Every Bird That Falls (two sparrows for a penny #3)

The Color of Sky and Stone (In the Shadows #1)

JANICE L. DICK

The Road to Happenstance (Happenstance Chronicles #1)

Crazy About Maisie (Happenstance Chronicles #2)

Calm Before the Storm (The Storm Series #1)

Eye of the Storm (The Storm Series #2)

Out of the Storm (The Storm Series #3)

DEB ELKINK

The Red Journal

The Third Grace

Vagabond Come Home

CHAUTONA HAVIG

Spines & Leaves (Bookstrings introduction)
Hart of Noel (Bookstrings "Noella")
Twice Sold Tales (Bookstrings #1)
Clock Tower Bound (Bookstrings #2)

MILLA HOLT

Into the Flood (Seasons of Faith #1)
Through the Blaze (Seasons of Faith #2)
Within the Storm (Seasons of Faith #3)
Amid the Ashes (Seasons of Faith #4)
After the Frost (Seasons of Faith #5)
Home Town Melody (Rhapsody of Grace #1)
Small Town Harmony (Rhapsody of Grace #2) (coming soon)

ANGELA D. MEYER

This Side of Yesterday
Where Hope Starts (Applewood Hill #1)
Where Healing Starts (Applewood Hill #2)
Where Joy Starts (Applewood Hill #3)

STACY MONSON

When Mountains Sing (My Father's House #1)
Open Circle

LORNA SEILSTAD

More Than Enough

Watercolors

CANDACE WEST

Through the Lettered Veil (Windy Hollow #1)

Among the Kindled Embers (Windy Hollow #2)

OTHER

Totally Booked: A Book Lover's Companion

CONTENTS

The Christmas Kiss

STACY MONSON

THE CHRISTMAS KISS

Stacy Monson

When Piper Devine's dream of opening her own chocolate store becomes a reality, her life turns upside down. She's tired. More than that, she's soul weary. Adding retail to her online business created a whirlwind of attention, orders, and chaos. Lots of chaos.

Someone is trying to sabotage her business. And also her burgeoning relationship with the handsome property manager who'd believed enough in her and her dream to help get the store up and running.

Who wants her out of the picture, and out of business? Is it the same person, or does she have a double target on her back?

To those who struggle daily in their work, striving against evil, facing obstacles, desiring to use the gifts God has given you to do the work you're called to—stay focused on the God who guides your steps. He will not leave you floundering. Be persistent in your work and lean on Him when things get tough. He will see you through.

"But I want you to keep your head no matter what happens. Don't give up when times are hard. Work to spread the good news. Do everything God has given you to do."

2 Timothy 4:5 (NIRV)

CHAPTER 1

Piper Devine tied the sparkling red-and-green plaid ribbon to the corded handles and handed the bag to Joseph Wahl. "She'll love it," she assured him.

He accepted it with a chuckle. "As she does everything I've bought from you."

"You have good taste."

"And you make good chocolate." He looked around the store, festive in its holiday finery, and nodded. "You've done a great job here, Piper. Very impressive. Not that I'm surprised."

She never tired of hearing positives about her store or her chocolates. "It was definitely a group effort. Including *you*."

His expression sobered. "There's nothing new about the fraud case yet, I'm sorry to say. I'm going to tap a retired FBI guy I know for a fresh perspective, but we might never nail whoever was responsible."

"Thanks for keeping the case open." Memory of the fraud that had closed down her cottage business still stung. And made her shiver. Just who was the guy she'd blindly allowed into her apartment six months ago? "Now, off you go. Say hello to your wife. And don't eat her gift on the way home."

"I never make promises I can't keep," he said over his shoulder as he left the store.

While the first health inspection had been a fraud, Joseph's inspections had been positive and encouraging. He'd become a regular customer since the grand opening in September. Piper turned her attention to two women approaching the counter. "Hello, ladies. Welcome to Pip's Divine Chocolates. Would you like a sample of today's Christmas special? Raspberry Grand Truffles."

Hours sped by as Piper offered samples, assisted customers, and replenished stock, humming along with the background music. Since her store's grand opening nearly three months ago, every day felt like Christmas. She couldn't wait to open the store each morning, greet customers, and revel in the joy of living her dream. Years of hard work had finally paid off.

"Closing time." The familiar male voice brought her out of the back production area with a smile. Finn McNally, the property owner she'd been crushing on since they met months ago at the library.

"A chocolate maker's work is never done," she replied, smoothing her apron.

"Concocting a new recipe?" His green eyes twinkled. "Can I get a peek behind the curtain?"

Piper folded her arms, trying to look serious. "Anyone who crosses the threshold into the production area is sworn to secrecy. Can you be trusted?"

"I've been back there about a hundred times, so I think so."

She grinned. "Good point. Lock the door and come on back." She returned to the production area, drawing a slow breath to quiet her racing heart. Finn had quickly become a good friend and her business mentor, but that was as far as the relationship had gone. "Stop acting like a twelve-year-old."

Resuming her spot at the worktable, she bit back a smile. A twelve-year-old with a massive crush.

Finn locked the store's door and flipped the decorative wooden Open sign to Closed, then stood for a moment in the popular retail shop, admiring the results of Piper's dogged determination. From shining glass display cases filled with meticulously made chocolates, to the retail area that carried his Chocolate Brews products, to the Christmas decor and music that invited customers to relax and browse—she'd put thought and planning into each decision.

He had to admit he'd learned a lot about business plans, marketing, and finance from his newest tenant. She was tenacious, focused, intelligent. And beautiful. She was also a bit of a mystery. She never talked about family, other than the grandma who had taught her to make candy, and she didn't seem to have a boyfriend. She was fiercely and frustratingly independent.

Shaking his head, he joined her in the production area. From their first telephone conversation months ago, she'd brought out his protective instincts. He was determined to find out all he could about her.

"So, what are we doing today?" he asked, accepting the camouflage apron she handed him. She'd had it sewn just for him, and it still made him smile like an idiot.

"*You* are watching *me* make a new fudge. You'll also be the official taste tester."

He huffed. "How will I learn to make it if I don't get hands-on experience?"

She shot him a grin. "The way I did—by watching first."

He continued his pretend irritation, happy to see the flash of her dimple as he pestered her. He took every opportunity to watch her making chocolate, or laughing with a shopper, or sharing new ideas for more cross-promotion between her store and Chocolate Brews, his coffee and cocoa bar. And to think he'd almost picked another business for this last spot in his building because he didn't want chocolate competition. She'd been right—they were far more collaborators than competitors.

She handed him a tiny tasting spoon, and he made a show of clumsily trying to hold it with his long fingers, drawing a laugh. As he dipped it into the bowl, she folded her arms and watched for his reaction. He took his time savoring the chocolate mixture, having learned from her the proper way to taste test. When he reached to take more, she slapped his hand.

"No double dipping," she scolded him. "Health regulations. Plus it's just...yucky."

He raised an eyebrow. "I'm not *that* gross, I hope."

Color touched her cheeks. "Of course not. But when I'm going to share this with other people, we need to keep everything clean." She handed him a new spoon. "One more taste."

He savored her blush as much as the fudge mixture until her foot tapped out a clear message. He set the spoon down. "Okay, sooo...it's very...what's the word...chocolatey."

She rolled her eyes. "I sure can't fool you. What else do you taste?"

"Coffee. And...cream. Like a cappuccino."

"How's the flavor balance?"

"Depends on what you're looking for. It's fine with the stronger coffee flavor, but maybe a bit more cream if you want a lighter cappuccino. You could promote this for coffee lovers or add the cream so it appeals to a lighter palate."

"Ooh, I like that idea." She made notes in what she called her "recipe bible," the ever-present, purple three-ring binder filled to overflowing. "How about texture?"

"I think it could be a little bit smoother, but I'm being picky for you."

Her shoulders relaxed and a smile filled her pretty face. "That's why you're my number-one taste tester."

"Because I'm rich, buff, and handsome?"

She laughed. "Because you're honest. I trust you to give me the truth."

"I'm not rich, buff, and handsome?" He let his shoulders droop. "I'd rather be that than honest."

"Trust me, you don't. Anyway," she added, moving the mixing bowl closer to the bar pan, "you're pretty well known for all of those traits. Now, will you hand me the green spatula?"

Unable to hide his smile, he handed the utensil to her, holding on when her fingers wrapped around it. She looked up and he winked. "I'm glad you consider me honest. And all those other things."

The pink on her cheeks deepened as she pulled the utensil from his grasp. "How about you wash up the last few items so we can get out of here?"

"Yes, ma'am."

Working in companionable silence, trading occasional comments that made them both laugh, they had the production area spotless within the hour. While she closed out the registers, he looked through the new Christmas items on the glass shelves. "You've added a lot of cool stuff."

"Gifts, not stuff."

"There's a difference?"

"Gifts are what you choose for someone. Stuff is what you find in souvenir stores."

"Ah. I stand corrected." He watched her check the locks on the double patio doors, making a mental note to get the outside camera set up and add security to the doors first thing next week. "Hey, what are these boxes?"

"My order finally arrived. Chocolate, flavorings, other ingredients. Can't wait to unpack it in the morning."

He held the door open, and she passed him with a smile, saying "Can you believe Christmas is just four weeks away? The gifts, the food, the joy. I'm so excited."

"Like a kid in a candy store," he mused, enjoying her laugh.

She locked the door, and they moved through the silent building to the front. "It's so quiet here when the other businesses are closed."

"One of my favorite things is opening The Depot in the morning," he said. "There's this peaceful energy, like it's waiting for the day to begin. It's a good time to pray over each business and what will happen there that day." He set the building security alarm and ushered her through the large front doors.

Their footsteps crunched on fresh snow. "You do that every day?"

"I do. And I'm happy to do it because I'm grateful these people have trusted me with their livelihood." He glanced at her. "I pray for yours too."

Brown eyes the color of his favorite dark chocolate looked up at him solemnly before a faint smile touched her mouth. "Thank you."

"My pleasure." She'd been clear about her disinterest in faith and God, which was one of the more specific prayers he said for her daily. "Let's get your car brushed off so you can go home and put your feet up. Saturday morning will be here before you know it."

Minutes later he waved her off and climbed into his nearby truck. He'd come in early tomorrow to help her unpack the boxes and get things organized. Pulling away from the curb, he chuckled.

Good thing he had such a great team working at Chocolate Brews, because he seemed to be spending far more time at Pip's Divine Chocolates than in his own shop.

CHAPTER 2

Morning did indeed arrive quickly, just as Finn had predicted. Perhaps because she'd replayed the evening endless times as she tried to fall asleep. She was enjoying the property manager's friendly attention far too much. Especially since he seemed to be in a relationship with the blonde girl who managed his coffee and cocoa bar. Joanie? Julie? Piper sighed as she collected her purse and tote bag and headed out to the car in the early morning silence.

Finn McNally was no doubt kind and funny to all his business owners. And as she delivered samples each week to the businesses, she heard plenty of comments about his green eyes and fabulous smile. She agreed with all of them. Even the married women had gushed about his willingness to do whatever was necessary to help make their businesses successful.

Parking next to his truck in the side lot, she sat a moment admiring the Christmas lights that sparkled around the property. He, too, was a new business owner, as well as new to property management. Each day he seemed to be everywhere around the train depot he'd renovated—helping, advising, going out of his way to make owning a business fun.

"Get a grip, Pip," she said aloud, climbing out of the car and starting up the freshly shoveled sidewalk. "Yes, he's been amazingly helpful getting the store up and running, but he's done that for everyone. He can't help that he's handsome and funny and—"

"Good morning, Miss Devine."

Finn's voice stopped her mid-step, her face instantly ablaze. He stood leaning on his shovel on the front platform of the building, smiling down at her. Had he heard?

"Oh my gosh! I didn't see you there. Good morning. Look at you out here shoveling so early on a Saturday morning." She bit her lip to stop the babbling.

He waited as she climbed the broad red brick steps, then pulled the main door open for her. "Well, somebody has to do it, so it's a good thing I like the exercise."

They stomped the snow from their boots, and he gestured toward his shop. "Since you're in so early, how about I make your favorite cocoa to get you ready for the big unpacking?"

"That's sweet. Thank you." She followed him into Chocolate Brews, breathing deeply. "It always smells so good in here." She waved at several of the building's tenants settled near the twelve-foot-tall windows. "And it's such an inviting atmosphere."

"Good to hear," Finn said, going behind the bar. Within minutes he returned with a festive red plaid mug from behind the bar. "Here you go—dark chocolate with a scoop of mint, topped with our famous Chocolate Brews whipped cream."

She accepted it with a smile. "You are by far the nicest property owner I've ever known."

"I'd be flattered if I weren't the *only* one you've known. Now, holler if you need help with those boxes. I've got a full staff this morning, so I can come anytime."

"I will, thanks. Here come your Saturday morning regulars." She passed a group of older men who had made Chocolate Brews their weekly Bible Study location, greeting them with a wave of her fingers wrapped around the mug.

Heading toward her shop at the end of one long hallway, she glanced at each business placard. Finn prayed for all of them? Every day? Even those not open on the weekend? He really was an interesting— She frowned as she approached her store. Why was water seeping out from under her door? Her breath caught.

"Not the sprinkler system!" She ran the final steps. "No, please no."

Dropping her purse and bag on the floor, she yanked her keys from her pocket, but a glance through the stained-glass window froze her in place. What in the world? A mess of items on the floor were surrounded and covered by white foamy stuff. That didn't look like a sprinkler system issue.

She dropped the keys twice before getting the door unlocked, pushing against it with her shoulder to force it open. Fumbling for a nearby switch, she stared at what the lights illuminated. The mug she'd been clutching hit the floor with a crash, showering her legs with hot liquid—a sharp contrast to the cold wind whistling through the shop.

"But...what..." Her brain struggled to make sense of the scene. The beautiful display cases smashed. Shelves of Christmas gifts emptied onto the floor. Foam sprayed everywhere, the fire extinguisher discarded in the middle of the room. The glass of the patio doors shattered. Large boot prints had mashed truffles onto the tile.

A deep shiver swept through her, and she dropped against the shop door, fighting a wave of nausea. Who would do such a thing? The Christmas decor she'd had such fun picking out with Mary was shredded, discarded around the room like candy sprinkles. Someone had destroyed her beautiful dream. Why?

Tears burned down her cheeks, and she turned away, glass crunching under her boots. Finn. Finn would help. She pulled the door shut behind her and wobbled down the hallway, blinking hard to stay focused and pausing to lean against the wall to pull in jagged breaths. It seemed to take hours to reach the center foyer, where she turned toward Chocolate Brews. More tables were occupied in the coffee shop, and the hum of conversation buzzed in her ears as she stopped in the doorway. *Finn. Help.*

The young man at the register looked up with a smile that faded when their eyes met. He moved quickly toward the backroom, emerging a moment later with Finn behind him. In a few steps, Finn was at her side, sliding an arm around her shoulders as he guided her to a bench outside the shop.

"What happened? Are you okay?" His warm hands wrapped around hers. "Piper, look at me."

His voice echoed down a long tunnel, and she forced her gaze up. His frowning concern swam in and out of focus. "I... My store."

"What happened?"

"I don't know." Why was it so hard to form words? "It's...gone."

He frowned. "Your store is gone? I don't understand. Are you hurt?" He examined her hands. "Did you break something?"

"It's all broken. Someone..." Tears spilled over. "Someone broke it."

"Okay. Can you stay here while I go look? I'll be right back."

As he withdrew his hands, her grasp tightened. "I'm sorry. For more trouble."

He squeezed her fingers and offered an encouraging smile. "You've never been trouble, Piper. I'll be right back, okay?"

She nodded and slumped against the wall, closing her eyes. This wasn't happening. She'd wake up any minute now. The uncontrollable shivering resumed, and she wrapped her arms tightly around herself, afraid she might literally break into pieces. It was just a bad dream. A nightmare she could never have imagined.

"Right." Finn's voice grew louder. He must be calling someone for help. "Yup, definitely a break-in. Doesn't look like any other businesses were hit. Okay, thanks."

His presence beside her on the bench calmed the shivering, but she kept her eyes closed. If she didn't look at him, it would stay a dream. His hand closed around hers. "Piper, I'm so sorry. This is my fault."

She turned her head slowly and opened her eyes. There were tears in his eyes.

"If I'd gotten the extra security set up sooner, this wouldn't have happened." He said something under his breath. "The police will be here in a minute, and I think the fire department, too, since they'll want to check out the foam. There will be a lot of questions, but take your time answering, okay? We don't want to miss any details that might help them figure out who did this."

"And why," she whispered. The knot in her chest made it hard to breathe. "They ruined my store. My company. It's all gone."

"No, it's not," he said firmly. "We'll get the store up and running as fast as possible. And you've still got the online business, so we'll use that to keep sales going."

She leaned against him and let him pull her close. His warm strength stilled the last of her shivering and calmed the fear that had clutched her heart with icy fingers. Moments later, when red lights flashed through the windows and swirled against the walls, Piper absorbed his strength and pushed to her feet.

"Hey." He stood beside her. "We'll do this together, okay?"

She pulled in a deep breath and lifted her chin. "You have enough to do without babysitting me. I'll be fine."

"I know you will, but I'm the property manager, Miss Devine. It's my building and your store that got broken into, so you're stuck with me."

His response allowed no argument, and she glanced up. It would be a lot easier to do this with him beside her. A faint smile touched her mouth as the lobby filled with people and noise.

Walking beside the police officer toward her store, Piper's stomach churned with each step of what felt like a death march. Finn's voice behind her as he talked with the fire chief kept her moving forward. She wasn't alone. Finn would help her through this...this...nightmare. But even he couldn't explain why someone was targeting her business.

Standing in the doorway, the disaster knocked the air from her lungs again. A hand at her throat, she took one step in and stopped. Such violence. Such utter destruction. Who would expend this much energy on a candy store? And why?

"Once the photographs have been taken," the officer said, "we'll need a list of everything that's missing, and what's been destroyed, which seems"—he looked around— "to be about everything. I'm sorry you're going through this, Miss. We'll do our best to find whoever did it."

"Thank you." She turned her gaze from the broken display cases to the shattered ornaments on the floor, and then toward the boxes that had been delivered only yesterday. Ruined. The front counter was empty. No point-of-sale machines, which meant no money.

"Here." Finn rested a hand on her back as he handed her a bottle of water. "Remember to breathe."

She accepted the bottle and drank deeply, eyes closed as the cold water ran down her throat. Maybe if she pretended she was on a beach somewhere... The nonstop click of the police camera shattered that silly dream. She wasn't on a beach. She was in frozen Wisconsin at the scene of a crime she didn't understand, couldn't even process. Christmas had been destroyed in so many ways by this brutality.

"Miss Devine, I want to cover some information with you." The officer's voice crashed into her whirling thoughts like a baseball bat against glass. She shuddered. Bad analogy. "Let's step into the hall, where it will be quieter."

"I'd like to join you," Finn said. "We can use my office in Chocolate Brews."

Piper followed Finn down the long hallway to his office, where they settled around a small meeting table. The officer pulled out a notebook and faced her.

"Miss Devine, do you have any idea who might have done this? Any disgruntled employees? Customers? Family members? Have you canceled any orders that made a supplier angry?"

She shook her head. "Not that I know of. I have a great crew of employees, and so far no customers have complained about anything. The store's only been open a few months."

"The fraud investigation is ongoing," Finn added.

"Fraud?"

Finn looked at her and she motioned for him to continue.

"Last summer Piper received a letter supposedly from the Health Department saying there would be an inspection on her cottage business. A guy showed up, reviewed her paperwork and equipment, then told her she had to shut down while he filed a report full of lies."

"He said that?"

"No," Piper said, knotting her fingers in her lap, "but he showed me his notes and *I* told *him* it was all lies. I keep excellent records, never had any complaints, and follow every procedure to ensure my products are safe to eat."

Finn nodded emphatically.

"What makes you think it was fraud?"

"When I leased this space, the health department came out for an inspection, and that agent told me there'd never been a complaint filed, they didn't write reports the way the fake guy did, and they didn't have anyone in the office with that name."

The officer wrote quickly. "No idea who instigated the fake inspection?"

"None. Joseph, the health department agent I work with, told me just yesterday that they're continuing the investigation."

"Interesting. Could be related, so we'll talk with the health department. What's Joseph's last name?"

The questions continued for another hour. Who was last out of the building and first in this morning? How did she relate to the tenants? He requested the building security tapes as well as photos of her store prior to the break-in.

As he wrapped up, the officer handed her a list of immediate action items. Calling the bank and the insurance company were at the top of the list. By the time they finished what he'd called the "first-round" interview, Piper was barely upright. If only she could go back to bed and start the day over. Better yet, repeat last night and change...something to prevent this.

Standing at the office door, Finn was focused intently on the officer, nodding. No hint of the cheerful or mischievous Finn she knew. Arms folded and feet planted, his stance emanated strength and protection, both of which she needed desperately.

After the officer left, Finn sat next to her. "Holding up okay?"

"I guess. It still seems like a dream." She met his concerned gaze, blinking against another burn of tears. "Why would someone do this? What did I do?"

He set his hand on hers. "You didn't do anything to deserve this."

"Well, I got on someone's bad side." She stood. "I guess I'd better start making a list of what's gone."

He stood up too. "Want help?"

"Thanks, but I can manage."

He grasped her shoulders gently, waiting until she looked up. "Piper, I have no doubt you can, but you don't have to do this alone. Let people help you."

As she'd been alone most of her life, she was more grateful for this assurance than he would know. "I will."

"Promise?"

The office door opened. "Oh, sorry." The female voice cut between them. Finn's blonde assistant.

"No worries," Piper said, stepping away from him. "I need to get to the store."

"I'm really sorry about what happened," Jodi said as Piper passed her in the doorway.

"Thanks. Me too."

Returning to the disaster her life had become, Piper pushed her shoulders back. She could do this. She had no choice.

CHAPTER 3

Finn watched Piper leave his office without a backward glance. Her resilience was astounding. She could easily have folded into a distraught mess. Instead, she'd pulled that determined independence around her like a cape and faced the issue.

"Hello?"

He blinked and turned his attention to Jodi. "Sorry, what?"

"Next week's order just came in." She studied him for a moment. "If you want to check it."

"I trust you to go through it. I need to get the security cameras set up in back, call the insurance company, and get the repairs started. Oh, and the cops want all our security footage from this past week."

Jodi crossed her arms and leaned against the door frame. "That one business has caused you so much trouble."

"She's had more than her fair share of issues." He neatened and stacked the papers the officer had left after the interview.

"But her issues keep costing you money. Money that should be going into our—*your*—business."

"She's also brought money and customers into Brew. It is what it is. We're learning as we go, right?"

Heading down the hall, he heard her loud huff. He was glad she was watching his back, caring about Chocolate Brews. And he was glad he could trust her with the shop while he attended to other things.

When he reached Pip's Divine Chocolates, the scene inside pulled him up short. Piper was moving around in the middle of the room, picking up items and putting them in the box she carried. Five of the other tenants were doing the same. His chest swelled at the sight. This was what community was all about.

Each person wore what looked like blue paper slippers over their shoes. Roberta handed him a pair. "So the foam doesn't wreck our shoes. Here are gloves to keep it off your hands." Pain in her eyes, she shook her head and added quietly, "I can't believe what this poor girl has gone through."

"Me neither." He watched Piper place a broken ceramic Christmas tree into the box, her brow pinched. "Thanks for helping. She needs to know she's not in this alone."

"Of course. We're already talking among the businesses about what else we can do, how to raise money to get her back on her feet."

"That's great, thanks." He met Piper in the middle of the room and reached for the box. "How about I do this and you make your list of what's missing."

She met his gaze with drooping eyes. "Okay. Thanks."

He took up her work as she went into the production area. Foam was visible on the back wall and on every piece of equipment he could see. Apparently, they'd trashed every inch of her space. Temples pounding, he gritted his teeth. Once the culprits were found, he'd want a few minutes alone with them. They'd better hope God restrained him from acting on his roiling emotions.

Outside the battered patio doors, several men set down large pieces of plywood. Finn returned their wave. After calling the police this morning, he'd called these guys to help cover the broken doors. Mark and Mike had assured him they'd take care of it before lunch. As always, his friends were true to their word. He'd been blessed a million times over by their lifelong friendship.

Soon the room vibrated with the whine of a saw and hammers pounding. Both of his friends were talented craftsmen and had the first piece of plywood in place quickly. Finn continued putting broken items in his box, glancing toward the production area where Piper had gone.

When she hadn't emerged after twenty minutes, he set the overflowing box on the counter and went to find her. She stood at the far end of the room, leaning on the worktable, her narrow shoulders shaking. He crossed the room and gathered her in his arms, where she sobbed against his chest. For the hundredth time, he silently asked God why. The answer would come eventually; in the meantime, he'd do what he could for her.

She drew a shuddering breath and stepped back, wiping her face with her sleeves. When she looked up, the anguish in her eyes made him wince.

"Thank you," she managed between hiccupping breaths. "I guess I needed that. I'm okay now."

"You're welcome. Anytime."

The corner of her mouth lifted. "Sorry about your shirt."

He glanced down at the wet spots on his Chocolate Brews shirt and shrugged. "Wash and dry."

"Good thing." She squared her shoulders. "Okay, back to work. Only a few things are missing from back here, which is a relief, but I'll have to find out if the equipment can be cleaned or has to be replaced. The worst thing is my recipe bible is gone. Why they'd want that, I have no—" She looked up at him, eyes wide. "Unless whoever was behind the fraud was behind this?"

Finn's brow lowered, eyes narrowing as he considered the idea. Even if he thought there was a connection, he'd voice his concern to the police and not her. "I doubt it. This is a very different crime from fraud." He ushered her into the retail area. "I'll check that the officer is following up on that thread. Did you make copies of the recipes?"

"Most," she said. "I guess I'll have to create new treats." Her flippant tone didn't match the clench to her jaw.

"Well, your premiere taste tester will be available at a moment's notice. What's missing out here?"

"Both point-of-sale machines are gone, as is my company laptop. Those are the big things. Everything else is ruined, including thousands of dollars of inventory." Her gaze moved to the boxes still sitting where they'd been delivered. "I was so excited to go through it today."

The hammering had stopped, and now one of the guys called, "Hey, McNally. Want to inspect our work?"

"Definitely," Finn called back. He looked down at Piper. "Come meet a couple of my best friends. They jumped in to help."

Piper let Finn direct her to the two young men standing beside the plywood wall now covering the broken patio doors.

"Piper Devine, meet Mark Dechovik and Mike Montrose. Guys, Piper is the owner of this store."

She shook their hands and thanked them for their quick work to secure her space. Their smiling generosity brought tears to her eyes yet again.

"Glad to help," Mark said. "Since there's so much cleanup to do, we got a little creative." He shot a grin at Finn as Mike lifted a long plank. "You'll need a dumpster, obviously, and it makes the most sense to put it right outside here in the back. So, we set up one side to be opened when necessary." He swung the plywood inward to demonstrate. "Then, when you're done for the day..." He swung it closed and Mike slid the plank into place to block the opening.

Grinning, Finn shook his head and gave them both an appreciative fist bump. "Leave it to you guys to come up with that. Thanks."

After assuring Piper they'd be back to help with construction of a new patio entrance, they gave her a warm hug, gathered their tools, and left through their makeshift opening. Piper looked up at Finn with a tired smile. "You have nice friends."

"Yeah. They've been around so long they're like family. I'll get the dumpster set up ASAP. With those guys helping, we'll have it cleaned up and a new door in place in no time. For now, what else do you need?"

Need? She sighed. The store back in one piece. Her life the way it was. "To know what to do next, I guess. I think I've accounted for everything missing or broken."

"That's a huge step. Have you called the insurance company yet? I've contacted mine and they're sending me an email with the information they'll need."

"I'd better do that now." She turned in a slow circle. Her amazing colleagues had picked up the last of the broken items and slipped out before she could thank them. "Then I guess cleaning up the foam will be next."

"The fire captain left a few sheets with clean-up instructions and some companies to call who know how to sanitize and restore things. I pinned it to the wall by the counter. But first we need lunch. I'll bet you haven't eaten a thing since you got here, and it's already 2:00, so let's go get a sandwich or a bowl of soup at the Brew."

Food wasn't even on her to-do list. "I'm not hungry."

"Me neither, but we'll force ourselves to eat something to keep our energy up. That's an order from the property manager."

The familiar twinkle in his tired eyes allowed a spark of light into her heart. "Since when does the property manager get to dictate when I eat?"

Turning her toward the door, he chuckled as he propelled her from the shop. "It was in the fine print of your contract, which you obviously didn't read. I'll let the police officer know where to find us if he needs something."

The gentle strength of his hands on her shoulders sent warmth down her arms, relaxing her tensed muscles. Unable to argue, she let him steer her toward Chocolate Brews and into a chair by the window.

"Soup, sandwich, or both?"

Chin propped on her hand, she lifted her gaze to his. "Whatever is easiest."

"Got it. Sit tight."

She watched him move toward the back of the shop. How had she been lucky enough to get him as a friend? He'd been a rock and a mentor from the beginning. She'd like to walk through life with someone like him. Leaning her head against the window frame, she closed her eyes. At least for now she wasn't alone.

CHAPTER 4

"Mary, you do not need to hover." Piper watched her bestie set the steaming mug on the side table beside a plate of cookies. Since Piper arrived home from the nightmare at the store, Mary had treated her like fragile glass.

"You need some old-fashioned hovering, my friend." She dropped onto the other end of the couch. "However, it would be more fun if you were open to accepting a little love."

Piper tentatively sipped the tea. Scorching—just the way Mary liked it. "I'm open."

Mary gave her a sideway glance and snorted. "Sure you are."

In the silence that followed, Piper battled another round of tears. Aside from Mary, she'd had no one to lean on for decades. Since her family's implosion after GeeMaw's death, she'd basically been on her own. Hovering wasn't something she was used to.

"I appreciate you being here," she said quietly. "I really do. I've just always been able to fix whatever problem came up. This one, though..."

"We'll fix it," Mary said. "All of us together. You, me, Roberta, Finn."

Her use of Finn's name always contained a note of mischief. Piper bit her lip to hold in a smile.

"What I wouldn't give to have someone like him in my corner," Mary added. "And you got him without even trying. The way he looks at you, girlfriend?" She fanned her face.

Piper rolled her eyes. "He's a wonderful friend, but he looks at me like he looks at all his tenants. When our businesses do well, he does well."

"He sure isn't looking at you with dollar signs in those green eyes. Nope. It's a lot more personal than that. And it's way better than how Ian looked at you."

"Seriously? *I* don't even remember how Ian looked at me, it's been so long."

"Four years isn't that long, Pip. I still remember how devastated he was when you broke it off to focus on your business. With the money that boy's family had, you could have had ten chocolate stores by now." She munched a cookie. "Do you ever hear from him?"

Piper shrugged, sipping carefully to not scald her tongue. "He pops up on my social media a few times a year. Sometimes I get a chatty email out of the blue. He always asks how the business is going." She shook her head. "He never understood why it was so important to me, why I needed to do it my way. He wanted to make it as easy as possible so I would have more time to focus on him, I guess."

"I'd have been happy to accept his help. He was the epitome of tall, dark, and handsome with boatloads of money thrown in." Mary finished her store-bought cookie. "But I'm not you and you're not me, and now you've got that gorgeous cowboy looking out for you."

"Cowboy?"

"You haven't seen him in his cowboy hat riding a gorgeous black horse just outside town? Oh, of course not, because you're determined to live in Halston while he and I live in the metropolis that is Lakeville."

Piper giggled at the description of the town with its 15,000 residents. Maybe it would be worth it to find an apartment closer to the store. To keep an eye on it, of course. "I'll bet he looks good in a cowboy hat," she mused, her heart skipping a beat.

"Good is hardly the word, but yes, he does."

She and Finn hadn't talked about their lives outside of The Depot. She had no clue where he even lived. She allowed herself another minute to picture him riding across the valley, then straightened on the chair. "Okay, let's get back to the to-do list. The email from the insurance company has twenty different forms for me to fill out, and I need to send before-and-after photos."

While Mary went along with the change of subject, Piper knew their conversation about Finn wasn't over. Her friend had always had lofty goals of love for their futures, but without her own prospect at the moment, she was single-minded in positioning Finn as the perfect candidate. It was fun to consider, but right now there were more pressing issues. Like all the lost revenue Piper had been counting on. And how she'd pay next month's rent.

Finn acknowledged the wave of his friend and pastor, Blake, and threaded through the crowded cafe. Settling across the table, he chuckled at Blake's wide-eyed expression. "What? Am I late?"

"I'm just surprised that you're not incognito. Aren't you feeling a bit traitorous patronizing another cafe?"

"Hey, I'm all about the community, so spending a little money elsewhere is good for business."

"Not to mention nobody can duplicate Annie's pancakes."

"God's truth," Finn agreed with a grin, "so it's appropriate that I meet the pastor here."

The waitress arrived with a bright smile to take their order, then moved away with a new blush in her cheeks. Finn leaned back in the chair and raised an eyebrow at his friend's smirk. "Now what?"

"As usual, the town hunk has the locals all a-twitter."

"A-twitter? You mean the local birds freak out when they see me coming?"

"The human kind. Which makes me wonder, are you ever going to settle down?"

"Just because you are?"

"Amy and I are on our way to the altar. I'm starting to think you have an aversion to simply going on a date."

The banter continued as Blake lobbed questions, which Finn expertly rebutted. They'd been friends since high school, and he knew Blake wanted only the best for him. Still, the prodding had become more pointed since his engagement.

"I'm glad you guys are happy, and I plan to celebrate loud and strong on the big day," Finn said. "But you may have noticed I've had a lot on my plate lately?"

"I have. Tell me about the break-in. That was awful news to get last night."

Finn provided a brief overview, pausing when the waitress brought their food. After Blake said a quick blessing, Finn continued with a description of everything that needed to be done. "That's all I know of so far," he added. "I'm sure there'll be more forms to fill out once the workweek starts."

Finishing a slice of toast slathered with jam, Blake asked, "How is the tenant handling it?"

"Like a champ." Finn cut up more of his plate-sized pancake. "Even so, she's hurting, and there doesn't seem to be any family around to support her. I think she's pretty much on her own." He'd been surprised she let him hold her while she cried. Surprised and touched. And a little off-balance ever since.

"That's tough. Does she have a church community?"

"She's pretty resistant to faith at the moment. I'm not sure it's ever been part of her life." He chewed the pancake slowly. "She knows I'm praying for her, but I think there's a lot of pain in her background that keeps her from even considering it for herself."

Blake focused on the last of his eggs, then leaned his elbows on the table. His expression was serious, although Finn caught a twitch at the corner of his mouth. "What's her name?"

"Piper Devine. Her friends call her Pip."

"And does Pip know how you feel?"

"About?"

Blake's gaze remained steady, and Finn briefly considered denying it. "No. At least, I don't think so."

"How does she feel about you?"

He'd asked himself that a million times. "I think I'm her big brother. The guy she can joke around with and who helps her out. I doubt it's anything other than that."

"Have you asked her out?"

"No! I'm the property manager." Not to mention he hadn't figured out a good way to ask. He'd always been a nerd when it came to dating.

"That doesn't make you her boss, you know." The twitch morphed slowly into a smile. "Even if you were, there's no law against it."

"I know." The words sounded more irritable than he intended, and he sighed. "She's been working so hard to get her retail business going, and now this..." He stared out the window for a silent moment. "Anyway, I'm wondering if the church can help. She's a chocolate maker, but she can't produce anything until the equipment is sanitized, the shop repainted, and the health department approves it. Could she use the church kitchen? We're licensed for commercial cooking, right?"

Blake nodded, eyes narrowed. "We are because of the community meals. Scheduling shouldn't be an issue. That would be a great opportunity for her and a good use of our kitchen. What does she need for equipment?"

"Not a lot, I don't think. She uses a stove, microwave, and specialized equipment like a grinder, a scale, and a tempering machine. And she'll need a fridge."

The smile returned. "You seem to know a lot about making chocolate."

"I run a coffee and cocoa cafe, remember?"

"Which is not the same as making candy," Blake countered.

Finn met his gaze. "Can she use the church kitchen or not?"

Blake laughed. "Yes, I think she can, but I'll clear it with Betty to be sure."

"Aren't you one of the head honchos?"

"I might be, but trust me, Betty's in charge. That's why the church is still standing."

CHAPTER 5

Piper stood in the hallway outside her shop Monday morning, staring at the door and searching for the courage to unlock it. Mary had been adamant that Piper stay home on Sunday, away from the store, to give herself a physical and mental break. Now she doubted the wisdom of that choice. She held her hands up, marveling at the tremble that had started when she drove into The Depot parking lot. She'd never been truly afraid of anything, but since discovering the break-in Saturday morning, fear had crept into her thoughts, into her dreams during intermittent sleep, into her very fiber, it seemed. And she hated it.

She stood at a crossroads because of that event. She could walk away from the store and find a new adventure. Or she could get focused and restart the retail side of her business. Walking away meant breaking the lease, which Finn would probably be relieved about after the issues she'd caused. It also meant she could reinvent herself and start something new. She could find somewhere new to live, try new things. But she'd be walking away from all she'd ever wanted to do—make people happy with special treats. And she'd be walking away from Finn.

"No!" The word spoken aloud in the silence startled her into action. She stuck the key into the lock and pushed the door open, then gasped. The space looked like it had before she started Pip's Divine Chocolates, except for the plywood covering the patio doors.

Her tentative footsteps echoed in the emptiness. She looked down—no shattered glass underfoot. No foam, no broken ornaments or gift items. She turned in a slow circle. No sign of the violent destruction, of her chocolates ground into the tile.

"Nothing like starting fresh." Roberta's voice came from the doorway.

Piper squeaked and spun around. "Sorry. I guess I'm a bit jumpy." She spread her arms. "But who...?"

"Angels? Chocolate fairies?" She wrapped Piper in a warm hug. "A bunch of us might have wanted to get it cleaned out yesterday, so you'd know where to start today. Sanitizing, painting, making samples for all of us."

The last comment pulled a smile from Piper as she stepped back and wiped her eyes. "Thank you. I can't believe you took your Sunday to do this. Tell me you didn't skip any open houses or client meetings."

"I didn't skip a thing." Roberta's words were reassuring. "Christmas time is notorious for few showings and even fewer buyers out looking. Now, this"—she held out a white envelope—

"is something we pulled together to help you get back in the game. And I will not hear any argument from you."

Piper looked from the offering to the broad smile and raised eyebrows that encouraged her to accept it. Opening it, she slid out a cashier's check. "What?" She gasped, stepping back with a hand at her throat. "Oh, no. No. You guys can't do this. Thank you so much, but I can't accept it."

Roberta nodded firmly. "Yes, you can and you will. We all know you'd do the same for any of us. This is our Christmas gift to you, to help you get started making all your yummy treats that will keep people coming to The Depot to browse your adorable store. It helps all our businesses. And we can use this as a tax write-off!" She turned for the door, waving long fingers over her shoulder. "Now get busy making more delicious things for us to sample. Ta-ta."

"But..." Piper stared at the empty doorway, then at the check still clutched in her hand. Ten thousand dollars? How could she possibly accept it? She pulled a piece of paper from the envelope and scanned the beautiful handwriting. Choking back a sob, she blinked hard to bring the words into focus.

Piper, we are so sorry you are dealing with such an awful crime. A hardship or difficulty for any tenant in The Depot is a hardship for all. We're a community of business owners, but we're also friends. And we're members of the Lakeville community with a commitment to keep our city safe and thriving. That means our businesses need to succeed.

This check is from all of your colleagues here in The Depot. We wish we could give even more. When a business does well, the rest of us do too. While the break-in makes us angry, we are also heartbroken that one of us has been dealt such a rotten blow. Please use this money to get your "sweet" store up and running as fast as possible. And please call on any of us at any time if you need help, ideas, or just want to chat a bit.

And Piper, while we love your treats, it's you that makes them so sweet. Know that we are behind you 100% and will do whatever we can to help. This WILL be a merry Christmas after all!

Each business owner had signed it, adding an encouraging word or symbol. Maybe she did have angels watching out for her. And walking the same halls she'd traveled with trays of sweet treats.

Eyes closed, tears on her cheeks, she pressed the letter and check over her heart and whispered, "Thank you."

Finn waited until 9:00 before making his way toward Piper's store. He'd seen her arrive at 7:00 and forced himself to allow her time alone in the space before the day kicked into gear. Her door was open, and he stepped in quietly. The crushed glass, broken items, and trampled chocolate had been swept away yesterday, providing a blank palette for her to start creating an even better store.

A noise in the production area pulled him toward the back. She stood at the stainless counter, papers spread before her. He cleared his throat and she jumped.

"Sorry," he said. "I thought you heard me."

She lowered the hand she'd slapped to her chest and shot him a half-hearted frown before turning back to the papers. "You might expect I'm a bit on edge."

"Didn't think of that." He gave himself a mental slap. "Insurance forms?"

"Lots and lots of them. How many do you have?"

"Around twenty-three, but who's counting. Need any help?"

She tapped the pen against her chin, frowning at the paper in front of her. "I'm a little confused about this one." She handed him a sheet with microscopic print. "Is this about raw inventory or finished product?"

"Let me get my magnifying glass," he said wryly.

They spent the next hour shoulder to shoulder reviewing each form. Her understanding of most of the requirements amazed him and yet wasn't a surprise. She had a sharp mind and a laser focus for details that put him to shame. He was more of a big picture guy, which was why Jodi was indispensable—she understood the fine print of business far better than he ever would.

Piper straightened from where she'd been bent over the counter and stretched her arms overhead. "Thanks for helping. It went a lot better with two heads."

He chuckled. "Not so sure about that. You've definitely got a head for business. But we do make a good team, hmm?"

She lowered her arms, her silence unsettling. Had he put his foot in it again? When she turned toward him, her eyes were shiny.

"Thank you," she said. "For helping me. For believing in me. For building such a great team here. And for...for the money." Her voice cracked. "I can't believe how generous everyone is being."

He released a silent breath of relief. "You deserve it, Piper. You've become an important part of this place."

Fingers pressed against her lips, she shook her head. "I just... How can I possibly thank you all?"

"Keep making your chocolate magic."

"But—"

He tapped her nose. "No buts. Just chocolate."

CHAPTER 6

Seated at the bar in Chocolate Brews, sipping her favorite mint white chocolate cocoa, Piper watched Finn chat with his customers. Listening, chatting, joking—obviously in his element. His smile was genuine, his attention focused. Each customer seemed to enjoy his undivided attention. She certainly did. She turned her focus back to her drink as her cheeks heated. Way too much.

Flipping open her notebook, she went down the checklist she'd created at her kitchen table last night. Cleaning up the shop to prepare for the sanitation process was at the top. Still stunned that her colleagues—no, her friends—had taken care of that, she crossed it off the list. And the money they'd given her? She didn't know how to process this nonstop generosity, let alone know how to repay it.

"So."

Finn's voice once again startled her. "Will you stop that?"

His grin was unrepentant. "I'm not doing it on purpose, but it's sort of funny seeing you jump."

"I'm glad you're having fun at my expense."

"Me too. Hey, I meant to tell you this earlier." He leaned his elbows on the bar, the mischief gone from his face. "Online orders are still coming in, right?"

The thought of those unfilled orders made her nauseated. Once again, her business was on the verge of collapse through no fault of her own. What did the universe have against her?

"Piper, look at me."

Stifling the runaway thoughts, she lifted her gaze.

"I've got good news for that. My church is offering the use of its commercial kitchen to make your candy. Once your equipment is sanitized, we'll move it to the church so the final cleaning and painting can be done at the store. You can fill the orders from the church until the store is ready."

She blinked, studying his expression. A church was going to let her use their kitchen? Right. For an enormous fee. "Why?"

His eyebrows rose. "Because we want to."

"How much will they charge?"

"Nothing. It's just until the store is back in order. And you'll be using your own food and equipment, for the most part. *Why not* might be a better question."

This was yet another debt she'd be unable to repay. "Will I have to start attending the church?"

"Not unless you want to. Piper, there's no ulterior motive here. It's a licensed, commercial kitchen that sits idle except Saturdays when we do a community meal."

"But…" The offer didn't make sense. They had to want something from her. "I'm not like you. I'm not sure I even believe in God, so why would they let me set up shop there for free?"

The frown that had gathered across Finn's brow relaxed, and he rested a hand on her arm. "We want to do this because helping someone in the community is the right thing to do. Believe it or not, a lot of people care about you and want to right this wrong. Let the church help you." His fingers tightened. "Let *me* help you."

The earnest light in his eyes and the reassuring warmth of his hand halted the growing panic. While each new offer threatened to bury her deeper under debt, that wasn't Finn. He'd proven that these past six months by leasing her his last space, by mentoring her as she set up shop, and by simply being a friend. He wouldn't make the offer with ulterior motives.

She bit her lip. Maybe this was what life was like for people who had friends and family around them. Maybe she didn't need to feel overwhelmed by unexpected generosity. Maybe she could learn to accept it, even enjoy it someday. Surely she could find ways to return the favors. "Wow. Okay."

The smile that filled his handsome face erased the doubts. If it made him happy to help her yet again, then she couldn't say no.

He squeezed her arm and straightened. "Great! Figure out what needs to be done to bring the equipment back to code, and get more product ordered pronto. You'll be back in business in a few days."

She nodded, and he moved away to help new customers. Watching him in action, she realized help wasn't the right word. He loved serving. His customers, his tenants. Her. She needed to pay more attention so she could learn how to apply that to her own life. Paying attention to him wasn't exactly hard to do.

Within a few days, Piper's divine chocolate making was ensconced in the Grace Church kitchen. Betty, the delightful church secretary, took her through a thorough training of their procedures, while Finn eavesdropped. Then Blake, one of the pastors, stopped in to welcome her and her candy making to the church. When he offered to do any necessary taste testing, Finn told him in no uncertain terms that *he* was the number-one taste tester so, unless Finn suddenly dropped dead, Blake would have to buy her chocolates like everyone else. Horrified by his stern tone toward the pastor, Piper started to intervene, but their laughter and Betty's wink revealed he'd been kidding. She rolled her eyes and turned back to her work.

Waiting for the new product order to arrive, Piper focused on making rock candy in Christmas colors, meringues, and Spritz cookies in a variety of shapes and flavors. Smiling at memories of learning beside GeeMaw, she put some of the old recipes to work. Betty had also trained her on the church's security system, so Piper could be in the kitchen as much as she wanted. And that was turning out to be eighteen hours every day.

Finn dropped by the first few afternoons, happily taste testing, encouraging her, and bringing her favorite cocoa along with bags of his unique trail mix. By late Friday afternoon, she had filled the refrigerators with trays and boxes of treats, completed the non-chocolate online orders, and prepared for the raw products that would arrive in the morning. Her arms and back ached from hours of stirring, measuring, spreading, and decorating. And her temples throbbed from the struggle to understand how her life had become a roller coaster.

The cleaning service called to report they'd finished and the refrigerators were ready. Relieved that the church would get their refrigerators back in time for the Saturday evening meal, Piper pulled her car to the front doors of the church, loaded as much of the inventory as she could, set the building alarm, and headed to The Depot. As soon as she got the store painted, she could move the equipment back. Just a few more days.

She cracked the window and breathed deeply. Aside from the drive to the church early each morning and back home long after dark, she'd barely set foot outside. The crisp air was invigorating. Twinkling Christmas lights filled the neighborhoods and her heart with brightness and even a touch of joy. Once the products were safely stored in the refrigerators, she would go home and get a solid night's sleep. She giggled. Right after a very long bubble bath.

At The Depot, she parked beside Finn's truck, loaded her arms with a few boxes of fragile treats, and headed to the front door.

Managing to get one door open, she propped it with her foot and backed carefully into the lobby. As she turned around, she squealed in surprise. Finn and his assistant stood a few feet away, dressed for a night out. Together, apparently.

"Here. Let me get those." Finn started toward her.

"No." She forced a smile to soften the sharp response. "I've got it. Well, you two look ready for a Christmas party." The words squeezed past the knot forming in her throat.

"Actually, my friend's wedding," Jodi said, taking Finn's arm. "We were about to lock up here before we dance the night away."

Piper stayed focused on the blonde's bright expression, unable to look at Finn. "Sounds wonderful. I love your dress." Sadly, she did. It was something she'd never be brave enough to wear, mainly because it belonged on someone like Jodi.

"Thanks. I needed something fabulous for a night out with this special guy." She beamed up at Finn, still clinging to his arm. "I guess we'd better get going so we're not late. Have a good weekend, Piper."

"Yeah. You guys, too." Piper managed a wobbling smile, including Finn with a glance. While his expression was unreadable, he looked amazing in his dark suit. "I'll lock up after I've brought the rest of my stuff in," she added, moving past them.

"Finn," she heard Jodi say, "could you help me with my coat, please?"

Tears burning, Piper hurried toward her store, kicking herself for hoping he might someday see her as more than a tenant. She brushed at her wet cheek with her shoulder and nearly dropped the top boxes of rock candy.

He'd been nothing but kind to her since they first met. *Nothing* other than kind. She set the pile of boxes on the counter and stood for a moment, eyes squeezed shut. It was none of her business that he was dating his assistant. She'd suspected it all along.

She stored the rock candy in the cupboard. Just because she had no life outside of her store didn't mean the rest of the world was that way. Other people had fulfilling relationships, enjoying friends and family and making lovely memories. That she didn't wasn't a reflection on anyone but her.

After putting the cookies in the refrigerator, she leaned heavily on the worktable. As Mary had pointed out, Ian had been willing to give her anything—on his terms. Finn was the opposite—caring, funny, encouraging. She'd been right to break things off with Ian, but to have gotten her hopes up over Finn was just plain dumb.

Drawing a sharp breath, she wiped her face, and retrieved the two-wheeler from the corner. She had so much to do to get her dream back on track that she didn't have time to be jealous. It was a waste of energy anyway.

Focus, Pip. This is your life.

CHAPTER 7

With his regular Saturday morning barista out sick, Finn couldn't get to the church to see Piper first thing, to explain about the date. Not that she had seemed to care, but he didn't want her thinking he and Jodi were a couple. While he might have considered it at one point, meeting Piper had blown those thoughts away. He'd tried to enjoy the evening with Jodi, but his mind and heart were elsewhere.

Piper hadn't answered his early morning text, so he would head over to the church as soon as his afternoon staff got in. They had to talk *today*. In the meantime, he'd flesh out the idea that had sprung up during his restless sleep—a Depot Christmas event to coincide with Piper's grand reopening. His tenants had been amazing in their response to the break-in, and he wanted to show them his appreciation of their sense of community. He had two weeks to pull together something simple and fun.

Between customers, he scribbled notes on a pad by the front register. Much as he'd be happy to skip the more secular part of Christmas, kids would want to see Santa, and since Mark owned a Santa suit... He put a check mark next to Santa. Mike could build pretty much anything, so hopefully he could throw a sleigh together. Another check mark. Plenty of people had wagons, so someone would no doubt offer a hayride around town. There was a group at church that might be willing to play Christmas music in the foyer of The Depot.

"What're you working on?" Jodi appeared beside him, slipping a Brews apron over her head.

"A Christmas party at The Depot."

"Seriously? It's a bit late to be throwing a party together, don't you think?"

"Nope." He'd twist a few arms if necessary. He would get it done for Piper. "Nothing fancy. Here's what I've got so far."

Over the next few hours, with ideas tossed in from the staff and even a few customers seated at the bar, the first annual Depot Christmas Party was set in motion. They'd check with the fire chief about a bonfire. Restaurants could offer specials for the night. A couple of local food trucks might be convinced to show up.

By 3:00, Jodi had a spreadsheet created with to-do items and assignments for follow-up, and a flyer ready to print and post around town. Roberta had stopped by and declared she'd scrounge up a handful of raffle items to raise money for the food shelf. What started as an idea in the wee hours had bloomed into a group effort of amazing proportions.

Struggling to contain his excitement, Finn drove to Grace Church with Piper's favorite cocoa in hand to share the news with her and talk about his non-date with Jodi. Blake greeted him from his post at the kitchen stove stirring vegetable soup. Of course! It was Saturday evening—community meal at the church.

"Piper helped with the setup," Blake told him before he asked. "Then she had somewhere to be by five."

Finn nodded, ignoring the disappointment that surfaced. For all he knew, she had her own date.

"She's pretty great," Blake added. "I can see why she caught your interest."

"Yeah." *Too bad I didn't catch hers.*

Piper laughed at Mary's comment as they painted side by side in the shop Monday afternoon. Sunshine sparkled on the glass of the display cases. Even the floor tiles squeaked as they walked across them. This second coat of fresh paint was all that remained before she'd start restocking the cases and shelves.

From atop the stepladder, she paused to gaze around the store. Two weeks ago, she'd been sure her dream had been destroyed. "I still can't believe it."

Mary continued rolling paint. "Amazing, isn't it? God worked through a whole lot of people to put you back in business."

Her casual mention of God didn't elicit the same recoil it used to. Nearly two weeks of working in the Grace Church kitchen had Piper rethinking her perception of church people and pastors. Even God. Pastor Blake had visited her daily to chat, sample the treat of the day, and encourage her when her energy lagged. No mention of God or the Bible, no scolding that she didn't attend church—any church. Just simple friendship and genuine curiosity about her work. The same was true for the various staff members who stopped by to introduce themselves and watch her work her chocolate magic.

"I think you're right," she said to Mary. "Without all of you, I'd still be frozen in the doorway staring at the mess. I honestly had no clue what to do."

Mary's sideway glance held a tinge of regret. "I still can't believe Finn is dating his assistant. Not with the way he looks at you. Have you talked to him lately?"

"I haven't even seen him in over a week." Missing the fun conversations they'd had still stung. "We're both crazy busy, so it's not surprising. I've been between here and the church, and he's had to deal with...stuff." Insurance. Security. Jodi.

In the silence that followed, she held back a sigh. Everything had changed.

"I saw some new gift items I think would be great in the store," Mary said.

As she chatted, Piper's mind wandered back to earlier last week, when she'd drummed up the courage to stop by his office. Finding it empty, she'd left a note near his phone inviting him to taste test a new recipe. No response. A few days ago, she'd left an invitation to a private event she'd decided to hold to thank her angels. Again, no response.

She couldn't blame him, since she'd done the same to him while working on candy production. Not to mention she didn't want to see him and Jodi hanging out together at Chocolate Brews. She flinched, wondering yet again if he'd known she'd been interested.

"Then I think we should sign up to ride the shuttle to Mars next week."

Piper looked at Mary, eyebrows raised.

"Finally, you're listening. I'm sharing all these great ideas and you're off in la-la land."

"Sorry. My brain keeps going a million directions with everything I still need to do."

"Knock knock." A male voice interrupted, and they turned in unison.

"Joseph! This is a nice surprise. Come in." Piper climbed off the ladder and set her paint brush aside.

Arms folded, he looked around with nodding approval. "This is an amazing transformation. Can't imagine how you got it done so fast."

Piper and Mary shared a glance. "Angels," Piper said. "What brings you by?"

"Good news. We've tracked down the health department imposter. Does the name Ian Schreiner ring a bell?"

"Yes, but what does he have to do with this?" She frowned. "He wasn't the guy who came to my apartment."

"That young man was Ryan Stevens, a friend of Ian's who agreed to play the fake agent."

"So, Ian was the mastermind." Mary's tone didn't hold the incredulity Piper was feeling.

Piper waved the statement away. "That's ridiculous. Why would he do such a thing after all this time?"

"Because he knows a catch when he sees one," Mary said, "but you dumped him."

Warmth touched Piper's cheeks. "I did not 'dump him,' and I'm hardly a catch." She rubbed her temples, then looked at Joseph. "Should I be worried?"

"I don't think so. The detective I spoke with said both young men now understand how serious their actions were and that you could press charges."

She put a hand to her stomach. "Did he—they—damage the store too?"

He shook his head. "Apparently they have air-tight alibis. The detective told me they're homing in on a couple of guys suspected of random break-ins locally and in nearby counties, so it seems you were just an easy target."

Piper looked past him to the new and secured patio door that looked a bit like Fort Knox with dead bolts and security wiring. Finn had suggested she go with a single door and overhead, half-moon window instead of replacing the French doors, to make the store more secure. Good decision.

She released a short breath, hands on her hips. "This wasn't at all what I expected, but I'm glad to have answers."

"If you press charges," Mary said, "that would tell him to back off and leave you alone."

She'd never thought she'd be a "press charges" kind of girl, but Ian had cost her a lot of money and clientele, her reputation, and many sleepless nights. "If he'll reimburse me for lost sales, I won't press charges."

"Piper—"

Her raised hand cut off Mary's protest.

Joseph studied her. "That might be enough to discourage him from any more behavior like this. I'll bring it up to the detective."

A strange lightness filled her chest, dissolving the dark questions that had haunted her since the fake agent's visit months ago. Ian would know now that she wouldn't be bullied back into that long-ago relationship. But let him get away with trying to destroy her dream? Too many people had helped her start and keep her business going. She wouldn't let them down.

CHAPTER 8

Finn turned from refilling the grinder and smiled. "Hey, Joseph! Great to see you." He reached across the bar to shake the older man's hand. "What brings you by the neighborhood?"

"Good news for your chocolate-making tenant and you, as well." He settled onto the stool, setting the folder aside. "Now I need a stiff drink. How about a cup of your strongest coffee?"

"Coming right up." Finn filled a mug and set it before Joseph. "What's the good news?"

"We caught the guys who were behind the fraud, and the cops have a solid lead on who did the break-in. Two different sets of people."

"That *is* great news!" He planted his palms on the bar. "Now tell me they'll all end up in jail."

Joseph took his first sip. "Woo. That's some strong coffee. Just what I need. Well, I suspect the thugs will be in prison for a long time, but the fraud guys won't be unless Ms. Devine changes her mind."

"She doesn't want to prosecute?" After all she'd been through?

"She requested monetary reimbursement. We'll see how that plays out." The corners of his eyes crinkled as he chuckled. "She's an amazing young woman."

Finn nodded. Piper was amazing, and he'd managed to scare her off. They chatted a few more minutes before Joseph headed to his next appointment and Finn went to his office. Dropping into his chair, he thumped his feet on the desk.

"Why isn't she prosecuting?" The silence didn't provide an answer. Financial reimbursement was a no-brainer, but to let them off with only that? He should talk to her, convince her the perpetrators needed to be taught a lesson so they didn't do the same to anyone else. Of course, he'd have to get her to speak to him again first.

He checked his phone, disappointed for the hundredth time that she hadn't responded. At lunch yesterday, Blake was surprised Finn didn't know she was wrapping up at the church and moving her equipment back to The Depot. In his gently direct way, he'd told Finn he'd be an idiot if he didn't pursue her. After Finn explained the awkward meeting when she'd seen him and Jodi going out, Blake had gotten that aha look on his face.

"You know what to do," he'd said, then changed the subject.

Finn leaned back in the chair with a sigh that burned with frustration. He'd understood her need to focus on making as much candy as possible, but when she didn't return his messages or answer his calls, it was clear where she stood. She had plenty of help getting back on her feet and didn't need or want his anymore.

"Fine. It's all fine," he grumbled, dropping his feet to the floor. He had plenty to keep him busy, like sorting through the paperwork piled on his desk. Starting at the top, he went page by page. Some he read and tossed; others went into the File bin. An hour later he'd made a good dent. He'd finish tomorrow. Shuffling the rest of the papers together, several smaller pieces fluttered to the floor.

"Hey, boss man." Jodi stood in the doorway. "Got a minute for an inventory question?"

"Sure. Let me pick this stuff up…" His voice trailed as he glanced through the papers. What the— Two were from Piper. No dates on them but clearly they were recent. One was a simple invite for taste testing at the church. His heart picked up speed. The other was a more formal invitation to a private party she was having at her store. Tomorrow!

He lifted his gaze to Jodi. "Did you put these on my desk?"

She stepped closer and glanced at them. "Nope."

"Did you know they were here?"

"I think I saw them, but they were right there, so I assumed you'd seen them too. With your filing system, or lack of," she added with an eye roll, "I'm not surprised they got buried. She didn't follow up with you?"

Finn studied her silently, pushing back a wave of anger. "No," he said finally. "What's your inventory question?"

They reviewed the report she'd brought in and briefly discussed where things stood for the Christmas event. When she returned to the bar, he turned his attention back to Piper's messages.

She *had* reached out. And no doubt thought he was upset or not interested. What a mess everything had become. Blake's words were almost audible. "You know what to do."

With sudden resolve, he nodded. Yes, he did. The rest would be up to her. Now to figure out the best approach.

"Slow down before you trip!" Mary's scolding held laughter.

"I can't help it!" Piper slid the last tray into the display case, then hurried around to study it from the front. "Isn't it pretty? I'm so happy I found GeeMaw's Spritz recipe. They look gorgeous right at the top, don't you think? And I love those darling boxes you found. They're the perfect size. I thought I might try another flavor—"

"Hey." Mary grasped Piper's shoulders. "Stop. Now breathe."

Piper closed her eyes and pulled in a deep breath, then another. The tension that had kept her wound up released like melted chocolate. "Okay. Yeah, that's good."

"You've been the Energizer Bunny for weeks. I'm afraid you'll crash before seeing the full results of that hard work." Mary turned her to face the store. "Take a moment to enjoy the fruits of your crazed labor."

"*Our* labor," Piper said, moving her gaze from the shelves re-stocked with gift items to the Christmas decor they'd found while shopping between the first and second coats of paint. It wasn't the same as before the break-in, but it was close. Better in a few ways.

The curtain they'd found on sale covered the patio door perfectly, adding a pretty flounce to that part of the room. She turned toward the display cases, three of the four now full, and they swam out of focus. For all of this to happen, God had to be in it. What that meant exactly she hoped to understand in the coming months. She blinked quickly against the burn in her eyes.

There were new photos on the walls—beautiful depictions of her finished products and of her in work mode. A hand pressed against her mouth, she looked at her bestie, and they burst into happy tears, falling into a joyous hug.

Completing the last items on her checklist, Piper hummed along with the Christmas music in the background. Tomorrow evening she'd host the tenant gratitude party. While Finn hadn't responded, the others had all given a resounding yes. With or without him, she couldn't wait to share the gifts she'd created for each of them.

After Christmas, she'd deal with her loaded credit cards, praying the insurance money would come through by then. For now, she would revel in the joy of new friendships and the inner strength that had grown these past weeks. She did indeed belong here among these amazing businesses. She could only hope Finn still thought so.

CHAPTER 9

Heart pounding, Finn entered the candy store, relieved Piper was not in the retail area. It gave him a moment to get a grip on his nerves. The store sparkled under Christmas lights strung around the room. Gifts lined the shelves, and the display cases were filled with an array of colorful treats. Instrumental music played softly in the background.

Piper emerged from the production room carrying a crystal pedestal plate with an ornate chocolate something on top. Her sudden stop when she saw him almost sent the large dessert off the plate. "Oh! Hi."

Standing in the middle of the store, Finn nodded. "Hi." He moved closer, hands in the pockets of his Dockers. "Is it okay for me to show up if I didn't RSVP?"

"Of course. I'm sure everyone expects to see you." She set the plate in the middle of the food table.

"Wow. That's amazing." As always, her creativity astounded him. "You did the decorating?"

"I did. I'm not the best at piping, but I'm getting better."

He studied the dessert. From the intricate icing bow on top to the tiny candy boxes gathered around the base, the treat sparkled with color and holiday joy. "You're the only one who thinks you aren't the best. I hear comments all the time about your beautiful decorating. This is your best work yet."

"Thank you. That's nice to hear." She straightened napkins and moved decorations an inch one way or another.

Finn cleared his throat. "I came early for a reason. If you haven't heard, we're hosting a community Christmas party here at The Depot on Friday to kick off your grand reopening."

Piper spun toward him, eyes wide. "But...you hadn't been planning anything before. Why now?"

"Because you deserve a truly *grand* grand reopening. You've been working nonstop to get the store back up and running, and I want to celebrate that."

Her chin quivered, and she pulled in a sharp breath. "Thank you. Still, to spend even more money when I've already cost you so much..."

"Well, that's true," he said.

She flinched and bit her lip.

"You *have* cost me a lot lately." He held up her messages. "I just found these yesterday. I didn't know you'd tried to get hold of me. So, you've cost me a lot of sleep, since I couldn't figure out why you've been avoiding me. And you've cost me hours of concentration because of the time I spend coming up with ways we can work together. And then, of course, you've cost me a lot of face time with my customers because I spend so much time here talking to you."

Her pinched brow softened as questions filled her eyes. She opened her mouth and Roberta's voice rang out.

"Hey, kids. Am I interrupting?" The realtor beamed at them from the doorway. "Looks like we're the first ones here for the shindig, hmm, Finn?"

He shot her a frown.

She winked. "Piper, hon, I think the store is even better now, and it was darling before."

The toy store owners joined them, followed by the flower shop manager, and the party was underway. Piper moved away from Finn without a backward glance, and he swallowed his frustration.

"Here you go." Roberta handed him a glass of punch, then leaned closer. "Sorry, but I couldn't un-interrupt once I was standing there. Looked like a serious conversation."

He took a swig of the fruity drink. "Yup."

"You know I've wanted you two to get together since I first met that sweet girl."

He nodded. He wanted the same thing, but he'd almost lost hope after the break-in. His gaze followed Piper as she moved among her guests, sharing hugs and laughter with each one. On impulse, he stepped into the middle of the room. "Welcome to Pip's Divine Chocolates," he said loudly.

The group quieted, turning toward him. He almost laughed at Piper's incredulous expression. "The reason I've called you all here..." He paused for the laughter. "Okay, seriously, I'm so glad

Piper provided this excuse for everyone to celebrate not only her grand reopening but also the success of pulling together as colleagues and friends after the break-in. You guys have been amazing.

"Before this party gets out of hand, I'd like to toast our hostess. Piper Devine, yours was the perfect business to complete this building. More importantly, you've been the perfect colleague and friend to all of us. I've watched you clear every hurdle thrown in your way, facing them with grace, grit, and determination." He lifted his glass. "I think I speak for all of us when I say here's hoping, *praying*, this next year brings the brightest success possible. You deserve it."

As the group raised their glasses and chimed in with "Hear, hear!" and "To Piper!" he met her tearful gaze across the room and winked. He'd managed to slip in the acknowledgment she deserved before she turned the focus of the evening on the people filling the store. He had a lot more to say, but it would have to wait. He hated waiting.

Piper laughed and hugged and chatted with her colleagues as the evening wore on, forcing herself not to keep looking for Finn. What he'd said before the party hadn't made sense—she'd cost him a lot, but mostly because he wanted to hang out here in the store? He hadn't gotten her messages until yesterday? She'd left them in plain sight. Of course, his desk was pretty messy. He wanted to work with her more but date his assistant? Not in her world.

Halfway through the evening, she rolled a cart to the center of the room, tingling with anticipation. She'd struggled to come up with something appropriate for each colleague, but without much time and with zero money, she'd been stumped. She hoped they liked what she'd finally landed on.

"If I could have your attention," she called, and the visiting quieted. "I have so much to say, but I know I'd cry through most of it, so I want to move right into the important stuff. My initial journey into retail has been interesting, to say the least. Once the store was up and running, I thought the worst was behind me."

"You thought wrong," Finn said with a grin.

She rolled her eyes. "Boy, did I ever. Now, though, because of all of you, I have the opportunity to start fresh and I am"— her voice cracked as tears welled— "so very, very grateful. You offered help physically to restore this space, and financially to restock the display cases. But most importantly, you offered friendship and support, which means more to me than you will ever know."

She swiped the wetness from under her eyes and took a deep breath. "Roberta, will you come here, please?"

Roberta moved forward and swept her into a warm hug, then stood beside her with lifted eyebrows, hands clasped in anticipation.

"There are twelve businesses up and down the halls here in The Depot," Piper said, "with Chocolate Brews being number thirteen and the anchor for all of us. Lucky for me, there are twelve months in a year. My math will make sense in a moment." The group chuckled. "Starting in January, I will feature each of your businesses for the month. I'll promote you in a number of ways including a spotlight in my newsletter, posters on the wall, and other marketing materials. And also..."

She handed a red-and-white chiffon bag to Roberta, encouraging her to open it and show everyone. Roberta carefully loosened the drawstring and lifted out a baseball sized chocolate truffle. A tiny Sold sign, copied from her actual realty signage, stood beside a tiny house, surrounded by swirls of piping in Roberta's favorite red and white. "Oh, my word! It's my own truffle! And look, the house is sold without me lifting a finger."

Piper smiled at the appreciative comments from the other tenants as they gathered around. "I'll feature a unique truffle every month decorated to represent your business. Each of you can pick the flavor you want for your month. Now, before you get so close you melt Roberta's chocolate, here are my versions of what each of your truffles could look like. I'm open to suggestions if you'd like something different. Cammie, you'll be February, since flowers are such an important part of Valentine's Day." She handed the floral shop owner a green chiffon bag.

She continued handing out the bags through the months to November, then paused to let everyone admire the decorated candy, a joyous ache in her heart. They seemed to genuinely like her idea.

"Okay, for December I have a treat for the Brews Crew owner and our esteemed property manager." She held up the tan chiffon bag and motioned Finn forward. She'd worked hardest on his, changing designs multiple times before asking Pastor Blake for ideas.

Finn joined her, his eyes sparkling with mischief. "I can't even imagine what this will be," he said, then turned to the group. "What do you guys think? A snow shovel? A cocoa mug? Light bulbs to represent all the ones I replace?"

They called out ideas—a train, a ledger, a ball and chain. He turned back to Piper, eyebrows raised. "Anybody even close?"

She laughed. "Nope."

He reached in and lifted out a white chocolate truffle, his smile fading. On top she'd created a tiny Bible and a gold key. Encircling the chocolate ball were delicately piped words. As the group crowded closer, he lifted an unreadable gaze to hers, and her heart skipped a beat. Maybe she should have done a train, like she'd first thought.

"The key represents The Depot," she explained, "and how, as the property manager, you've unlocked the potential of each of your tenants. The Bible represents your faith. While it's not something you proclaim in words all the time, we see it in how you treat your customers, your tenants, and the many visitors who come into The Depot. The words on there are things I've heard people say about you."

He read some of the words aloud. "Amazing. Reliable. Supportive. Fun. Encourager." His gaze moved back to hers. "Me?"

She nodded.

He offered a crooked smile. She couldn't read his expression or his silence. After a long moment, Eli from the staffing business said, "Wow. Finn McNally speechless. That's a first!"

Laughter erupted, as did color on Finn's face, and Piper released a sigh of relief. That her gift idea seemed to be so well received pushed aside the weight of repayment that she'd wrestled with since the break-in. These were her friends. She didn't have to repay them for acting out of kindness and compassion. It was what friends apparently did for each other. She was learning so much from all of them.

CHAPTER 10

As if having his conversation with Piper cut short by Roberta hadn't been bad enough, there wasn't another moment when Finn could catch Piper alone. He'd been running like crazy to finish the final details for The Depot Christmas party, and she'd had a long line of customers since her soft opening on Monday. The few times they'd passed in the hallway, she'd smiled shyly but kept chatting with whoever she was with. Was that good? Or was she making sure she wasn't alone in case he brought up her debt again?

Friday arrived sunny, bright, and not as freezing cold as it had been, perfect for an outdoor Christmas party. He made the rounds through the building, checking with each business to see if they were ready. Spirits were high as they shared their plans for welcoming the community, giveaways they'd prepared, and treats they would offer. By the time he headed to Piper's store, their excitement had rubbed off on him.

He entered the crowded chocolate shop and paused to enjoy the aroma and the buzz of conversation. Piper stood behind one of the display cases, offering a sample to a customer. Her gaze touched his, and pink filled her cheeks. He hid a smile. That had to be good. Right? A moment later she joined him near the door.

"Looking for something special?" she asked, hands behind her back.

"Not anymore. I've found everything I was looking for right here."

The color on her face deepened, but before she could respond, a woman's voice interrupted them. "Excuse me. Do you have any more of these candles?"

"I'm happy to check." Piper looked at Finn with an apologetic lift to her brow. "To be continued?"

Her simple question calmed his frustration, and he nodded. "Tonight."

The smile that broke across her face as she turned away gave him hope. Humming the tune he'd heard in her store, he returned to his café. A glance out the front windows made him pause mid-step. A large, green sleigh with red trim was sitting just off the front walk, a bulging burlap bag on the seat. Mike had come through again. Santa Mark would no doubt be delighted.

As dusk settled over Lakeville, Finn made sure all of the outside Christmas lights came on, then greeted his musician friends from Grace Church and showed them where to set up in the lobby. The bonfire, monitored by the fire chief, lit the night sky and the faces of people gathered around it.

Standing on the expansive front step of The Depot, Finn laughed out loud when Santa Mark strolled up the sidewalk in his Christmas finery, the red hat sitting at a jaunty angle on his head.

Instead of a reindeer, he was accompanied by his trusty old mutt, Jabba, who hobbled up the steps to Finn.

"Hey, old boy." Finn gave the dog a solid pat. "You behaving yourself?"

"Ho, ho, nooo," Santa Mark replied. "Unless you count chewing a hole in one of my boots behaving."

"Jabba, you did that?" Finn leaned down and whispered loudly, "Good job."

"Hey, he doesn't need encouragement. They were sort of my favorite boots. Now, do you want me outside in the sleigh or inside somewhere?"

"Will you be warm enough out here? We can move the sleigh a little closer to the bonfire."

Together they positioned it to provide warmth for Mark, then cheered when local farmers Bob and Nancy approached leading a reindeer.

"Rudy loves attention," Nancy said, "so we figured this would be a good way for him to get some love."

"He's the perfect addition to our setup. Thanks!" Finn left Santa Mark chatting with the couple and jogged into the building. The hum of voices and laughter in Chocolate Brews made him smile as he threaded through the crowd to his office. Before the evening ended, he had one more thing to do.

Once the Christmas party ended, the building emptied, and her store was back in order, Piper pulled out the pan of brownies she'd baked that morning. Far too wired after the fun and chaos to go home, she'd get some decorating done first.

Thirty minutes later she put the final flourish to the frosting and stepped back to admire her handiwork. It was actually fun doing more complicated patterns now. She smiled as she washed out the icing tips. GeeMaw had always gushed about Piper's knack for flavors, but she was disappointed that Piper hadn't inherited her flair for design.

"At least it's better than passable," she said.

"What is?" Finn's voice came from behind, and she spun around.

"Are you going to do this forever?"

He chuckled. "I just might if I keep getting reactions like that."

She shook soapy water off her hands at him before turning back to the sink. "I'll have to figure out how to put a bell on your shoes."

"That would be pretty festive this time of year. How did tonight go for you?"

"It was wonderful. With Christmas only a week away, I wasn't sure how many people would come, but I think half the town showed up." She dried her hands and faced him. "Everyone seemed happy to be out visiting and doing last-minute shopping."

"What'd you think of Santa Mark with his real reindeer?"

She smiled fondly. "He's such a great guy. The kids loved him, although they might have loved Rudy more." She'd stolen a few minutes to step outside for a deep breath and ended up having a lovely chat with Mark. And with Mary, who stood beside the sleigh smiling brightly. "I don't know how you did it, but the whole event was a fabulous success. From my perspective, anyway."

"The idea was a lot simpler in my head, but everyone jumped in to help plan and make it work."

"You're someone people like to rally around. The Pied Piper of Lakeville."

He laughed. "No, that'd be you. Look how you rallied The Depot tenants."

His praise warmed her, while his presence sent a tingle along her arms. "Finn, I really appreciate you setting the event up with my reopening in mind, but if you do this for all your tenants, you'll go bankrupt."

"True." He leaned back against the stainless table and folded his arms. "So, it's a good thing I only do it for you."

He was standing too close, sending her insides into a jumbled knot. She covered the bars and slid them into the refrigerator, then busied herself cleaning the workspace. Anything to stay focused elsewhere.

After a prolonged silence, he said, "We've started several conversations over the past few days that we haven't had a chance to finish. I don't like loose ends, so I'd like to wrap things up."

"Okay." Both conversations had left her confused, hopeful, and sad. He didn't seem to want to boot her business out, but he'd said she had cost him so much.

"You should never play poker." His comment interrupted her racing thoughts. "Every possible emotion just moved across your face."

She set the rag and spray bottle aside and turned resolutely toward him. Might as well get it over with. "How would you like to finish those conversations?"

He chuckled. "Cut to the chase. Got it. Okay. The other day we were talking about how much you've cost me these past months."

"Yes, we were." The one debt she couldn't repay. "I didn't have a chance to apologize for being such a pain, so I'd like to do that now."

He waved a hand in dismissal. "Don't bother. The debt is too great for a simple apology."

"Oh." Her heart slammed against her ribs. "Do you want a cut of my profits? Would that help?" She'd never get ahead at this rate. Or be able to break even.

"What? No!" He shook his head. "Piper Devine, you are something else. I have a plan for repayment, and it starts this weekend." He pushed away from the counter and faced her, making her feel small and insignificant under his gaze. "We'll start with dinner tomorrow evening at Manny's. I'll pick you up at 6:30."

Without waiting for a reply, he continued. "Then I have a bunch of gifts for my nieces and nephews, so you can help me get those wrapped on Sunday."

She tried to blink clarity into the chaos in her head. Did he want her to work off some of the debt? "I don't understand. You want me to pay for dinner?"

With an exasperated snort, he put his hands on his hips. "You're determined to make this as hard as possible, aren't you?"

"No." She had no clue what was happening. "At least, not on purpose." Her throat knotted, and she willed the tears back.

"Piper, I'm asking if you'll have dinner with me, and then hang out with me while I wrap presents on Sunday."

Her mouth dropped open. A date? An image of him and his assistant dressed up for their night out flashed before her. She snapped her mouth shut and lifted her chin. "I don't date people who are already in a relationship."

"The only relationship I have with Jodi is professional. We met as baristas at another coffee shop about five years ago. She's got a great head for business, she's a go-getter, and she's my friend." His intense gaze locked on hers. "But we are not now, nor have we ever been, a couple. I went with her to the wedding as a favor, since she didn't have a date. She's my right hand in Chocolate Brews, but it's strictly business."

"Oh." Not only was he not dating Jodi, he was asking *her* out!

"You and I also have a professional relationship," he said, "but I'd like to see it go a lot deeper. Piper, will you have dinner with me?"

It was really, truly happening. Her heart danced in sweet relief. "I thought you'd never ask."

His frown relaxed into the most gorgeous smile she'd ever seen. "I'm not very good at the dating scene," he admitted. "Blake told me I'd be an idiot if I didn't ask you out. I'm hoping this is the start of an amazing partnership—you, me, and God."

"Me too," she said. She'd already gotten the impression God was going to be a big part of her life going forward. Having Finn guide her along that new path was comforting. And exciting.

Finn looked up at the ceiling overhead. "Well, would you look at that?"

She followed his gaze and giggled at the sprig of mistletoe stuck to the ceiling, her cheeks warming.

He stepped closer and held his hands out. Long, warm fingers wrapped around hers, sending warmth up her arms. "Do you know the tradition of mistletoe?"

Every nerve tingling, she shook her head.

"Way back, men were allowed to steal a kiss from any woman standing under it."

"Oh, really?" She looked up at him with a raised brow, her heart spinning. "What if the woman declined?"

"Oh, it was considered bad luck." A smile tugged at the corners of his mouth as he moved even closer. "Very, very bad luck."

It was getting hard to breathe. "Well, I don't need any more of that."

His green eyes, sparkling with the mischief she'd come to love, held hers for an interminably long moment. When his lips met hers, she slid into his embrace and sent a prayer of thanks to the heavens. The sweetest thing in her life was no longer chocolate—it was this man who exuded strength, faith, and calm. Her sweet dream had come true in the form of Finn McNally.

A NOTE FROM STACY

After four years of caregiving for my husband, to have the ability and desire to write once again, along with the excitement of creating characters and new worlds, is an amazing, unexpected gift. Thank you, Sweet Jesus, for allowing me to serve you and the Kingdom once again in this way.

I'm currently working on book 2 of the My Father's House series – *"When Valleys Mourn"*. I'm excited to continue the story of the Gordon sisters and their search for answers about their family history. Watch for the release spring 2025!

Thanks so much for staying on this journey with me. I pray for all of my readers and thank God for being allowed to share my love for Jesus and my desire for all to know Him through my stories.

Blessings,

Stacy

About Stacy Monson

Stacy Monson is the author of the award-winning Chain of Lakes series and is a founding member of The Mosaic Collection. She lives outside the Twin Cities metro area with 15 chickens, an old dog, and lots of wildlife (which includes 7 grandchildren).

Learn more at www.stacymonson.com

Titles By Stacy Monson

Stories that reveal an extraordinary God at work in ordinary life.

THE MOSAIC COLLECTION: NOVELS
My Father's House Series
When Mountains Sing

When Valleys Mourn (Spring 2025)

THE MOSAIC COLLECTIONS: ANTHOLOGY STORIES
"Mountaintop Christmas" in *Hope is Born*

"A Summer of Reckoning" in *Before Summer's End*

"The Sweetest Sound" in *Song of Grace*

"Whispered Miracle" in *A Whisper of Peace*

The Chain of Lakes series
Shattered Image

Dance of Grace

The Color of Truth

Standalone
Open Circle

Unremarkable Sue

ELEANOR BERTIN

Unremarkable Sue

Eleanor Bertin

Fresh out of high school, Sue has no plans for college, no full-time job, no boyfriend, no life. All she hopes is that her future includes Glen, the son of her dear friend, straight-laced Mrs. Evelyn Hardy. When a crisis hits the Hardy family, the value of the girl they've taken for granted for years comes clear.

CHAPTER 1

"I hope she will prove a well-disposed girl," continued Mrs. Norris, "and be sensible of her uncommon good fortune in having such friends."
~Mansfield Park, by Jane Austen

1980

Sue Roundell bopped and hummed along with the radio while she cleared the noon rush tables in the empty diner. *"Gonna hear some funky disco, Langford—"* Good thing the clink of dishes and the whirring of the café overhead fans drowned out her singing. Who was Langford? No idea, but the Doobie Brothers sure could get a girl moving.

She had more reasons than just the singable Doobies to feel good this afternoon. As soon as VeraLyn came in to take over the supper shift, Sue had four days off to look forward to. More than that, her friend Mrs. Evelyn Hardy had invited her out to the farm for a couple of days until her next shift at the café. Sue never went out there without being invited, but she was invited often, even after her friendship with Myra Hardy had cooled to next to nothing. Through high school, Evelyn had frequently invited Sue for dinner after church, obviously hoping she would be a good influence on Myra. This made for some awkward Sunday afternoons.

"I would appreciate a helping hand during the busy harvest season," Evelyn had said the last time Sue was there. "As you know, my girls are no longer home to help." The corners of her mouth had tightened. "You may sleep in Myra's room."

The sight of the older woman trying so hard to put on a brave face after Myra's departure wrenched Sue's heart. One morning, directly after graduation, Mrs. Hardy knocked on her daughter's bedroom door to wake her and discovered her bed empty. Empty, but for a note saying Myra was sick of living a lie and needed time to find out who she was without religion continually crammed down her throat.

Myra's brother, Glen, quoted the note verbatim when he gave Sue the news at church the next day. "'Sick of living a lie.' As if. The Kid's got some nerve, hurting Mother and Dad this way," he said with a snort and an angry scowl. "Betcha ten to one she'll be back in fall just in time to collect her education fund. Selfish little twit. Good thing you two aren't friends anymore."

In another way, Myra's departure was a relief for both Sue and the older woman. Now that her former friend was no longer present to mock her with Suzy Homemaker taunts, Sue felt free of the burden of trying to smooth over Myra's animosity toward her mother. A weight of worry seemed to have lifted from Mrs. Hardy's knobby shoulders, too.

The other advantage was that, with Myra away and his older sisters moved out, Glen and Sue were the only two young people left. Sue had spent more time at their place than at her own home this summer.

Thinking of Glen put a smile on her face. She dumped a handful of soiled cutlery into a gray plastic bin, singing along with a Fleetwood Mac tune. Unlike Myra, who had become a shameless flirt in the last couple of years of high school, Sue wouldn't be caught dead throwing herself at a guy. At the diner, the other waitresses made more in tips by flirting, but Sue couldn't bring herself to do it. What kept her from stooping that low was the dignity and self-respect Evelyn Hardy had instilled in her. Still, Sue wasn't above enjoying the time she and Glen got to spend together.

Now, as she worked her way to the last table in the row of booths, a bent piece of paper sat in the centre, propped against the saltshaker. When she snatched it up, coins clattered, and a few dollar bills fluttered. Sue read the scrawled message while gathering up the tip with one hand.

Great service. Your cute. Call me sometime.

She rolled her eyes. Like she was going to chase after some guy who couldn't spell. Not only that, he didn't even have the nerve to speak to her in person. Or leave his name. Another meathead like the rest of the guys who made passes at her. She stuffed the note and the money into her pocket before stacking the dishes in the bin and wiping down the table. Humming along with the Top 40 hits on the radio, she worked on cleaning until VeraLyn, the other waitress, burst through the rear entrance, letting in a welcome breeze. Sue wheeled her trolley back to the kitchen where she emptied her pocket into the tip jar, then started scraping plates.

VeraLyn hung her jacket and washed her hands before tying on her apron. Heading to the fridge, she paused to peek into the tip jar. "What's this?"

Trust VeraLyn to home in on the counter where the crumpled note still lay next to the tip jar. She smoothed out the words, then smirked. "Let me guess. You're not going to call him."

"Not interested."

VeraLyn's lip curled as she waved the page at Sue. "Was he cute?"

Sue rolled her eyes and turned back to loading the dishwasher. "I seem to attract all the wrong kinds of guys." She could have added, *and never the one I really want to notice me.*

"You're way too picky." VeraLyn grabbed several bags of fresh vegetables and patted Sue's shoulder as she passed by on her way to the prep counter. "Like, going to prom alone because the guys that asked you weren't up to snuff. What are you waiting for, anyway? You don't wanna end up like me—in my forties and everybody decent is already taken."

Sue concentrated on her work without answering, though she glanced at the clock with its coating of greasy dust atop its rounded plastic dome. She kept meaning to do something about that. Mrs. Hardy would be aghast. Why not now? Half an hour until her shift was done. She would have a couple of hours once she got home to shower and get herself ready before Glen picked her up to take her out to the farm. Again, a smile worked its way onto her face as she unfolded the step stool and reached for the clock. Looking down, she found VeraLyn staring at her.

"What are you grinning about? You got plans for your days off?" The woman could suck the truth out of a Soviet spy.

"Going out to the Hardys' to help out." Sue lifted the clock off the wall and brought it down to scrub it clean.

"You beat all, you know that?" VeraLyn paused, one hand on her ample hip. "Why a cute, young chick like you wants to go hang out with old farm people is beyond me. You should be out with kids your own age, having fun."

Sue blushed, feeling defensive. "I like them, okay?" She wiped the wall and rehung the clock, unwilling to mention Glen to VeraLyn, who would be sure to tease and pressure her unmercifully.

"Whatever." VeraLyn turned to squint at the board listing the menu specials for the week. "Do you mind grabbing me another bag of carrots from the cold room?"

Sue wiped her hands on a towel and hurried off to the storage room she'd recently reorganized. It still gave her pleasure to be able to walk straight to the freezers or cold storage area without the obstacle course of buckets and boxes of supplies in the way.

When she first started working for Mel Duthie in the summer after tenth grade, the diner's inefficiency and disorganization was hard to miss, but she wouldn't have dared offer suggestions. Over time, however, she'd gotten bolder, straightening the cleaning supplies closet, finding faster ways to bus tables, and even taking the initiative to toss the unused, cracked dishes that were taking up prime shelf real estate. Mr. Duthie hadn't noticed, but VeraLyn mentioned the improvements to him, and he raised her wage to four dollars an hour. She began looking for other ways to perk up the place. Posting the written list of weekly specials was one of her innovations. Anything she'd accomplished here she had learned by watching Evelyn Hardy. Certainly not from her own mother, whose idea of cooking was opening a can of Alphagetti. Was that why she liked hanging out at the farm?

She grabbed the bag of carrots as well as a box of chicken patties and the scissors VeraLyn would need to open the packages.

"Good thinking. Thanks." VeraLyn grabbed the scissors and set the goods on the stainless steel table. "Now, isn't it time you were out of here?"

"Right." Sue untied her apron and tossed it into the laundry hamper before lifting her purse off the hook near the back entrance. "See you next Wednesday. Have a great weekend."

Walking home to the tiny house where she and her mother had lived since they had moved here when Sue was eleven, VeraLyn's comments played in her head. Why *did* she spend every spare minute at the Hardys'? It wasn't only her long-time crush on Glen.

Mrs. Hardy fascinated her. Her certitude, her stability, her wise authority. Sue loved Evelyn Hardy with all her heart. Why?

When Sue was a flighty, foolish, easily swayed preteen, Mrs. Hardy had been patient. When she was a clumsy know-nothing, the older woman had educated her. When Sue was caught in wrongdoing, Mrs. Hardy had looked through the excuses and deception and forgiven her. Sue would never understand why Myra, with a mother like that, would have rejected her so blatantly, would have walked away from the faith.

The stale smell of tobacco smoke assaulted her nostrils on her arrival home. Sue tried not to feel irritated by the clutter and mess of the little house. Mrs. Hardy would never show annoyance the way Sue felt like doing. Mrs. Hardy would calmly tidy up. So that's what Sue did. Her mother would be home from work shortly after five, about the same time Glen would be showing up to take her to the farm. She swooped through the small front room, emptying the ash tray, straightening, tossing out trash, bringing dirty dishes to the cramped kitchen. She washed, dried, and put them away, cleared the counters, and wiped down the spilled tomato soup on the stove element.

Finally, with an undercurrent of excitement, she turned her attention to cleaning herself up. After showering and blow-drying her hair, she did it up in hot rollers, brushed on a touch of mascara and blush for that natural look, and began agonizing over what to wear. She was going there to work, but she still wanted to look good. Her green pleated skirt and short-sleeved cream blouse with the neck bow would be good for church on Sunday. Wistfully, Sue pulled out her new red jumpsuit. It looked so good on her but would only get ruined by dirt or grease if they were digging potatoes or frying doughnuts. She rehung it, then put a couple of pairs of jeans, T-shirts, and sweaters in her bag, along with other essentials.

When she turned around, Mom was standing in the door, lighting a cigarette. "Going somewhere, Susie?"

Sue stopped packing to face her mother, trying to keep a guilt-wince off her face as she explained. "Mrs. Hardy asked me to help out at the farm this weekend."

Mom took a drag that pulled her round cheeks into hollows. "I thought we could have a girls' night this weekend." Her eyes brightened. "*Charlie's Angels* is on. And after that is *Dallas*. Don't you want to find out what J.R. is up to? Plus, I bought your favourite snackies."

Sue tipped her head to one side, feeling lousy. "I already promised, sorry."

The corners of Mom's mouth tightened. "You're always going out there. This is the third weekend in a row. What about me?" She inhaled again, her eyes narrowing before she exhaled a cloud of blue smoke. "Besides, what do you want to hang around with old people for? You should be out having fun with kids your own age."

Sue stifled the urge to point out that her mother had just suggested she spend the weekend hanging out with her—also an old person. But Sue felt guilty enough even without her mom's wounded tone. She promised her mother she would carve out some time for the two of them to watch their favourite shows next time she had days off. Glancing out the window to the street in front, she watched for Glen's old green truck.

From the corner of her eye, she caught the heavy steps of her mother's disappointment fading from the room.

CHAPTER 2

He was not pleasant by any common rule: he talked no nonsense; he paid no compliments; his opinions were unbending, his attentions tranquil and simple.
~ *Mansfield Park,* by Jane Austen

Glen stashed his lunch box behind the seat of his 1970 GMC pickup and hopped inside. His mother had asked him to stop by Sue Roundell's house and bring her home. When he fired up the old beast, the radio came on to a Top 40 station.

He swung around the corner from the seed plant where he worked and down the street of small, shabby houses where Sue lived. She must have been watching for him because he'd barely pulled to a stop when the front door flung open and she hurried down the sidewalk, trundling a stuffed duffle bag on one shoulder.

He got out to help her heft it into the box of the truck, then opened the door for her. "You're in a good mood."

She smiled at him, a smile that surprised him by what it did to his insides. *C'mon, she's your kid sister's friend, barely out of high school.* He hid his response by circling around to the driver's door and hopping inside. Putting the truck in gear, he started down the street toward the highway.

"Next up," the radio DJ was saying, "we've got the Bee Gees with 'Stayin' Alive.'"

"Oh, can I turn it up? I love this song."

"Go ahead." Glen wasn't much of a Bee Gees fan, but he kept time, tapping on his leg.

Sue nodded and grooved to the music, singing, *"You can tell by the way I use my wok, I'm a walrus man, no time to talk."*

He turned to gape at her, laughing out loud.

"What?" she asked, her eyes all innocent.

"Are you serious? Walrus man?" He pulled his gaze back to watch the road, slapping the steering wheel and chuckling.

"Well, who knows what they're saying? Now hush and let me listen." She bounced to the beat, picking up the next lines. *"When I'm making a loaf, and I get hired, a cat get in, I need a trike."*

Unbelievable. Whether she was a certified dingbat or a comedian, his shoulders shook as he listened, fascinated as she invented an entire songful of bizarre lyrics. How different she was from his sullen kid sister. He missed the old Myra, the way she was before she got to be a boring, money-hungry flirt. But it was nice to have Sue around to tease.

Once they got to the secondary gravel roads, he slowed to a stop. "You ever learn to drive stick?"

Her clear blue eyes widened as she shook her head warily.

"Time you learned. Slide over here."

"Uh, okay."

Glen shut off the engine and got out the driver's door to let Sue take over. He came around and settled himself on the passenger side.

She gripped the steering wheel, eyeing the gearshift with a frown.

"Don't worry. It's easy. Just takes practice, is all." He pointed to the four pedals on the floor. "That far left one is the emergency brake. Ignore it for now. Next, you've got your clutch, brake, and accelerator. Step on the clutch before you start the engine. Go ahead and turn the key."

The engine roared to life. Sue frowned, concentrating. He made his instructions as simple as he could. For a first timer, she was doing alright, but with all the jerking and lurching his poor truck was subjected to, Glen was sure his brain was rattling loose. Still, they were short of help on the farm, and he figured they could use another driver over the next few days. Finally, she got the truck moving smoothly enough to reach a decent speed and let him relax a notch.

He cut off a yawn with his hand. "I'm kind of looking forward to getting back to school. Working full time and farming in the off hours is wearing me out."

Sue tossed her curls to glance at him briefly. "Will your boss let you have a few days off for harvest?"

"Yeah. I'll be home tomorrow and Monday. We've got John Flanders and his boy, Bruce, helping out this weekend so, as long as this weather holds out, we should get most of the crop off." He eyed her, trying not to stare at the gentle curve of her cheek. He'd always liked the clear and clean look better than Myra's goopy, made-up face. "So, how about you? Any plans for college?"

"Not really. For one thing, on my mom's bookkeeping salary, there's never been extra money." She shot a quick smile his way. "But it's okay. You can still keep learning outside of a classroom."

"True." He pointed ahead to the next turn, walking her through the steps of shifting down for the corner. The truck stalled, drifting, and she had to start over again. More pitching and heaving before they were off again.

Glen sat back in his seat as they picked up speed. "This summer, I've had a chance to think over my first two years of college and realized what I loved best was the studying. I'm starting to think what I'm cut out for is an academic career, teaching at a college somewhere." He watched the golden fields pass by his window for a half mile or so. "Which isn't at all what Mother wants for me. She's got it in her head I should be a missionary. But I'm not hearing that calling." He pulled his ball cap off and pointed it at the right turn ahead. "Engage the clutch and shift down."

Sue managed to shift to second gear, but they still took the corner at a terrific speed.

"Whew!" He ran his hand through his hair. "You might want to brake a bit more for the turns."

"Sorry," she said, accelerating and shifting up to third again, this time smoothly. She turned up the radio for an ABBA song. "Oh, I love this one."

He watched, amused, as her head started nodding in time to the beat.

"Watch her scream," she sang, *"kicking the dancing queen..."*

"You kill me!" Glen laughed.

At least she was keeping her eyes on the road. Finally, after only one more harrowing turn, she pulled into the Hardy farm.

Once they'd jerked to a stop in the shaded driveway, Glen explained the emergency brake to her, and she shut off the engine. They both leaned back against the seat, exchanging glances and laughing. Her cheeks were flushed with excitement, her eyes sparkling.

"Other than the corners, you didn't do too bad," he said, nodding approval at her.

"Thanks, I guess. I hope I don't have to do that again any time soon."

"Why do you think I taught you? We'll likely need you to shuttle us around from one field to another over the next few days."

She tipped her head back and gave a small moan but didn't protest.

CHAPTER 3

Fanny, being always a very courteous listener, and often the only listener at hand, came in for the complaints and distresses of most of them.
~Mansfield Park, by Jane Austen

While Glen lugged her bag into the house, Sue sat behind the wheel of the old truck for a few moments recalling her first visit to the Hardy farm. She'd been eleven years old and skittish as a barn cat about meeting Myra's formidable mother. By Myra's account, Mrs. Hardy was super strict, no nonsense, and humourless. But the woman had warmly welcomed Sue into their home and shaken her plump hand as if she were a distinguished guest.

Except for a bit more wear on the painted trim, the house remained much the same as it was seven years ago—a neat, classic, white two-story farmhouse that beckoned to her, inviting in its predictable orderliness and serenity. Only now, she knew its people and their hearts so much better. She knew Myra's chafing under the strictures of her upbringing and Glen's scholarly dreams.

She had noticed Mr. Hardy's reluctance to read the Bible or pray and observed Mrs. Hardy's knitted brows and murmured worries over her husband's spiritual state. Sue had noted Evelyn's prayer requests at church and knew her resistance to suggestions that Walter be put on medication for his depression. Weren't prayer and relying on the promises of God good enough, Mrs. Hardy had demanded.

Walter hadn't hidden his annoyance with Evelyn on account of her concern. "I'm every bit as much a Christian as she is, but sometimes I just don't have the gumption to show it," he had once wearily confided to Sue. "Only don't tell *her* that."

Over time, Sue had collected their secrets, reverently gathering them to pray about them, tending and guarding them in her heart.

Glen poked his head out the screen door, jolting Sue back to the present. She opened the truck door and climbed down. Evelyn's gladiolas were in full, glorious bloom, their extravagant reds, oranges, and deep pinks a flagrant blaze of colour next to the worn porch step Sue passed on her way to the front entrance.

"Planning to sit there all day?" He held the door, standing aside for her to enter. "See you later," he said as he strode down the step and hopped back into the pickup to take off down the driveway. Sue remained alone in the doorway, her senses left to cool after the heat of his presence next to her. As always, he'd been nice to her without a clue that she was any more to him than his sister's friend.

She hallooed the empty kitchen where the loud-ticking clock presided over a sink full of canning jars, a green mesh sack of corn cobs resting on the floor nearby.

"Welcome here, Susan." Mrs. Hardy emerged from the rear of the house, tying her apron behind her. Her face relaxed into a brief smile. "We are so grateful your mother could spare you."

A pang of guilt darted through Sue. It wasn't as though she had asked Mom.

The work began immediately and only let up at 9:00 p.m., once the last dish was washed and counter wiped down. The weekend flew by with husking, blanching, and freezing dozens of cobs of corn, preserving quarts upon quarts of dill pickles, and preparing meals for the harvesters. Evelyn was beginning to trust Sue in the kitchen. She let her handle most of the meal on her own.

Mr. Hardy surprised them all by participating in the fieldwork heartily, as though he had never spent hours staring sightlessly at the living room wall, the weight of the world stooping his lanky frame. Sue's heart warmed to see him coming in at the end of the day tired, hungry, yet with a light in his eyes. She felt Mrs. Hardy's quiet satisfaction at this development, too.

Mid-Saturday afternoon, Glen radioed to ask that supper be brought to the field. Evelyn was ladling salt and vinegar brine over jars filled with bright green mini cucumbers when the call came. Steam from the large cauldron had loosened white tendrils of the hair around her ears from her carefully pulled-back bun. She nodded at Sue. "You will have to do it. I simply cannot leave the stove with these jars still processing." She bobbed her chin at the microphone next to the two-way radio on the counter. "Ask him what field they're on and get directions."

Sue crossed the room to the end of the kitchen counter, her mind racing with the responsibility. She held down the button and said, "Sue here."

Glen's voice crackled through the speaker, giving rapid-fire directions to the south quarter section on the old McKnight farmstead. Sue scribbled down the route with growing misgivings. She'd done so little driving in the country and wouldn't know a section from a bushel, but she stuffed the note into her jeans pocket hoping for the best. Then she packed lawn chairs, dishes, serving utensils, napkins, and condiments into the pickup truck. She tucked towels as insulation around the food to be kept warm, wedged all the jars and pots and pie plates into the large wooden crates that Mrs. Hardy indicated and loaded them next to the other supplies. Finally, she brought out the cooler with salad and drinks.

She started the engine with a good deal of trepidation. All it would take was some wild lurching for that beautiful dinner to end up splattered across the inside of the truck box. She chanted the directions to herself down the three miles of road, turned right, and watched for the evergreens of an abandoned farm site. Feeling like it was a sort of test, she wanted to do this right.

At the approach to the field, she had a moment of doubt. No sign of the machinery Glen had said would be in view. She bumped across the stubble in low gear, scanning the horizon until she spotted a red grain truck next to the huge combine receiving a bronze stream of grain into its box. The combine operator motioned for her to park a short distance ahead of the truck, probably to avoid the grain dust blown by the wind. Sue managed to stop the truck in the spot indicated and breathed a relieved sigh. So far, so good. She stepped down from the pickup and paused in the dry heat for a second, enjoying the light cool breeze. The faint, nutty smell of wheat in the air was overpowered at times by the smell of diesel fuel. Coppery wheat poured out of the combine's augur in a magnificent rush that gleamed in the sunshine. Slippery stubble stalks underfoot, the deep blue of the sky—all of it struck her as overwhelmingly beautiful.

Glen stepped down from the grain truck as she was laying out the serving dishes on the tailgate of the pickup. With a sudden inspiration, she raised the container of rich, brown sauce at him and sang, *"You made the rice, I made the gravy."*

"Billy Joel would not be impressed, butchering his song that way," he said, shaking his head and grinning.

As the men gathered, Sue presided over the meal, serving out meat and potatoes, ladling gravy, serving ears of corn, and reminding everyone there was salad, pickled beets, fresh-baked rolls. Coffee? Lemonade? Which kind of pie—saskatoon, apple, or a little of each?

The workers munched in silence while Sue watched in satisfaction, jumping up to provide whatever they needed. Within twenty minutes, they gave her their thanks and compliments on the food, then returned to their machines, saying they aimed to finish the field before dusk. Sue gathered dishes, replaced lids on food, and repacked the gear in the truck. She sat in the cab finishing her own plate, knowing one thing for certain about her future. She was born for this life.

CHAPTER 4

*Till she had shed many tears over this, Fanny could not subdue her
agitation; and the dejection which followed could only be relieved by
the influence of fervent prayers for his happiness.*
~*Mansfield Park*, by Jane Austen

Throughout high school, Sue had had no clear direction for what
her future held, though her grades were usually above average. The
university or career plans of other girls failed to inspire her, and the
guidance counsellor's suggestions left her feeling inadequate.

Harvest had now come and gone, and Sue had picked up only
a few more shifts at the diner, but she didn't mind, and Mom was
content to have her at home. Her education under Mrs. Hardy,
especially over the past summer, though, had been priceless. Even
after Glen had returned to school, Sue had continued her visits.

She had discovered the vagaries (a word that Evelyn had used
and insisted Sue look up) of jam making. Pectin or none, jam or
jelly. There were differences, and a woman ought to know them.
Sue had learned, was still learning, the sensitivities of yeast and

the delicate temperate zone it required. "Just below the point of pain" evidently meant something altogether different to a seasoned baker's hand than it did to an inexperienced one like Sue's. At last, her dinner rolls had come out fabulously. Mr. Hardy had had two with his supper, which was saying something, given his half-hearted appetite.

Besides baking, learning the fine art of mending ("a stitch in time saves nine"), and the wisdom of waiting to dig the carrots until after a killing frost when they would be sweeter, Sue often simply sat with Mr. Hardy. She knew that Evelyn would have liked her to read to Walter, especially the Bible, but Sue sensed this would have smothered the poor man. He had his low times, what his wife called "the Slough of Despond," and Sue respected these seasons, instinctively knowing what he needed. The day the buns turned out so well, his gaze had met hers, and he'd surfaced out of his dark vortex just long enough to say, "You'll make someone a good wife someday." Then he'd continued slathering on the fresh plum jam. His rare praise made the heat rise in Sue's cheeks.

With time, Sue made herself indispensable to the Hardys. One day before she left town to come to the farm, Mrs. Hardy telephoned, asking her to pick up the mail from the post office and bring it to them.

Sue was happy to run such errands since the Hardys had graciously lent her the old green GMC while Glen was away at school. She'd become quite adept at shifting gears for corners. When she arrived at the farm, Sue held up the letter from Glen.

Evelyn had her hands in dough. She waved her sticky fingers. "Would you please read it to us?" She called toward the living room doorway, "Walter, come listen to what Glen has to say."

Slowly, Mr. Hardy shuffled to the kitchen table while Sue sat across from him and opened the envelope.

Dear Mother and Dad;

You're probably wondering if I've dropped off the face of the earth by now since you haven't heard from me in so long. Sorry about that. My only excuse is the workload. Let's just say it's a bit heavier than high school was, with a whole lot more writing. By the way, Mother, your being a stickler for spelling and grammar is standing me in good stead. I just wish I'd taken a typing course. It takes me forever to type my papers.

Thanks loads for the care package. Were you expecting a pipe bomb on the mail truck? The parcel was bundled up like the Crown jewels. Anyway, everything arrived in perfect condition. You can pass on my thanks to Sue as well, since you said she helped with the baking. Sadly, all the cookies and fudge got devoured in about two days and the guys on my floor are clamouring for more. Hint, hint.

Another reason it's taken me a long time to put pen to paper is that I've been doing some soul searching over the past few weeks. One of our chapel speakers challenged us with making every minute of our lives count. Along with a lot of the other guys in my dorm, I've come to the conclusion it's best if I stay single to serve the Lord the way He wants.

I'm amazed how freeing it is. No more checking out girls, no more angst over dating, no pressure to find "the right one." Instead, I'm simply focusing on my studies, waiting to discover whatever God's plan for me is.

With one more paragraph still to go, Sue faltered in the reading. Her grip on the paper tightened and she fought to bring her wavering voice under control. Evelyn's hands stilled in the large, yellowware dough bowl as she peered strangely at Sue.

Clearing her throat, Sue read the remainder of Glen's letter. He would not be home for Christmas this year but instead was heading for Mexico on a mission trip to renovate a seniors' facility. He did hope to be home during Reading Week next February.

Evelyn stopped kneading and straightened her back. "Well now. With both our older daughters working over Christmas, that will leave us on our own for the holidays."

"Unless Myra comes home," Walter murmured.

Evelyn frowned before silently continuing her kneading.

Sue folded the letter, struggling to set aside Glen's news until later, when she could sort out what she thought of it all. With a deep breath, she looked up and smiled at Evelyn. "What can I help you with today?"

A chill wind had begun to blow as Sue finished digging the last of the potatoes and lugging them down to the cellar that afternoon. She dumped them into the bin and shut the cold storage room door behind her before joining the Hardys in the kitchen.

"Thank you for your help, Susan." Evelyn glanced out the window. "And not a moment too soon. The forecast is for an accumulation of six inches tonight." She returned her gaze to Sue. "No doubt you will want to get home before dark. I have supper almost ready, so if you lay the table, we can begin momentarily."

Evelyn's devotional for the day spoke to Sue with a reminder to trust God even when things didn't turn out the way she hoped. After their prayer, Sue rose to clear the table.

As Evelyn was helping Walter back to his recliner in the living room, the phone rang. "Would you answer that please, Susan?"

Sue crossed the kitchen and picked up the receiver. "Hello?"

"Sue?"

"Myra! What a surprise!" Sue stretched the short cord of the wall phone to peek past the doorway to the living room. "Long time no hear."

"I'm surprised, too. What are you doing there?"

"Oh, this and that. I try and help wherever I can."

A pause in the conversation made Sue cringe. Myra's pauses meant only one thing—she was taking time to fit an arrow into her verbal bow. "I can't believe you. You must be nuts, wasting your life hanging around with old people."

Sue backed into the kitchen, afraid Mr. and Mrs. Hardy might hear their daughter's loud voice.

Myra talked on. "But I guess you always were the favourite. Anyway, it's just as well you answered. Listen, you can tell my folks I won't be home this Christmas. I have to work almost every day over the break."

"But your sisters won't be home for Christmas, either, and your parents just got word from Glen that he's not coming. Your mom will be so disappointed."

"I doubt it." Myra sniffed. "You'll let them know?"

"I guess so."

"Okay. See you around." Click.

Sue hung up and paused, watching the Hardys seated in the living room, listening to an evening radio sermon. It seemed a shame to add to their cares. Sighing, she headed toward them, ashamed to be bringing them the upsetting message from Myra.

CHAPTER 5

"I can never be important to anyone."
"What is to prevent you?"
"Everything. My situation—my foolishness, my awkwardness."
"... There is no reason in the world why you should not be important where you are known. You have good sense, and a sweet temper, and I am sure you have a grateful heart, that could never receive kindness without wishing to return it. I do not know any better qualifications for a friend and companion."
~Mansfield Park, by Jane Austen

1982

Glen read over his Greek-to-English translations on the final exam one last time before turning it in. He was unsure of several of the verbs, but he'd never done himself any favours by over-thinking. He left the lecture hall less than confident but relieved. That was a wrap for his second-last semester before graduation. He'd promised his parents he'd arrive the next day, home for Christmas for the first time in two and a half years. He'd spent last Christmas in Mexico and the previous summer in the Yukon satisfying his mother's craving for him to get a taste of cross-cultural missions. His mind hadn't changed. It still wasn't for him.

Back in his dorm room, Glen burst in on Kevin, one of his roommates, sitting on his bed, staring down at his hands with a lopsided smile.

"What's with the stupid grin?" Glen asked, stretching out on his top bunk and cupping his head with his hands. When Kev didn't immediately answer, Glen shot him a look.

Kev shrugged sheepishly and held up a small, open, blue velvet box.

Glen sat up, gawking at the sparkling diamond ring. "What's the deal with that?"

"Asking Karen to marry me. What else?" The hint of a smile still played at the corners of Kev's mouth as he snapped the velvet box closed.

Now it was Glen's turn to stare. "But what about our pact? What about staying single to serve God?"

"C'mon, man." Kev shrugged, laughing like nothing could touch his happy mood. "That was just a self-protective mechanism in case we didn't find someone. You know what the Word says. 'It is not good for a man to be alone...' Besides, Stephen and Doug went shopping for rings with me, too. They'll both be engaged by the time we all leave for the summer."

"The brotherhood is dropping like flies. The betrayal cuts deep!" Glen clutched his chest and flopped back onto his bed, only half joking.

He managed to offer congratulations to his three exultant buddies as he packed up his room that evening and loaded his belongings into his Honda Civic. Driving home the next day, he consoled himself with the thought of one more semester with the guys, but the strong sense of the end of an era hovered heavily upon him. Kev wasn't entirely wrong. The pact had served as a protection, at least for Glen, from the formidable task of finding a woman who would pass muster with Mother.

A blue dusk had crept over the landscape by the time he pulled up the lane leading home. No string of coloured lights festooned the porch eaves. Not even a porch light lit his way to the front door. He let the gloomy house swallow him whole, almost tiptoeing up the stairs with a suitcase and backpack to his old room. The silence and the dark were depressing. He had rarely returned home to find it so empty. After the tinsel and high spirits of the college cafeteria and common room, the lack of a Christmas tree left a forlorn vacancy. Downstairs, the porch door squeaked open. He trotted down to greet his folks.

But it was Sue Roundell. She let herself in as if she lived there, fumbling in her rush to unzip her knee-high boots. When she finally noticed him, she stopped short. "You're home!" Her forehead crinkled in concern, her eyes wild. "Listen, I've just come from the hospital. I didn't know what else to do—your mom asked me to take care of your dad for the day while she was at the ladies' sewing circle."

"What are you talking about? Since when does Dad need a babysitter? And what is it you've done?"

She gave him a look before hurrying toward the living room. "You haven't been around much in the last couple of years," she tossed over her shoulder. "You don't know how things have been."

He trailed her halfway up the stairs. "What do you mean, how things have been?"

She charged out of the bathroom clutching a razor, shaving cream, and deodorant in the crook of one arm. Next, she was in his parents' bedroom. Drawers were opening. He barged in as she was piling undershirts and socks onto her armload. "What's going on?"

She tucked the clothing and other items into a bag she carried under one arm. "I took your dad to the hospital. It was the only thing I could think to do. He's been doing poorly for months, but today, when I walked into the porch, he was handling a gun. I got scared. It looked like he might harm himself. I managed to coax him to the truck and—"

"Harm himself!" Now he was worried.

Sue was already out the bedroom door and heading down the stairs. "Yeah. So I got him to Emergency"—she turned back to face him—"and called your mom. Who is definitely going to kill me for getting him involved with a psychiatrist."

"Mm. You got that right." He flicked his chin at her bag. "What else does he need?"

"His healthcare card from his wallet. I'll get his meds." She crossed to the kitchen cabinet to the left of the sink. "And you'll come with me, right?"

"To the hospital?" He searched for his father's billfold in the basket of keys and vehicle registration folders on the counter near the door.

"To face your mother. I called her just after lunch once they admitted your dad, so she'll have arrived there by now."

"Ah, for moral support." He smirked, dropping the wallet into her bag. "Sure thing. Wouldn't miss it."

Sue drove the two of them to town in the old green GMC and managed rather well, he had to confess. "You've improved a lot since that summer I taught you to drive standard."

"Thanks."

He reached for the radio knob, but she stopped him with an outstretched hand.

"Just...don't. I can't handle that right now."

That was when he picked up on her concern. Her tension must mean she cared deeply about his father's well-being and not only about Mother's disapproval. "Did the hospital staff say what they thought the problem might be?"

She shot him a brief glance. "You know how it is. You don't get a clear answer until you talk to the doctor." As if she knew all the ins and outs of the medical system. As if she had her own ideas about his father's condition but was too discreet to offer the diagnosis.

Glen was beginning to see she'd been right. He didn't know how things had been here at home. Last spring, he'd left for a four-month volunteer trip up north directly after his last exams. Before returning in time to start the fall semester, he had met his mother only briefly at a restaurant. The odd weekends he'd been home, he'd failed to notice his father was any worse than usual.

To be listened to and borne with, and hear the voice of kindness and sympathy in return, was everything that could be done for her.
~Mansfield Park, by Jane Austen

Evelyn Hardy was not angry with Sue. She felt, in fact, too weary for anger or any strong emotion. For years now, Walter's deteriorating mental health had been pulling them both slowly, relentlessly down into a quagmire of shared misery. An eruption of some sort seemed inevitable. Evelyn felt almost too tired to care.

The call from the hospital, therefore, had not surprised her. What had come as a surprise was that little, unassuming Susan had been the one to wrangle the unbudging Walter into the hospital. What would she do without Susan? The girl had turned out to be an unexpected yet unmitigated blessing. With her, Evelyn believed she could face whatever might come.

At one time, Evelyn might have been ashamed that her family was reduced to seeking the world's solutions for her husband's dark nights of the soul rather than relying on God alone. Now she was long past resisting any help from professionals. All her prayers and efforts with Walter had failed. Despite her despair, she was profoundly relieved to now hand over the load to others.

CHAPTER 6

*She was of course only too good for him; but as nobody minds having
what is too good for them, he was very steadily earnest in the pursuit
of the blessing...*
~*Mansfield Park,* by Jane Austen

Two days later, Glen and Sue entered the large psychiatric hospital
an hour from their hometown. Glen, who worked at his old job
for the day to pull in a few extra dollars, had brought Mother there
in the morning to spend time with Dad. After work, he picked up
Sue who wanted to see Walter again. They met Mother and Dad
in his ward room and followed his father as he shuffled alongside
the nurse to one of the family lounges. A guy could almost lose
his balance doddering at that pace. "Smoke on the Water," the
old Deep Purple song, popped into Glen's mind. Recalling Sue's
penchant for misheard lyrics, he leaned over and sang quietly into
her ear. *"Slow-walkin' Walter..."*

She pulled away abruptly, making Glen ashamed of himself.
"Sorry."

"I'm sorry, too." She grimaced. "It's just that I've never seen him so bad." She cleared her throat, then whispered. "Makes my heart hurt."

Once they got his father seated in a recliner, Glen was surprised to see Sue sit on the arm of Walter's chair and begin gently stroking his hair. None of Glen's sisters would have ever felt so free. But Dad closed his eyes, apparently content with the attention. How did she *do* that?

His mother entered the room after her brief consultation with a nurse. She gave a quick shake of her head when Glen sent her a questioning look. They were waiting on word about whether Dad would be able to come home for Christmas.

Walter's blank, unresponsive stare made for a rather silent, short visit. Before driving home, Glen first dropped Sue off at her house in town. He and his mother had been out all day and, for different reasons, they were dead tired.

When they turned into the lane, the twinkle of multicoloured lights beckoned them home. He glanced at his mother. "When did you find time to put those up?"

She turned toward him in wonder. "I thought you must have done it. But if not you, then who?"

"Sue. Susan," they said in unison.

The fragrance of shortbread and pine met them when they entered the house. From the door, the sparkle and shine of a small Christmas tree glittered from the front room window. The outline of a few gifts lurked beneath it. He half-expected choirs of angels to burst into joyful song.

"The dear girl. She has used all my old decorations, but the effect is... so different." An odd wobble sounded in Mother's voice.

"Okay if I have one of these?" Glen had a shortbread cookie poised at his mouth.

...and it was not possible that encouragement from her should be long wanting.

~Mansfield Park by Jane Austen

The doctor signed Dad's release the day before Christmas Eve. Glen drove his silent parents home, his grim mood lifting when he saw Sue's old pickup in the driveway. He parked as close to the front door as he could.

"Watch your step," he said, helping his father out of his small car. "The fresh snow is going to make things slippery." The three of them made their slow way into the house as a few feathery flakes still fell.

Glen grabbed the push broom to clear the fluff off the sidewalk and Sue's truck. The air was fresh with the cold and the stillness peaceful, but he looked forward to Sue's company over dinner. Mother and Dad weren't exactly lively fellowship these days.

Finishing the task, he propped the broom against the house and entered the porch, leaving his coat on a hook and his boots beneath it. He slipped into the kitchen, surprised to find it empty, though the savoury aroma of something beefy came from the oven.

Murmured voices from the living room made him pause out of their sight. Sue was saying goodbye to his parents.

"Will you not stay until Glen comes in?" his mother asked. "You should join us for the supper you have gone to the trouble to prepare."

No answer came from Sue, but perhaps she made a facial expression because Mother's next words surprised him. "I am aware you have feelings for him. You have my word I will not embarrass you."

Another murmur and the rustle of an embrace. "Thanks for the invitation," Sue was saying, "but I'll come visit again in the new year. I'm not all that interested in pairing off. What I've been learning is that being single gives me a lot of freedom to serve the Lord. Now, I promised my mom I'd spend more time with her while she's off work for the holidays, so I should get going. You folks have a wonderful Christmas."

Her quick steps brought her to the kitchen. Glen stood frozen to the floor, unable to think of a thing to say. She gave a little gasp at the sight of him, flushed. Then, head down, she made a beeline for the door.

Dazed by what he had overheard, Glen stepped into the living room. Mother and Dad looked up, wearing identical frowns.

Evelyn's eyes widened. "You've been eavesdropping?"

Walter sat up straighter. "Don't be a fool, boy. Go after that girl. She ought to be part of this family."

Glen looked to his mother to protest as she always had at any hint of matchmaking. She did nothing of the sort.

"You heard your father. The girl is a national treasure." She tilted her head at the door. "Off you go, then."

Scarcely realizing the momentous step he was taking, Glen grabbed his jacket and made for the door. Sue had feelings for him? He cursed himself for a witless moron. His pace increased when he got outside, finding Sue had reached the old pickup and was opening the driver's door. "Wait!" he called, hurrying toward her.

She turned back, her red-mittened hand still on the door handle. Glen stopped, taking in the festive picture. Sequins of snowflakes sparkled on her red tam and scarf, bright against the faded green of the truck, cheeks rosy where the frosty air had kissed them—how had he never realized how beautiful she was?

With his eyes fixed on hers, he loped forward. The look on her face told him all he needed to know. She had feelings for him, his mother had said.

His father had practically pushed him on the girl, his mother's exacting standards were more than satisfied in her, and his own vague notions of a celibate future had abandoned him with the revelation that she felt something for him. By the look on her face, he figured she had meant all that rot about staying single as sincerely as he had meant that misguided letter to his parents two years ago.

More misheard lyrics sprang into his head. *"Young and sweet, only seven teeth..."* He drew near to her, chuckling.

Her eyes sparkled like the diamond in Kev's blue velvet box. "What?" she asked, lips parted, ready to smile.

EPILOGUE

How wonderful, how very wonderful, the operations of time, and the
changes of the human mind!
~*Mansfield Park,* by Jane Austen

2009

Glen's tie pressed against the lump in his throat as his gaze
followed Sue moving about the crowded church hall after dinner
in her floaty, pale blue dress. Dinner was over, embarrassing slide
show finished, humourous and sentimental speeches by their kids
complete, yet Sue was still hugging old friends, pressing a hand
here, offering a word of encouragement there.

What would he be without her? He shuddered to think. Nor
could he kid himself. It may be their twenty-fifth wedding an-
niversary, but all these people—weren't they really here for Sue's
sake? His throat lump thickened. The giggly, clumsy kid who
had become a fixture at the Hardy home ever since his sister had
brought her home from school had blossomed into— Now Glen's
eyes began to swim. All that she meant to him thundered through

his mind with an accompanying shame. When was the last time he had paid tribute to her, wife of his youth, lifeblood of his heart, custodian of his soul? He cleared his throat and picked up the microphone.

"Folks...folks, can I ask that you find a seat for just a bit more of your time?" He beckoned everyone back to their chairs. While they settled, he asked the servers to refill the punch glasses. Then he picked up the goblet next to his plate. "Sue and I are grateful to each one of you who came to celebrate with us today. No one stays married without a community's love and support." He smoothed a wrinkle in the white cloth covering the table in front of him.

"I have more reason than anyone for gratitude. Somehow, through no deserving of my own, God has blessed me with a wife who has exceeded every expectation I could have had. She has always been there with a smile of encouragement and a listening ear, a hot meal or a tasty treat, making our house a home, putting me and our four kids ahead of herself, making me look better than I am. And all of this without expecting thanks." He looked down at Sue who was blinking back tears and, again, something clogged his throat.

"Will you join in me in a toast to honour Susan Hardy, a woman of inestimable worth, whose price is far above rubies." He motioned to have the guests stand, then raised his glass toward his wife. "To you, my lovely Sue, a rare and most remarkable woman."

A Note From Eleanor

Dear Reader,

Many fictional heroines are larger-than-life –witty, bold, and brilliant. They are strong women, high achievers, recognized and celebrated. But I wanted to feature a character whose lifelong ambition was to play second-fiddle, someone quietly and contentedly in the background, someone like Fanny Price in Jane Austen's *Mansfield Park*. I re-read that great novel and fell even more in love with Fanny.

An early reader of my novel, *Flame of Mercy,* called Lynnie's mom, Sue Hardy, a "bland character." I had to agree. Sue was there, but in the background, nondescript. Her calm presence in a home where a grim woman like Grandma Hardy loomed so large needed an explanation. How could such a mother-in-law be borne by any young woman? My award-winning story "Christmas at the Crossroads" in Mosaic's 2022 *Whisper of Peace* Christmas anthology has already revealed the background of their relationship. Now, I wanted to tell the love story between Sue and her husband, Glen.

I hope you enjoyed my "modernization" of Fanny, the famously shy Austen character, and have had some of your questions answered about Sue from *Flame of Mercy* and *Flicker of Trust.*

Your friend,
Eleanor Bertin

Acknowledgments

The Mosaic Collection is a treasury of books but, more importantly, a collection of women of faith. We inspire and encourage one another in our walk with Jesus, but also in the art of writing. I wonder what would have become of my writing aspirations if not for such a wonderful, international group. I am beyond grateful to belong.

My gratitude to Deb Elkink and Brenda Anderson for their keen eyes and insightful input, and to Sara Davison for her artful cover design.

As always, all praise to my Saviour, Jesus.

About Eleanor

From her home in central Alberta, Canada, Eleanor Bertin writes fiction that ponders the depths of God's love and mercy to humanity. Before raising and home-educating a family of seven children for thirty years, Eleanor received a college diploma in Communications and worked in agriculture journalism. She returned to writing in 2016 and has since published five novels, as well as the memoir, *Pall of Silence*, about her late son, Paul.

She and her husband of more than 40 years are the grandparents of ten amazing grandchildren. Along with their youngest son, Timothy who has Down syndrome, they live in the Before of a beautiful century home. www.eleanorbertinauthor.com

Titles By Eleanor Bertin

THE MOSAIC COLLECTION: NOVELS
The Ties That Bind Series
Lifelines

Unbound

Tethered

Burning Bright Series
Flame of Mercy

Flicker of Trust

THE MOSAIC COLLECTIONS: ANTHOLOGY STORIES
"Like Wool" in *Hope is Born*

"Love & Unexpected Stress Responses" in *A Star Will Rise*

"How Life Begins" in *All Things New*

"Christmas at the Crossroads" in *A Whisper of Peace*

"Grounded" in *Before Summer's End*

"A Portion of Grace" in *Song of Grace*

"Who Sends the Rain?" in *Dancing in the Rain*

"No Night There" in *The Heart of Christmas*

"Meg and the E-Monster" in *A Thrill in the Air*

"Not by Chance" in *Sounds Like a Plan*

NON-FICTION

Pall of Silence: My Journey from Tragedy to Trust

Love, Christmas

A Whisper of Grace Story

Johnnie Alexander

Surprise gifts from "Love, Christmas" bring hope and peace to the world-weary residents of a rural Ohio town.

When a middle-aged widow sorts through her deceased mother's holiday ornaments, she finds a wooden box labeled "Love, Christmas" and recalls a long-buried memory. Inspired by the discovery, she pays a decades-old good deed forward by giving an anonymous gift to a young woman struggling with her own grief. As the box is passed from one weary person to another, so is "a thrill of hope...led by the light of faith" ("O Holy Night" lyrics).

For Patty Young

A lovely friend who's never too weary to be a blessing to others.

"A generous person will prosper; whoever refreshes others will be refreshed." (Proverbs 11:25; NIV).

"To ease another's heartache is to forget one's own."
(Abraham Lincoln)

Chapter One ~ Shannon

December 11ᵗʰ

Shannon Tracey placed the old-fashioned gold star on top of the petite Douglas fir, then stepped back to assess the decorated tree. And to swipe away the tears she failed to hold inside. Only one of her mother's holiday totes still needed to be emptied before this nostalgic, happy-sad trip down memory lane could end.

Mother's most treasured ornaments, a few from Shannon's childhood and others marking special occasions, now adorned the lighted evergreen. An oval blue frame held a miniature photo of JT when he was only a few months old. A similar frame, this one pink with a photo of baby Gina, hung close by. The white script along the bottom of each frame read: *Baby's First Christmas*.

"Where did the years go?" Shannon murmured. Twig, her mother's aged Brussels terrier, responded with a loud snore. JT and Gina were adults now and too busy with their lives out on the West Coast to come home for the holidays.

At least they'd flown in for their grandmother's funeral. Which, to add to the family's heartache, had been almost a year to the day since their dad's unexpected death.

"Not going down that lane." Shannon directed a watery smile at Twig. The grizzled dog relaxed in a pillowy, round bed on the fireplace's broad hearth. If her grief got out of control, Shannon feared she'd spend the rest of December curled up in her own empty, lonely bed.

Eager to finish the difficult task, she placed the last tote on the wide coffee table and removed the lid. Most of these items appeared to be holiday craft remnants, probably from the years when Mother taught third and fourth grade Sunday school.

Shannon sorted through the tote, adding usable items to the *Donate* box and tossing the rest in a black trash bag. She set aside a pack of gift tags along with a couple of boxes of unopened greeting cards for her own use.

Beneath a strand of ragged green garland, she discovered a square, wooden box with an ornamental square attached to the lid. Inscribed in a scripted font were the words:

Love, Christmas

A memory, long buried, stirred inside Shannon's heart. She perched on the hearth beside Twig's bed and opened the box. A sheet of crumpled purple tissue paper was inside—nothing else—but once upon a time a surprise gift had lifted her parents' sagging spirits.

Twig sneezed, then rested her chin on the furry edge of her bed. The tip of her pink tongue protruded beyond her toothless mouth as she stared at Shannon with her expressive, bulging eyes.

"I must have been six or seven when I found this box on our porch swing," Shannon said as if answering Twig's unspoken question. "It was in a gold bag, and Mother's name was written on the tag."

Shannon scratched Twig behind her soft ears as the memory came into sharper focus. Dad delivered pizzas in the evening instead of heading off to the factory each morning for his shift. Her parents talked in low voices, stopping abruptly whenever she entered the room.

Her stomach now tightened with the same heavy knots she'd experienced as a child. Those unsettling days before Dad found a new job had cast a shadow over the excitement of Christmas.

Then the mysterious box appeared on the porch swing.

Tears, happy tears, shimmered in Mother's eyes as she stared at the gift certificate she found inside. Thanks to their anonymous benefactor, her parents had bought a large enough turkey to invite their elderly neighbors to join them.

Shannon put the lid back on the box and traced the scripted letters with her finger. "I wonder if Mother and Dad ever found out who pretended to be 'Christmas.'"

In what Shannon could only describe as a holy nudge, her thoughts drifted to a conversation she'd had a year ago about favorite holiday memories. She'd spent Christmas Eve at the Granite Grill for a dinner arranged by, of all people, Mac Calloway, the cemetery's eccentric caretaker. Another guest, a young foster teen, confided her secret wish.

Perhaps it was time to pass along the box to someone new.

CHAPTER TWO ~ CASSIDY

December 12th

Giant elves, wreathes, candlesticks, and toy soldiers adorned each historic street lamp along Lafayette Street, while the downtown sound system filled the air with holiday music. Cassidy Piper wished with all her heart she could hibernate through the festive season. She'd give her meager life savings to retreat to a cave before Thanksgiving as long as she didn't have to emerge until after New Year's.

Not a day went by that she didn't think of Courtney, but the heartache was most intense during the holidays. "Time heals all wounds," said the nameless *they.* Cassidy begged to differ. This, her fourth Christmas without her sister, scraped her heart raw.

But hibernation wasn't an option. Neither sleep nor grief were luxuries Cassidy could afford while juggling three part-time jobs and studying for finals.

She stamped the slush from her boots as she neared the Granite Grill. Strands of garish, multi-colored bulbs outlined the picture window, and cartoonish holiday stickers surrounded the diner's logo.

The overhead bell jangled as Cassidy entered, and Vince called out a gruff greeting from behind the cash register. A black sweatshirt bearing the diner's logo covered his broad shoulders and middle-aged paunch. The streaks of gray in his thick, dark hair complemented the gray patches in his short beard.

"The usual good enough for you today, Cass?" Vince's voice boomed over the hum of conversation from the few other diners seated at tables and on the stools lining the counter.

"That's why I'm here." Her forced cheerfulness hit an obviously false note, and she inwardly groaned when Vince squinted at her. Not much got past his acute gaze. He seemed to have a knack for reading his customers' moods—no doubt honed by all the years he'd spent behind the Grill's counter.

"Frog sticks, hot and fresh, and a cup of chocolate mud coming right up." Vince waved his spatula toward the kitchen.

Cassidy smiled her thanks, then headed toward her favorite booth. The row of windows on this side of the building faced the town square. A late-nineteenth-century, two-story brick municipal building and community center stood in the exact spot where the Sterling family, early settlers in the area, had erected a wooden church and schoolhouse in the early 1800s. War memorials and park benches were scattered around the center's snow-covered lawn, while the first bell from the long-gone church was on display near the entrance. Footlights shone on the bell and the nearby flagpole, where Ohio's unique, swallowtail flag hung below the Stars and Stripes.

On the opposite side of the center's entrance, beside the white-washed bandstand, stood an enormous fir tree decorated with large baubles and lighted garlands.

A live Christmas tree.

Cassidy sighed with longing as she stood beside her booth. Only one of the foster homes where she and Courtney stayed for a time had a live tree for the holidays. The sisters had dreamed of staying with that family forever, but circumstances changed and so did their placements. More than ten years had slipped by since then, and the two girls were never placed together again.

Before the childhood memories could overwhelm her, Cassidy took off her heavy jacket and removed her laptop from her backpack. Once settled in the booth, she opened the computer. As the screen came to life, a chair scraped against the tiled floor.

Cassidy glanced that direction as two men, both wearing EMT uniforms, rose from their seats. The older one, Doug Chapman, acknowledged her with a nod. Despite the warmth of his gentle smile, his eyes reflected concern.

"Studying hard?" he asked as he retrieved his coat from the back of his chair. "You look tired."

So did he, but Cassidy refrained from saying so. He'd been among the first to arrive at the scene of Courtney's accident, and what he'd seen that night seemed to affect him still. Not that he ever talked to Cassidy about it. His silence told her more than words ever could.

Vince had introduced them at the Christmas Eve dinner he and Mac hosted at the Grill last year. Since then, the Chapmans provided an occasional helping hand when Cassidy needed one. Once she'd started her freshman year at the community college located in the next town over, however, she hadn't spent as much time with them.

"Please tell Sarah thanks again for the reference," Cassidy said. "I love working at the library. It's like all the books there belong to me."

Doug's smile deepened. "Spoken like a true bookworm."

"Nah," Cassidy bantered. "I'm a book dragon."

Vince arrived with a basket of French fries in one hand and a mug of hot chocolate smothered under a cloud of whipped cream in the other. "That's why she's gonna make the dean's list."

"Only if I finish this art history presentation by tomorrow." Cassidy still needed to proofread the text on each of the slides she'd created and read over the accompanying research paper one more time. Plus study for her finals in math, history, and literature.

"We're praying for you," Doug said as he shrugged into his coat. "Once the semester's over, be sure you take a good, long nap."

"That sounds lovely. Please don't forget to tell Sarah hi."

Doug lowered his gaze as a shadow seemed to age his features. "I'm sure she'll say hi back." He held up the check with his scrawled order. "I'll meet you up front, Vince."

"Be there in a minute." Vince set Cassidy's fries and the mug next to her laptop as Doug and his partner headed for the cash register. "I'm guessing you didn't know Sarah's gone," he said, keeping his voice low.

Cassidy widened her eyes. "She left him?"

"No, no," Vince assured her. "Nothing like that. She's in Cincinnati taking care of her mother. First the dear soul broke her ankle, and then she had a stroke. Doug's a good man, a good father, and we can thank the Good Lord that the twins are teens instead of toddlers. But it's been a strain on all of them to have Sarah away."

Vince moved the ketchup from the condiment holder to the side of the basket. "Eat your fries while they're hot."

Cassidy's gaze followed Vince as he rounded the counter by the cash register and rang up the transaction. Poor Doug. He worked such long hours, and now he needed to fit his feet into Sarah's impossible-to-fill shoes. And poor Sarah. She must be feeling torn in two, needing to be with her mom while missing her family.

I wish there was something I could do.

A couple of hours later, Cassidy's art history presentation was revised, proofed, and ready to present to her class the next day. As she put away her laptop, Vince returned to the booth with a plain cardboard package wrapped with a red ribbon. A label affixed to the top had her name printed in a block font.

"Strangest thing," he said, his tone gruffer than usual. "Nicolás ran upstairs for a minute, and when he came back down, this here package was in the kitchen." The young fry cook, who lived above the diner, worked long hours to help support his Honduran parents.

"Someone knows you're here," Vince added.

"What is it?" Cassidy asked.

Vince shrugged, then folded his arms in a bouncer's stance. "No telling till you open it."

Cassidy turned the package over, but only the manufacturer's name and bar code were on the bottom. "It's too light to be a bomb," she joked.

"See what it is. I don't have all day."

The mysterious gift had apparently caused Vince to unleash his inner Papa Bear. Not necessarily a bad thing, Cassidy mused, as she removed the ribbon and opened the lid. A square wooden box, nestled in silver tissue paper, rested inside. Inscribed in a scripted font on an ornamental square affixed to the lid were the words:

Love, Christmas

"Curiouser and curiouser," Cassidy murmured.

"Who's Christmas?" Vince asked.

Instead of answering, Cassidy removed the lid from the wooden box and found a gift certificate inside.

"It's for the Christmas tree farm. Out by Archer's Marsh. For a live Christmas tree." Cassidy wrapped her arms around Vince in a spontaneous hug. "Thank you, Vince. This is the best gift ever."

He awkwardly patted her shoulder as he gently extricated himself. "Wish I could take credit for it then. But it's not from me."

"I wonder who then?"

Vince pressed his finger against the scripted words. "There's your answer."

CHAPTER THREE ~ DOUG

December 14th

Doug Chapman signed out of his shift while debating the family's supper choices. Venison chili always hit the spot on a cold winter day, but he'd forgotten to move the container from the freezer to the fridge last night. His other options were a stop at the grocery store on the way home to pick up a frozen lasagna, all the fixings for a taco bar, or a roasted chicken from the deli. None of those options seemed appealing, especially not when those items had already been on their family menu multiple times since Sarah had left.

Cincinnati was only a couple of hours away, and the family exchanged frequent texts and phone calls. Yet Doug and both boys felt her absence as if she'd gone to the moon. Kind of like Nicki, their oldest. Same age as Cassidy's sister and almost as troubled during her teen years. At least, unlike Courtney, she still lived and breathed. He only wished Nicki did her living and breathing closer to home instead of two time zones to the west.

"Hey, Chappy. Hold up a minute."

Doug turned to greet his supervisor, who strode toward him with a snowman gift bag dangling from his fingers.

"Whatcha got there, Buzz?"

"No idea, but your name's on the tag." Buzz's cell rang as he handed over the bag. "Gotta take this. See you tomorrow." He headed back to his office with his phone to his ear.

"Thanks," Doug called after him, then peered inside the bag. He pulled out the square wooden box and read the words inscribed in a scripted font on an ornamental square affixed to the lid:

Love, Christmas

Was this some kind of joke?

No "from" name on the tag. No card tucked between the sheets of tissue paper.

Doug took one glance at the gift card he found inside the box and broke into a huge smile.

He still didn't know about supper, but he and his boys were playing paintball this weekend.

CHAPTER FOUR ~ SHANNON

December 19ᵗʰ

As she did most Thursday mornings, Shannon drove to the cemetery for her weekly visit to her mother's and her husband's graves. This close to Christmas, she'd mentally braced herself for heart-wrenching tears and slipped a tissue pack in her coat pocket before leaving her house.

Instead she couldn't help smiling as she passed through the iron gates. Her first stop at Granite Grill for a to-go cup of Vince's dark roast blend had blessed her beyond imagining. The morning regulars were all abuzz with the mystery of the anonymous gifts.

"It's the craziest thing," Vince said as he rang up her order. "Cassidy Piper's gift certificate was in a wooden box." He leaned forward and lowered his voice. "Pretty sure she passed it on to Doug Chapman. But our buddy Mac got a gift card to the hardware store inside of a miniature stocking. Not only is the wooden box being passed around, but folks are finding gift cards in all kinds of things."

Shannon blinked in surprise. She'd hoped to honor her mother's memory and bring a bit of joy into a hard-working student's life, but she'd never expected this wondrous multiplying of her simple act.

"No one knows who started all this generosity," Vince continued. "Just like in Cassidy's box, there's never a note. Only two mysterious words."

The same words I leave with you, treasured reader:

Love, Christmas

A Note From Johnnie

Dear Treasured Reader,

Two simple words, "Love, Christmas," sparked within me a few years ago, but I had no idea what to do with them. From the get-go, the phrase appeared to be the closing of a letter. But who was Christmas? And who was this mysterious person writing to?

We never find out who blessed Shannon's parents during her dad's unemployment, but I imagine the secretive Christmas would be delighted to know that Shannon's generous gesture inspired an outpouring of anonymous gift-giving in her rural community.

God promises that "whoever refreshes others will be refreshed" (Proverbs 11:25b).

My prayer is for a Love, Christmas season where we prayerfully seek to refresh the weary and rejoice in God's blessings.

Hugs,

Johnnie

ACKNOWLEDGMENTS

Special thanks and a virtual chocolate orange to:

· Sara Davison, who encouraged me to pursue my "Love, Christmas" story idea when I was unsure what to write;

· Deb Elkink, whose editing know-how smoothed out a few wrinkles;

· Jill Lancour, who put her design skills to work to create my story's cover.

I'm also handing out virtual candy canes to each one of my Mosaic sisters ~ you bring so much heart and wisdom to our MC group. To walk this crazy writing path with you is a joy and a blessing.

As always, all my love to Bethany and Justin, Jill and Jacob, Nate and Bre, and the grandest of grands ~ Jeremy, Jedidiah, Kaydi, Josey, and Presley.

About Johnnie

Johnnie Alexander is a wannabe vagabond with a heart for making memories. As a bestselling, award-winning novelist, she has written more than thirty works of fiction in a variety of genres. She serves on the Mid-South Christian Writers Conference Executive Board, co-hosts Writers Chat, a weekly online show, and writes monthly posts for the Heroes, Heroines, and History blog. A fan of classic movies, stacks of books, and road trips, Johnnie shares a life of quiet adventure with Rugby, her raccoon-treeing papillon.

Connect with her at JohnnieAlexander.com.

Titles By Johnnie Anderson

THE MOSAIC COLLECTION: NOVELS
The Mischief Thief

THE MOSAIC COLLECTIONS: ANTHOLOGY STORIES
"The Caretaker's Christmas" in *Hope is Born*
"A Stranger Comes to Springlight" in *Before Summer's End*
"Paper Trail" in *Song of Grace*
"Souvenir in My Pocket" in *All Things New*
"Christmas Comes to Springlight" in *A Thrill in the Air*

WORLD WAR II NOVELS
The Cryptographer's Dilemma
Echoes of War Series
Where Treasure Hides
When Memory Whispers (Mosaic)

MISTY WILLOW SERIES
Where She Belongs
When Love Arrives
What Hope Remembers

NOVELLAS

"The Healing Promise" (Courageous Brides Collection)

"Journey of the Heart" (Erie Canal Brides Collection)

"Match You Like Crazy" (Resort to Romance Series)

"Blue Moon" (Homefront Heroines)

"The Thistle Rings" (Love's a Mystery in Gnaw Bone, Indiana)

"The Potter's Design" (Love's a Mystery in Crooksville, Ohio)

"Three Dog Knight " (Mystery of Cobble Hill Farms Series)

SHORT STORIES

"Beneath the Christmas Star" (in *A Cup of Christmas Cheer—Tales of Joy and Wonder for the Holidays*)

ANNIE'S FICTION

Novels in the following series:

Victorian Mansion Flower Shop Mysteries

Hearts of Amish Country

Inn at Magnolia Harbor

Sweet Intrigue Mysteries

Love in Lancaster Country

Mysteries of Aspen Falls

GIFTING
Christmas

Angela D. Meyer

GIFTING CHRISTMAS

Angela D. Meyer

One snowstorm. Ten stranded travelers on Christmas Eve. What could go wrong?

With her bed and breakfast closed for the holidays, Karen is looking forward to a tranquil Christmas with her husband. But when a snowstorm forces them to take in several stranded strangers, Christmas cheer quickly unravels, and a young family becomes the scapegoat for the other guests' frustrations. How will this stress-filled holiday forever change Karen's perspective on Christmas?

"Gifting Christmas" is a between-the-books short story occurring between books 1 and 2 of my Applewood Hill series.

Praise be to the LORD, for he has heard my cry for mercy. The LORD is my strength and my shield; my heart trusts in him, and he helps me. My heart leaps for joy, and with my song I praise him. Psalm 28:6-7 (NIV)

GIFTING CHRISTMAS

Karen wiped the frost from an upstairs window. Pulling her sweater snug around herself, she watched the snow fall on the grounds in front of their bed and breakfast, drifting deeper by the minute. Tomorrow would reveal a very white Christmas. When the weatherman had forecast almost blizzard-like conditions, their guests left early. James, the on-site manager, opted for spending time with family in Kansas City, and Barry sent the rest of the staff home. Karen looked forward to a quiet, just-the-two-of-them Christmas.

She rubbed her oversized belly as she abandoned her vigil. "Don't worry, baby. Daddy will come back from the store soon." She glanced at her watch. He had left shortly after lunch at noon, and it was approaching two o'clock. An image of him stuck in a ditch flashed through her mind, but she chided herself for worrying. "God, please keep Barry safe."

Seven months ago, she had been prepared to end their marriage, but by the grace of God, she had forgiven her husband. She wished the healing didn't take so long, though. They still met with a counselor once a week, and Barry was part of a men's group from church, yet there had been a couple of times when he had fumbled in his recovery, and all his old offenses had flooded her heart. She had fought the anger and chosen forgiveness all over again. She hoped the next few days would nurture the healing in their relationship.

Enjoying the peace found in the emptiness of their usually bustling bed and breakfast, Karen checked each room upstairs and ensured they were ready for guests arriving after Christmas. She lingered in each room and admired the holiday decorations. She might leave them up for a while and let the next round of guests enjoy Christmas in January.

After shutting off a forgotten light, she meandered to the rear window to check on her and Barry's house situated across the employee parking lot behind the bed and breakfast. As soon as Barry returned, they would trudge through the snow to its promised warmth and begin their Christmas retreat. She envisioned a calm evening in front of their fireplace, snuggling next to her husband. With no one demanding anything from her.

She rubbed off the frost thickening on the glass and peered outside. Wind gusts were blowing the snow into deep drifts against their house. She should have gone over before Barry left. Like he had insisted. But she had been adamant that each room be rechecked.

On the main level of the bed and breakfast, a door slammed against a wall, and the wind howled inside, carrying Barry's voice with it. "Karen?"

His voice urged Karen down the back stairway and deposited her near the kitchen. "I'm coming." She hurried down the hallway, past the formal dining room and library. She rounded the corner into the foyer and halted, staring at the couple near the front door. A slightly overweight man she guessed to be in his late forties stood a few inches shorter than the woman beside him. A Marilyn Monroe wannabe, she seemed quite a bit younger than the guy whose arm she held onto. Relief that Barry was no longer out in the storm warred with unease at the sight of the couple.

Barry pulled off his knit hat, revealing his dark hair, thick to the touch, that she had always loved. He strode across the floor and pulled Karen close. "I'm glad I made it back before the snow got any deeper." He placed a hand on her stomach and leaned down. "See, baby, Daddy's safe and sound."

Karen looked behind Barry at the strangers. Her muscles tensed. "Are you going to introduce me?" She cringed at the tart sound of her voice.

He gave her an empathetic smile. "Honey, these folks were stuck near the end of the drive."

The man doffed his cowboy hat, revealing a bald head. "I'm Jared, and this here's my wife, Dotty. Pleased to meet you." The man's southern drawl fit with his stout appearance and pulled her into its warmth. "We slid off the road partway into a ditch. Good thing your husband came by when he did."

The woman plopped her right fist on her hip and glared at her husband. "I told you we should have left earlier. Why you wanted to be at that party way out here in the country in the first place on a night like this is beyond me." She threw her hands up in the air, her blond hair bobbing in time with her gestures. "But I'm never right. How could I be right? It's not like I listened to the weather forecast or anything." She flashed a conspiratorial smile at Karen. "Men. Right?"

Karen grimaced inwardly at the woman's whiny complaint as she proffered a slight smile. "The weatherman did nail it this time."

Barry put his arm around Karen's shoulders and kissed her cheek. "They need a place to stay till the storm blows over."

"Well, I..." Karen stopped at the sound of banging on the front door. What now?

Barry opened the door, and the wind caught it, blowing it against the wall. Snow flew inside along with four individuals. Barry urged them to come in, then secured the door before he faced the newcomers as they dusted the snow off their coats and removed their winter gear.

Tiredness threatened to overtake Karen as she acknowledged that a restful Christmas with Barry was moving far out of reach. Why couldn't God send these people somewhere else? With one hand she gently kneaded her lower back. *Lord, give me strength.*

A woman about the same age as Karen unwrapped her scarf from around her neck. Sporting long, jet-black hair, she met Karen's gaze through a pair of red-rimmed glasses. "I'm July." She appeared serene, but the austere notes of her voice offered a different version. "This is my husband, Thomas. And two of my employees, Ben and Jeannette." She took off her fogged-up glasses. "I hope you have some rooms available. Our client we were meeting with gave us directions for a shortcut to the airport, but I'm afraid we're lost. And now with the snow we can't possibly catch our flight." The woman looked around and seemed to notice the lack of activity. "You are open, aren't you?"

Karen shifted on her feet, swollen after a long day. "Actually, no. We're..." Karen stopped. They couldn't refuse them shelter. "We've sent the staff home. My husband and I are the only ones here." She clenched her fists, overwhelmed by the intrusion.

"You have to let us stay here." Thomas's clipped tones demanded obedience. His long overcoat, now unbuttoned, revealed an expensive suit, dress shirt, and tie. His entire manner spoke of someone who was accustomed to the boardroom, controlling the meeting. He held his gloves in one hand and slapped them into his other. His arrogance aggravated her.

Karen stiffened and glared at the man. "We don't *have* to do—"

"Nowhere else is open." Dotty took a stance in the battle for a place to stay. All the others murmured their agreement.

Karen glanced at Barry. She wanted a hot bath. And tranquility. But she couldn't deny that these people needed a safe place in this storm.

He smiled and leaned closer. "Don't fret. I have an idea."

Karen wrinkled her brow and nodded.

He faced the stranded travelers. "Take a deep breath. We won't kick anyone out into the snow, so settle down." He chuckled. "But my wife is right. We are closed. And we don't *have* to let you stay." He looked pointedly at Thomas. "Hear me out. All our staff is gone. No housekeeping. No chef or other kitchen staff.

And as you can see, my wife is very pregnant. I don't want her taking care of all of you on her own and going into labor early." Barry smiled. "Here's the plan. For Christmas Eve, there will be no charge. Tomorrow, we'll deal with tomorrow night. If you haven't caught our names, this is Karen and I'm Barry."

Brilliant. Karen smiled.

"What's the catch?" Jeannette, one of July's employees, slipped to the front of the group. The young woman wore her blond hair in a pixie cut and sported a green coat. Her tone was light and perky despite the worry in her voice.

Karen stifled a chuckle when an image of one of Santa's elves at the mall flitted through her mind.

Barry smiled. "You don't have to scrub any toilets, but you do get to neaten up after yourself. Clean up your own spills, strip your bedding before you leave, that sort of thing. Food will be whatever we pull together. Leftovers, cold cuts, and such. It won't be fancy. Be considerate of each other and, please, don't abuse our hospitality. That work for everyone?"

The group of strangers all nodded in agreement.

"Then it's settled. After you retrieve what you need from your cars, I'll give you a tour and then take you to your rooms. Karen and I will be staying in the manager's apartment near the kitchen if you need anything."

Karen breathed easier. Barry's plan was great, even if she couldn't spend the night before Christmas in her own bed. They could use up food they had already prepared for their original

Christmas guests that would otherwise spoil. And they still might carve out some time together.

The guests all trudged outside for their belongings and then, after a few minutes, Dotty ran back in. "Someone spun out on the road. I think they hit a light pole."

Barry grabbed his coat and took off. The others trickled back into the bed and breakfast and visited amongst themselves while they waited. Dotty and Jared stood in front of the window arguing. July and Thomas talked together almost secretively. The Christmas elf and Ben, her apparent significant other, sat on the bottom stair holding each other's hands while they watched everyone else.

Tired, Karen leaned against the check in desk. "Could someone go check if my husband needs help?"

All of the guests averted their eyes.

Seriously? If they weren't willing to help Barry in this situation, what did that forebode about their stay? She paced the length of the foyer, anxious for Barry to be safe inside again.

July joined the younger couple. Bits of conversation about Christmas bonuses floated Karen's way. The woman gave the younger couple each a card, nodded, and walked away.

A thud sounded against the front door, and Karen hurried to open it. Barry trudged inside, a young child in his arms. A woman followed with two kids bundled in winter wrappings, peeking over the top of their scarves. The one on the woman's left stood almost as tall as she did, the one on the right was barely big enough for school. Karen secured the door and helped them with their coats.

"Not kids!" July's voice morphed into the controlling tone of a schoolmaster. "So help me, if they cry all night and make a bunch of noise, I will not be happy."

When the woman just in from the cold choked back a sob, Karen stared at July. "Really? After we welcomed all of you? I suppose you would be happier in the cold?"

July opened her mouth, then shut it.

Karen turned away from the hot-headed executive. As she hung the newest arrivals' damp outerwear on the coat rack, she assessed the bedraggled family.

"Mamá!" The youngest child squirmed out of Barry's arms and ran to his mother. The taller of the other two, a boy, glared at Karen as though daring her to send them back outside. She smiled at him, then watched the little girl, eyes wide open in wonder as she looked around at all the Christmas decorations. Brown hair hung in one loose braid almost to her hips.

"Barry, we should put them in the honeymoon suite."

"*No puedo* ... I can't ..." The woman pulled her children closer. "I can't pay."

Thoughts of sending everyone away fled Karen's mind. Still tired to the bottoms of her soles, some of the emotional exhaustion lifted. "Didn't my husband tell you? No one pays tonight."

"Really?"

Karen smiled. "Really. What's your name?"

"Isabella. And these are my kids. This is José, he is three, María is six, and the tallest one, Jesús, is ten." She grinned. "I always liked Christmas."

"They're beautiful names for beautiful kids."

Barry checked his watch. "All right everyone, follow me. You can leave your luggage here till I show you to your rooms." He reached for Karen's hand, then led the way to the right of the foyer and down the hallway. "The first room down this hall is the library, the perfect place to experience a bit of holiday cheer." He flung open the double doors and switched on the lights, revealing the seven-foot-tall Christmas tree fully decked out. Stockings hung from the mantelpiece on either side of the fireplace. Poinsettias stood sentinel in the corner to the right. Fairy lights twinkled in and out and around well-placed decorations. "You'll also find plenty of books, movies, and games for entertainment during your stay. We do have internet, though I hope it doesn't go out. There's a landline if needed. For non-entertainment purposes only. "If you'll follow me, I'll show you the dining room."

Barry led the way out the door and down the hall. Karen waited till they all left the room and turned off the lights.

Jeanette joined Karen and walked with her.

Karen glanced at the young woman. "What's on your mind?"

"Is it possible for Ben and me to stay in separate rooms? We're not...we aren't..." She took a deep breath.

In a world that expected every dating couple to cohabitate, Karen found it refreshing when someone went against the cultural norm. "Of course you can. And no need for an explanation."

Jeanette brightened at Karen's assurances.

"Your relationship will be stronger for the choice you're making."

"Thank you."

They caught up with the rest of the group as Barry led them into the dining room. Murmurs of delight rippled among the group as they entered the room decorated in a style reminiscent of Christmas in Narnia. Karen's sister had outdone herself this year when she decorated the bed and breakfast for the holiday.

"This is where we'll serve food while you're here. Your first meal will be an early supper in about three hours. Now, let's get you to your rooms so you can settle in for the night."

Karen leaned closer to Barry. "I can show them to their rooms while you grab what we need for the night from our house."

"Great idea." Barry kissed her on the cheek and headed out through the kitchen.

Karen led the way back to the foyer and took the keys for five rooms off their hooks while everyone gathered their belongings.

Half an hour later, everyone settled, Karen joined Barry in the apartment for a few hours respite before preparing supper. He welcomed her with open arms. Maybe their Christmas wasn't spoiled after all.

Barry filled a basket with bread. "So, Mrs. Marino, shall we feed the troops?"

Karen laughed. "Next time, could you give me a little more warning before you invite guests over for dinner?"

Barry wrapped his wife in a hug. "I'm sorry Christmas won't be what you were hoping."

She leaned against his chest and listened to his heartbeat for a moment. "At least we're together."

"That's what matters. By the way, I ran into your dad at the store earlier. He had a letter for you, but with the storm incoming, he asked me to deliver it. You distracted me from giving it to you earlier."

"I did, did I?"

"Yep. It's all your fault." Barry sobered. "In all seriousness, though. He wanted you to have it for Christmas." He pulled out an envelope from his back pocket. "It's from your mom."

She gasped as she accepted it and looked at the elegant handwriting on the front of the envelope.

He kissed the top of her head. "She must have written it before you returned from New York but died before she could give it to you. Your dad found it in her things."

She held it against her chest. Sniffling, she slid her finger under the flap.

"Hey, where's the food?"

Barry and Karen twisted around. Thomas glared at them from the doorway into the kitchen. Karen stuffed the letter in her jeans pocket.

Barry chuckled. "You can go to the store, since you're in a rush."

Thomas sputtered. "Do you know who I am?"

"Someone we welcomed in from the cold when he was stranded in the snow."

Thomas huffed and left the kitchen.

Karen picked up the platter of deli meats. "You ready, Mr. Marino? We better supply our lodgers with sustenance before we get mobbed." She led the way into the dining room. Barry followed and helped set up the buffet with sandwich supplies along with some chips and dip as well as a variety of fruit and pop.

Once everyone had taken a seat at the table, Barry clinked his fork against his glass. "Before you dig in, I'll offer grace."

"You can't do that in a public place." July crossed her arms.

Barry raised his eyebrows.

Dotty laughed. "July, honey, tonight we're not paying customers. I think he can do whatever he wants. Got it?"

July scowled. "Fine."

Barry bowed his head. "Lord, bless this meal tonight. Bless those at our table as they take refuge from this storm. Show each one of them your light this Christmas. In Jesus's name, amen. Dig in!"

A gentle buzz filled the air as they lined up for food. The children, now comfortable in their surroundings, played together at one end of the room, laughing and giggling. Karen helped Isabella fill plates for her kids, enjoying the mix of Spanish and English the little family used amongst themselves. Barry talked with Ben and Jeanette.

After all the guests had dished up their food, Karen and Barry filled their own plates and sat at one end of the table. Sadness and worry infused the Spanish chatter to Karen's left while Thomas led an apparent business meeting of sorts with his crew at the opposite end of the table. On Karen's right, Jared and Dotty were in a heated debate about who was at fault for their predicament.

There was no spark of Christmas joy at the table. How could she make it more real for them in this moment? Maybe singing Christmas carols or sharing Christmas memories?

The noise crescendoed and disrupted Karen from her plotting. Dotty's voice shrilled out above the others. "It's your fault we're stuck here. If you had listened to me, we would be home right now, not here with a bunch of kids running all over the place making such a racket." She gestured wildly at her husband.

The room grew silent.

Dotty raised her hands palms out as though she were fending off an attack. "What?"

"She's right. How can we think with all this commotion?" Thomas sneered at the young family.

July's voice joined the clamor. "And why should they get the honeymoon suite?"

The whole room erupted with accusations and complaints. Barry whistled, but no one paid any heed. He shouted a plea for them to quieten down. Nothing made a dent in the uproar.

Isabella's shoulders slumped, and after a couple minutes, she stood. María cried, stood on her chair, and reached for Isabella. The older kids crowded next to her.

The room slowly quieted as Isabella's voice rose. "You have so much, and you don't even see it. My little *família* ..." She touched the heads of her kids as they clung to her. "... *tenemos nada* ... we have nothing. Tonight, I can't believe your generosity." She nodded at Karen and Barry. "But we will leave the dining room now, so you have your precious quiet."

Karen stood. "You don't have to do that."

"I think it is best. For us." Isabella guided her children out of the room.

Karen looked around the table at each person there, but they all avoided eye contact. She placed the family's still-full plates along with fruit and cupcakes on a tray. Following the outcast family up the stairs, she paused every few steps to catch her breath. She had made her peace with hosting unexpected company, but she would be perfectly content if their only guests were Isabella and her kids.

As she reached the landing, the lights flickered then went out. What else might go wrong before their guests were gone? She kept her arm against the wall as a guide and arrived at the honeymoon suite without any trip-ups. She knocked on the door. "Isabella, it's Karen. I have food, and I'll start a fire for you."

The door opened, and Karen eased inside. "You are each a tiny shadow." A couple of giggles greeted her ears. "Isabella, there's a flashlight on the shelf in the closet. Can you find it?"

"I'm trying. Ah, here it is." The spotlight it cast on the ceiling gave the room a warm glow. "Thank you, Karen. But you don't need to bother with us."

"It's no bother. Anyone hungry?" Karen set the tray on the coffee table, then walked over to the fireplace. "I have no idea how long the power will be out." She placed wood on the rack, then struck a match. Holding it close to the kindling, the fire quickly grew. "Add logs as you need them. You should stay warm even if the power doesn't come on." She closed the screen in front of the fire and stood up. "And Isabella, please know that you're welcome in our home."

"I'm sorry for the way I spoke to the others. I am *cansada* ... tired. This has been a rough year."

"Do you want to talk?"

"You have time?" Tears rimmed Isabella's eyes.

Karen nodded and put an arm around the young mother. "Everyone needs a shoulder now and then." They sat on the couch and leaned close together, talking while the kids ate.

An hour later, using her phone's flashlight to illuminate her steps, Karen marched down the stairs and into the library, where the other guests were visiting. She cleared her throat and waited till everyone was focused on her.

"If any of you knows what it's like to do without, it isn't obvious. Did you know that Isabella's husband died six months ago? That two days ago they were kicked out of their apartment because they couldn't pay rent? Who does that at Christmas, anyway? Without a phone, she came to Westfall thinking they could stay with friends, but her friends weren't home. Isabella and her kids were headed to a shelter in Kansas City when she crashed into the ditch. She has no money for car repairs or for travel to her family in Florida." Karen paced in front of the group. "We opened our home to you, and all you've done is complain. About our generosity and her presence. I think if you end up here tomorrow night, we may have to double our normal rates." Karen looked around the room, pausing her gaze on each person before she left.

Barry followed her into the hallway. "We'll make sure Isabella and the kids are okay." He tried to pull her into a hug.

She stiffened. "That wasn't my point. Those people..."

"Are our guests."

Karen squinted at him. It annoyed her when he so pointedly hit the mark. She looked at her feet. "You're right. I need to treat them well, no matter what. But how do I do that and stand up for Isabella and her kids at the same time? Maybe a good night's rest will help my attitude." She relaxed into Barry's embrace.

"It's been a hard day for everyone. Sleep will probably help us all." He cupped her face in his hands. "God has this. You go on to bed, and I'll take care of closing up for the night."

The lights flickered in the apartment and then remained on as Karen dressed for their unusual Christmas Day. Thankful they had power, she pulled on her favorite oversized, burgundy sweater as she contemplated their unexpected Christmas companions. She knew she needed to change her attitude. Her own thoughts hadn't been far off from their guests' when Isabella's family first showed up at the doorstep of the bed and breakfast. "God, please forgive me. I really need your help showing kindness even when I don't feel like it, or when the others treat Isabella and her family badly. Help me walk out the meaning of Christmas. You loved us when none of us deserved it. Help me do the same."

With her attitude adjusted for the day, she ran a brush through her hair, then neatened up her mess. When she picked up her jeans from the night before, an envelope fell out of her pocket. Her mother's letter. How had she forgotten about it?

Curling up in the overstuffed chair in front of the fireplace, she opened the envelope and pulled out a single sheet of paper. The scent of lily of the valley wafted into the air, reminding her of when she was young and her relationship with her mom was good. Her mom's handwriting was wobbly, evidence of her state of health at the time she wrote it.

My dearest Karen,

If you're reading this, you didn't make it back in time and I'm already gone. I am so sorry for turning my back on you. You deserved so much better. Will you please forgive me? I hope someday you can.

I don't have much energy, so I'll keep this short. If I could encourage you in one thing, it is this—to trust God always. He'll always have your back, even when it feels too rocky to be true. Hang on to that. With so much love I'm bursting,
Mom

Karen reached for some tissue as the tears came. A few minutes later, a crash startled her. It sounded like pots and pans in the middle of meal prep. Barry must be cooking breakfast. She tossed the tissue in the trash, then folded the letter carefully and placed it with her clothes from yesterday. After she splashed water on her face, she headed to the kitchen, but laughter drew her down the hallway.

She stopped in the doorway of the library, not believing her eyes. The Christmas tree she and Barry had put up before the storm now had gifts around it. The three couples who were gathered in the library looked up when Karen entered, then glanced at each other nervously.

July approached Karen. "We've been horrid. You opened your home, and we treated you like a servant instead of our gracious host. We know it couldn't have been easy for you to give up your Christmas plans for us, and after what you shared about Isabella, we decided we needed to be more grateful. We talked it over and put together some gifts for Isabella and her kids. Barry found your stash of gift bags. I hope you don't mind."

Wrapping her mind around the shift in attitude, Karen shook her head. "Not at all. This is so kind of you all."

Barry hurried in from the hallway. "Breakfast, anyone?" He grinned at Karen, then

glanced around the room. "Where's Isabella and the kids?"

"I'll get them." Jeannette jumped up from her window seat and scurried out of the room. A few minutes later, she returned with the small family. "Can we do gifts first?"

Isabella stepped back. "Gifts? I didn't ... I can't ..." Fruitlessly, she tried to stop the kids from rushing to the tree.

"Mom, these all have our names on them." One by one, Jesús examined each package. "Can we open them? *Por favor?*"

"I don't understand." Isabella joined the kids.

Jared cleared his throat. "We were awful to you last night."

"You were right. About all of us." Dotty slipped her hand through her husband's arm.

Thomas nodded. "What we want to say is that we're sorry."

"But the gifts. Why?" Isabella looked around the room at each of the guests who had been so unwelcoming.

"Giving is the best way to discover what you're searching for." Ben sat down at the piano and tapped his fingers across a few keys. "My gran used to remind us of that every chance she had. Christmas music anyone?"

Jeannette laughed. "After Isabella and the kids opens their presents."

Karen touched Isabella's arm. "What about it?"

Isabella looked at her kids. "What do you say?"

The kids jumped up and down. "Yeah! Gifts for Christmas!"

Thomas picked up a gift bag and gave it to Isabella. "From July and me."

Isabella sat on the couch and pulled out the tissue paper. At the bottom of the bag was a piece of paper folded up. She unfolded it. "An airline's mileage report? This doesn't make sense."

July smiled. "We've earned so many miles from our various business trips that we want to provide each of you with plane tickets to Florida, where your family is."

Isabella covered her mouth with her fingertips. "I can't believe this."

José snuggled next to his mama. "*Abuela y Abuelo?*"

Isabella nodded as tears streamed down her face. "*Sí*. We get to see Grandma and Grandpa."

Dotty handed her another bag. "From me and Jared."

Isabella pulled out more tissue paper and an envelope with the words "for your family" written on the outside. She pulled out a brochure and gasped when she saw the pictures of a resort in southern Florida. "What is this?"

Dotty clapped. "Do you like it? We planned the trip for after Christmas, but Jared really didn't want to go." She punched him playfully. "When we found out July and Thomas were providing a way for you to go to Florida, I decided to give him what he really wants. Me and him, alone at home for a whole week. No friends or family. No nights on the town." She winked at her husband. "Isabella, it's all covered. The room, the food, transportation, and admission to area attractions. Fortunately, we haven't made all the reservations yet, so we'll talk later and figure out what's best for your family, then tomorrow we'll make all the necessary phone calls."

"I don't know what to say." Isabella covered her face. "No one ever has given us so much."

"Here's one more." Jeannette held out another bag.

"More?" Isabella looked inside the bag and pulled out a couple of gift cards. She examined the back of each and gasped. "A thousand dollars? This is too much." She tried to return the cards to the young couple.

Jeannette sat next to Ben. "We thought it might help you get settled. Or for whatever else you need."

Isabella clutched the cards to her chest. "How can I thank you all enough?"

Jeanette kissed Ben. "You were right. It does feel good to give away our bonus."

"Mamá, Mamá. Can we open our gifts?"

Isabella nodded and the kids tore into the other packages. A remote-control car for Jesús, a doll for María, and a stuffed dog for José.

Barry sat down on the floor with the kids. "We had a few things stashed away for Karen's niece and nephew." He looked up at Karen, who nodded. "If they were here, they would have shared the gifts themselves."

José jumped up from the floor and wrapped his arms around Barry. He held the youngster close.

Isabella watched the interaction, then whispered to Karen. "He misses his daddy so much. You have a wonderful husband, you know."

Karen laced her fingers together and rested them on her baby bump as she watched Barry interact with José. He was going to be a good father. Her eyes misted over. Although this Christmas had turned out differently than Karen expected, contentment flooded her heart.

Barry stood up. "Anyone who wants a Christmas feast this morning, follow me." He lifted José to his shoulders and led the way to breakfast.

Karen felt God heal her heart as a new memory overwrote more of the bad ones, and a quiet joy replaced the weariness of their unexpected Christmas. She and Barry still had their own gifts to exchange, but giving away her Christmas had been the best gift she could have received.

A Note From Angela

The world offers a type of joy that is attached to our circumstances, but God offers true joy that we can have regardless of what's happening around us. Even when we are weary or grieving, we can experience His joy. Finding joy can be counterintuitive. Like Karen discovered in "Gifting Christmas," when we trust God with our expectations and relinquish them into his hands, he fills us with joy that lasts far beyond the gifts under the tree. This Christmas season, no matter what you're facing, I pray you are filled with his joy that will give you strength.

ABOUT ANGELA D. MEYER

Angela D. Meyer writes fiction that showcases God's ability to redeem and restore the brokenness in our lives. Now that her two children, whom she homeschooled, are grown, she works the front desk in a chiropractor's office. When she's not at work, she stays busy writing, serving in the kids' ministry at her church, and learning how to grow things. She enjoys sunrises and sunsets, hanging out with friends, a good laugh, and reading. Someday, she would love to vacation by the sea.

Titles By Angela D. Meyer

THE MOSAIC COLLECTIONS: NOVELS

This Side of Yesterday

The Applewood Hill Series:

Where Hope Starts

Where Healing Starts

Where Joy Starts

THE MOSAIC COLLECTION: ANTHOLOGY STORIES

"The Jukebox Café" in *Hope is Born*

"Returning to Christmas" in *A Star Will Rise*

"Jillian's Refuge" in *Song of Grace*

"Reinventing Josie" in *All Things New*

"Reclaiming Tomorrow" in *A Whisper of Peace*

"Rekindling Her Dream" in *Dancing in the Rain*

AN *IN THE SHADOWS* NOVELLA

The
Back Door
Christmas Tour
Company

SARA DAVISON

THE BACK DOOR CHRISTMAS TOUR COMPANY

an In the Shadows story

Sara Davison

When an unexpected letter arrives in his box, Rav Temauri's carefully ordered life is turned upside down. In a wildly uncharacteristic move, Rav makes the spontaneous decision to abdicate his responsibilities and set out on a quest to discover where he belongs.

It takes flying halfway around the world—and encountering, under mysterious circumstances, the unlikeliest group of people—to show Rav that *home* is somewhere he never could have imagined.

"If we find ourselves with a desire that nothing in this world can satisfy, the most probable explanation is that we were made for another world." - C.S. Lewis

DECEMBER SEVENTEENTH

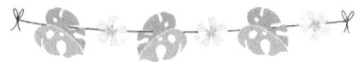

Rav Temauri did not make rash, impulsive decisions. Ever. Until the Christmas when he was twenty-six years old and made a wild, crazy, completely unplanned one. Likely he would regret it, but in any case, it was done, and he couldn't undo it now.

For as long as Rav could remember, his life had been so wildly out of control that from the moment he'd left home at eighteen he had poured every bit of his focus and energy into making sure he knew exactly what was coming and when.

Which made the fact that he had grabbed a last-minute flight to a country halfway around the world with zero planning or preparation extremely surprising. To Rav, anyway. No one else was surprised because no one else knew what he had done. And—he reflected in a rare moment of self-pity—he doubted anyone would care if they did.

Leaning over the paint-chipped metal railing of his three-star hotel, he strained to catch a glimpse of the brilliant blue-green Pacific Ocean between the fancy hotels that lined the waterfront in front of him. Not the greatest accommodations. Given that he hadn't tried to book accommodations in the tourist mecca of Tahiti until a couple of days ago and Christmas was a week from tomorrow, though, he really couldn't complain.

The paper he'd stuffed into the front pocket of his jeans crackled, reminding him why he had come. Or, rather, why he had left home in such a hurry. He dug into the pocket and pulled out the unexpected letter he'd received from his oldest brother, Tane, three days earlier.

Their family was a mess. Their father, who had abused their mother whenever he drank, which was often, had been in prison since Rav was six for driving through a stop sign while drunk and t-boning a car, killing the kid in the back seat. *Maman*, beaten down physically, emotionally, and psychologically, had barely been able to take care of herself after that. Tane, who was nine at the time, had stepped in to raise Rav and their middle brother, Alain.

Tane, in the truck with their father, had been thrown through the windshield when they struck the car that killed a classmate of his. Still, he'd managed to keep it together enough to be the anchor for the family.

Rav owed Tane everything.

With their brown skin, Tane, Alain, and Rav didn't look like the other kids in Pemberton, the small town north of Vancouver, British Columbia, where they'd grown up. That meant the other kids had been mean sometimes. Nothing they couldn't handle. At least, until the accident. Then the bullying became merciless. It didn't get better until Tane went to high school and became friends with Beck and Johnny. The three of them made a formidable team, and when Rav and Alain started tagging along after them wherever they went, the elementary school kids gradually backed off.

After high school, Beck, Johnny, and Tane went to the police academy together. When they graduated, all three of them disappeared into what Alain and Rav guessed was some kind of undercover work. Tane wouldn't—or couldn't—confirm or deny that, but the bottom line was they'd rarely seen him since. He'd been gone this time for almost five months, and Rav missed his big brother terribly.

So, he'd been counting the days until Tane came home for Christmas. Which was why the letter Rav had received hurt so much. With a heavy exhalation of breath, he unfolded the paper torn from a notebook and scanned the words again.

Hey little brother,

I'm really sorry to do this to you, but I won't be able to come home for Christmas after all. I wish I could explain why, but I can't. I'm good, though, and so are Beck and Johnny. I hope you and Alain and Maman are as well. I will come see you as soon as I can in the new year.

Tane

It wasn't the first time Tane had failed to show when they were looking forward to seeing him, but this time it struck Rav harder than ever. With Alain doing his Ph.D. and working as a professor's assistant at UBC in Vancouver, Rav had stayed in Pemberton to be there for their mother. She'd gradually recovered over the years and was okay on her own. Still, as much as he would have loved to move away from the place filled with such bad memories, he'd found an apartment in town so he could be close to her if she needed anything.

Rav folded up the worn notebook page and shoved it into his pocket. He needed to call Alain, let him know that neither of his brothers would be around over the holidays. Alain, who'd been planning to spend Christmas with his girlfriend, Carly, and her family, would have to check in on *Maman*. It was a little mean, messing up his brother's plans like that, but Tane had messed up Rav's, so maybe Rav could relinquish his responsibilities for once, dump them on someone else.

A motorboat, bobbing in the waves, caught Rav's eye. It wasn't that far from shore, but it did appear to be buffeted from the whitecaps crashing into and curling over its aluminum side. Had something happened to the motor? Or had it, like Rav, lost its anchor?

He shook his head as he pushed away from the railing. No need to get all melodramatic. He hadn't exactly lost Tane, although—given his brother's job and whatever it might involve—Rav did live in perpetual fear of that. Still, it felt as though the words of his brother's letter had severed the thin rope attached to whatever passed for a stabilizing force in their family.

Tane had been that for him and Alain, as much as he could be. Still, Rav's oldest brother had scars from the accident on more than his face and chest. Maybe it was time for Rav to stop asking Tane to give more of himself to them than he could.

Except that setting Tane free left Rav bobbing about as wildly and without direction as that boat out on the ocean. Exactly why, in a crazy, uncharacteristically impetuous act, he'd booked a flight to Tahiti, a country he had never set foot in but in which his family roots ran deep.

If he couldn't find a new anchor here, in the homeland of his people, then he would have to resign himself to bobbing and weaving his way through the crashing waves of life as best he could without one.

December Eighteenth

Rav had hoped that being in the land of his family would provide him with a connection to ... something. As though he'd come home. Instead, he felt more alone than ever. And *home* felt very far away.

The problem was he had no real idea what he was looking for, which made the elusive *thing* he sought difficult to find. He had rented a car for a day and taken the five-hour drive around the entire island. The scenery was breathtaking, no question, but he was a tourist here.

A fact emphasized sharply when he returned to his dingy hotel room and stood staring out the window, desperately seeking that sliver of green-blue water between buildings.

Rav had never been fully comfortable in Canada either. So where was home? One thing was for sure—he wasn't about to find it wandering aimlessly around the island on his own. On impulse—apparently that was his thing now—he grabbed his phone and did a quick search for tour groups in Tahiti. Likely they'd be all filled up, but maybe he'd get lucky and someone's flight had been canceled or a spot had opened up for some other reason.

He didn't get lucky. Although he called every tour company on the island, asking about their three- or four-hour tours, every single one he tried was completely booked. By the time he hit the button to connect with the final company—Golden Island Tours—he'd pretty much resigned himself to returning to his hometown as empty inside as when he had left.

The company spokesperson, who spoke English with a light, Tahitian accent, was nice enough but firm in her insistence that, like all the other companies, their tours over the holidays were full.

Rav drove his fingers through his hair. Might as well see if he could catch a flight home tomorrow, let Alain off the hook. Pick up his life where he had left off and carry on as though this crazy little spontaneous blip had never happened.

The thought depressed him enough that he decided to take one more shot. "I'm sorry to hear that. You were my last hope. You wouldn't consider adding one more person if I paid extra?"

After a brief pause, the woman spoke. "Just one? Are you saying you are all alone for Christmas?" As though afraid of anyone overhearing her, the woman had lowered her voice enough that Rav pressed the phone harder to his ear and closed his eyes, straining to catch the words. Words that suddenly brought his bleak situation into sharp focus.

He sighed. "Yeah. I suppose I am."

"What is your name?"

"Rav Temauri."

A clicking sound echoed through the phone, as though the woman was inputting something into a keyboard. Looking him up? His muscles tensed, but then Rav relaxed. He didn't have much of an online presence, and he certainly didn't have anything in his mundane life to hide. What difference would it make if she did a little research on him?

After a moment, she murmured, "So, you're the one."

Rav raised his eyebrows. The one? What did that mean?

Before he could ask, she spoke again. "Look, Rav, I can't allow any more tourists in our groups, but if you want to come here in person, say at six tomorrow evening, I believe I have another option for you."

Rav frowned. That sounded a little sketchy. Why did he have to show up in person to book a tour?

When he didn't answer, the woman cleared her throat. "If that doesn't suit you, then I wish you all the—"

Before she dismissed him entirely and the opportunity vanished, Rav rushed to cut her off. "No, it's fine."

"Very good. I will send a cab for you. Where are you staying?"

He hesitated. Should he be giving her that information? Despite his misgivings, his curiosity had been piqued. "I'm at the Blue Heron in Papara."

"Excellent. The taxi will be there at five-thirty. When you arrive, come to the back door. And make sure no one sees you."

"Why—?"

The line had gone dead. Rav pulled the phone from his ear and stared at it a moment before tossing it onto the couch next to him. Everything about that had been weird. No way he was going to some unfamiliar location in a strange country all on his own for a clandestine appointment with a stranger. And right around sunset? That would be foolhardy at best and utterly stupid at worst. If Tane found out ...

Rav straightened, the letter crinkling in his pocket. Tane wasn't around to find out anything about his younger brothers, was he? Which meant he'd forfeited any say in what Rav did or didn't do.

Besides, something about the conspiratorial tone in the woman's voice intrigued him. He tapped his fingers on the worn arm of the couch. He didn't carry a weapon like Tane or have his brother's training, but he'd learned the hard way in school to hold his own in a fight. Should this set-up turn out to be questionable or even dangerous, he'd do what he had to do to protect himself and get out of there. And then he would head home.

December Nineteenth

The next evening, the taxi pulled up in front of Rav's hotel at five-thirty on the dot. When Rav slid onto the back seat, the cabbie, an older gentleman in a red beret and a white T-shirt with a worn Coca-Cola logo on the front, turned to give Rav a scrutinizing look. After a few seconds, he nodded and pulled away from the curb.

Rav furrowed his brow as he settled in the back corner of the cab. Another strange reaction. What, exactly, was he getting himself into here?

He gazed out the window as they drove on the Circle Road from Papara toward the capital city of Papeete, twenty minutes away. They chatted a little, the driver offering information about the sites they passed by. As interested as Rav was, the man taxed Rav's limited French with his inability—or refusal—to converse in English. Although Rav could understand French pretty well, since that was all his parents had spoken to him as a kid, he didn't speak much of it. Maybe because, when his father was drunk, he screamed at them in French, usually as he was hitting them or their mother.

The route took them along the west coast of the French Polynesian Windward Islands. Rav leaned forward and used the manual handle to roll down the window a few inches to let the cool, salt-laden air and the cry of the seagulls wash over him, blowing away the vestiges of horror from his childhood that clung to him like cobwebs.

Mountains loomed before them as they drove past bamboo huts and one-story wooden houses painted bright red, yellow, or blue. Window boxes lining the top of a wall on one side of the road were filled with bright red flowers, and palm trees dotted the landscape, massive fronds waving gently in the breeze.

As guilty as Rav might feel about abandoning Alain and their mother for the holidays, he didn't miss the cold and snow of Pemberton one bit.

An old stone church ahead caught his eye, and Rav contemplated it as they grew closer. Christianity was the predominant religion in Tahiti, so it wasn't unusual to see churches dotting the landscape, but he hadn't paid much attention to them until now.

When was the last time he'd gone to church? *Maman* had taken him and Tane and Alain when they were kids. After the accident, they'd stopped going. Rav had few memories of Sunday school, other than hazy details like sitting cross-legged in a circle singing and the teacher holding up pictures as she told them stories. He recalled one about a giant and another about a whale. If he really thought about it, he could see a huge boat filled with animals. A kind of graphic one—of Jesus on a cross covered in blood—lingered in the recesses of his mind, but not much else.

Still, as they drew even with the stone building, the sight of the cross on top of it like the one in the story sent something rippling through him like the tiny waves of the clear, teal-colored South Pacific Ocean lapping against the shore mere feet from the other side of the car. Rav turned his head to keep his gaze fixed on the church until it disappeared behind them.

Patches of blue sky broke through the mist draped over the mountains as they entered the outskirts of the capital. Traffic was much heavier in Papeete, where the tour company was located, and Rav gripped the door handle as the cab picked up speed and cars and scooters roared by them.

After several minutes of maneuvering the taxi along busy streets, the cabbie turned into a small parking lot in front of a two-story, concrete building with a red-tiled roof. Light poured from the large front windows, and a fluorescent sign above the door announced that this was the *Golden Island Tour Company*.

The driver stopped the vehicle and grasped the top of the passenger seat as he peered around at Rav. "*Porte d'entrée ou porte arrière?*"

It took Rav a moment to translate in his head and realize the man was asking if he wanted the front door or the back. As welcoming—and not sketchy—as the front entrance looked, he said, "The woman I spoke to said to come to the back door."

"Ah." The cabbie contemplated him the way he had when Rav first climbed into the car. Then he nodded again before turning around and guiding the cab to the side of the building, stopping at the rear corner.

The dual-currency meter said seventeen American dollars or two thousand French Pacific francs. Rav tugged two thousand-franc and one five-hundred-franc notes from his wallet and held them over the seat. "*Merci.* Thank you for the ride."

The man waved away the money. "*Non, merci. C'est un cadeau.*"

Rav stared at him. A gift? Really? Why?

Before he could ask, the man grasped Rav's forearm and said, in heavily accented but flawless English, "I hope you find what you are looking for, my friend."

Getting to the back door of the business involved first glancing around to make sure, as the woman on the phone had requested, that no one other than the cab driver was watching him. Then he picked his way carefully along the uneven concrete. Tufts of weeds poked out here and there, although the lot didn't appear overgrown or completely neglected. It was almost as though it had been intentionally left just wild enough to discourage uninvited guests. Strange for a business, but no stranger than anything else that had happened thus far.

Dusk had settled over the city, leaving the property in murky twilight. Enough illumination glowed from the occasional lamp-post and the strings of lights in the trees that he could make out a low wall at the back of the lot with a metal railing running along the top of it. The steady rolling of waves hitting the shore hummed in the air.

When Rav reached the door, set halfway along the building, he stopped and assessed the situation. This entrance, lit by a single bulb next to the opening, looked nothing like the front. No windows graced the concrete wall or the wooden door desperately in need of a fresh coat of blue paint. Words engraved on a metal plate screwed into the wall next to the door and nearly lost behind dangling vines read *The Back Door Christmas Tour Company.*

He frowned. So, not part of Golden Island Tours? Then what was this place?

Although Rav had dismissed his eldest brother's opinion earlier, his voice echoed in Rav's mind now, as it had his entire life. Tane the cop would likely have a lot to say to Rav about coming to a questionable place like this alone. And not leaving. Which, despite the urging of the voice of reason in his head, Rav didn't appear to be doing.

The thing was, as unorthodox as these circumstances were, he was curious. Curious enough that a tingling sensation had spread along his arms and legs. So, without giving himself time to talk himself out of it, he reached for the rusted metal handle. Surprisingly, the knob was warm to his touch. Could be from the sun, although the day had been cool, and shadows stretched across the back lot here on the east side of the building.

Strange. And, oddly, somehow even more welcoming than the light from the windows around the front. Drawing in a deep breath, thick with the scent of lilies woven into the wreath, Rav took a last glance around the empty lot and then rapped his knuckles lightly against the wood as he pushed open the door.

When he stepped into the room, a Tahitian woman who looked to be in her sixties rose from behind a desk and rounded it to come toward him, both hands held out. "*Monsieur* Temauri. I am Maeva Amaru. My sister, Vaheana, sent you to us after the two of you spoke on the phone earlier. Welcome."

Rav hesitated. His *maman* had never shown them a lot of physical affection, so he wasn't sure how comfortable he was accepting it from this stranger. Still, the woman's smile, the tiny laugh lines extending from her sparkling brown eyes, drew him in, and he placed his hands in her soft, warm ones. "It's Rav."

"Rav." She gripped his hands firmly. "You are here at last."

"At last?" This *was* the time her sister had given him for his appointment. Wasn't it? "Am I late?"

Her laugh was light and tinkling, like water rippling over stones. "Late? No. There is no late. You arrive when it is the right time for you. As you have done."

His forehead wrinkled as he attempted to decipher what she was saying—was it a language issue? Although she did speak with a slight Tahitian accent, she was clearly fluent in English, so that likely wasn't it. In any case, nothing about the situation felt dangerous, so he'd ride it out, see what this *option* was that her sister had mentioned on the phone.

With a gentle squeeze of his fingers, she let him go and held out a hand toward a plush leather chair in front of the desk. "Please. Sit."

Rav knew few Tahitian words—hello and please and thank you but not much else. He did know that this woman's name, Maeva, was also a Tahitian greeting that meant *welcome*. Which fit her perfectly. Rav followed her across the room. As rundown as the place looked on the outside, in here lamps set on every table cast soft light on the gleaming wooden walls. Several paintings of sites from around the world hung on string from nails, and the wood floor was covered in a large blue rug with gray lines that looked like waves. It felt almost as though they were on a ship about to depart for unknown worlds. The twin longings to stay in this place forever and strike out immediately on some grand adventure twined through him like rigging from that ship, and Rav shook his head. What was happening to him?

As he settled on his seat, the woman rounded the desk with a soft flaring out of her floral skirt and lowered herself onto the black chair on the other side.

"So, you are looking for something." Maeva tugged her laptop closer and began typing on the keys.

Kind of a strange way to put it, but okay. "I am, yes. A tour of the island. Your sister mentioned you might have an available spot for me?"

She looked up, surprise flaring in her eyes. "Of course we have a spot, Rav. We have been saving it for you."

"Okay, great. Which day is available?"

"Actually ..." Maeva hit a few more keys before jumping to her feet and striding to the printer sitting on a table against the wall behind her. The machine whirred before she snatched the paper it spewed out and returned to her desk. "Our only tour lasts seven days beginning tomorrow and ending on Christmas Day."

"Seven days?" Rav had never heard of a tour that long on this little island. Most were three or four hours. The longest he'd seen was eight hours. And they were typically in the two-hundred-dollar range, Canadian. How much would a seven-day tour cost? Rav shifted on his seat.

He hadn't been at his chartered accountant firm long enough to make a decent salary yet, and he'd already spent a thousand dollars on the hotel and more than two thousand on his spur-of-the-moment flight here, which blew his vacation budget for this year. And next year. He sighed. "That's likely more than I'm looking for, so if that's all you have available, I guess I'll have to pass. Thanks anyway." He slid to the front of the chair but stopped when Maeva folded her hands on the desk, her brown eyes meeting his.

"More than you are looking for? How can you know that when you have no idea what it is you are seeking, Rav Temauri?"

For a few seconds, he only gaped at her, a tendril of heat coiling in his gut. How on earth could she know that?

"Ask yourself this." Maeva's features softened as she unclasped her fingers and lifted her hands. "What do you have to lose?"

It was a valid question. Rav was tired of living with this gaping ache inside. So tired he'd traveled halfway around the world to see if he could fill it. If he left now, he'd have wasted a lot of time and money with absolutely nothing to show for it. Other than even more money, he really did have nothing left to lose.

"All right." With a heavy exhalation of breath, he tugged the wallet from his back pocket and flipped it open. "How much is it?"

"Nothing."

He looked up, the credit card he clutched between two fingers pulled partially from its slot. "Nothing?"

That warm smile crossed her face again. "That's right. This particular tour is always free. A gift."

"A gift?" Although he was aware that he was contributing little to this conversation beyond repeating what Maeva said, Rav couldn't seem to form any coherent sentences on his own. In any language.

"Yes. In fact, as soon as you agree to join us, I will contact the Blue Heron, cancel your reservation there, and have your things brought over. That should result in a refund showing up shortly on your card, which will mean, if you are keeping score, that you will come out ahead. Financially, anyway. The rest is up to you."

Her words were getting all scrambled up in his head. Rav made another attempt to make sense of them. "There's no cost."

Her smile broadened enough that a deep dimple appeared in each cheek. "I didn't say that. Only that you will not have to pay any money."

A light shower of tingles danced over his skin, but nothing about the woman was ominous. "Where would I stay?"

"Here." She waved a hand toward another blue door, this one freshly painted and leading into an interior room. "This is our home, Rav. My husband Nino's and mine. And you are invited to share it with us. It will be your home as well over the holidays."

A home for the holidays. Those words, at least, were clear. The mysterious longing that had ignited when he'd first entered the room—to stay here forever—intensified. He *could* stay here. If not forever, at least for seven days. The sense that he actually might find what he was looking for if he did agree to stay filled him with the same glow of warmth radiating from that rusty door handle.

What do you have to lose at this point? He tucked the card back into the slot and closed his wallet. "Okay then. I accept."

"Wonderful." Maeva clapped her hands. "Simply sign here and then I will take you to meet the others." She slid the piece of paper from the printer tray across the desk to him.

The others? Rav didn't ask, only scanned the form, which didn't appear to be asking him to confirm anything other than his name and the fact that he intended to participate in the Back Door Christmas Tour this year. After scrawling his signature on the line at the bottom, he stood and trailed after Maeva as she crossed the room to the other blue door, turned the knob—which Rav suspected would be every bit as warm as the one outside—and pushed it open.

Although he hadn't heard a sound coming from the room while he'd been sitting at the desk, the moment he reached the threshold, the hum of conversation, tinkling of dishes, and soft Christmas music playing in the background filled the air. Rav counted six other people in the large room, three men and three women, holding plates and standing around talking beneath a large, glittering chandelier. Strings of lights twinkled from the rafters, and potted palm trees were everywhere, loaded down with ornaments and more lights. The tantalizing aromas of roast pork, coconut, and nutmeg drifted in the air. Rav's senses went into overload as he attempted to take it all in.

One of the men glanced over and then detached himself from the conversation he'd been having with a gentleman in a Hawaiian shirt. When he started in their direction, Maeva touched Rav's arm lightly. "Here's Nino."

Maeva's husband wore knee-length cargo shorts and a dark blue shirt with white ferns printed all over it. He strolled toward them, one hand outstretched, his eyes and smile as welcoming as his wife's. "Ah, *Monsieur* Temauri. Welcome. We have been waiting for you. Now we are all here." Like his wife, Nino spoke excellent English with a light Tahitian accent.

Rav allowed the man to take his hand in a firm grip and pump it up and down. "It's Rav, please. I'm sorry if I kept you waiting. I thought my appointment was for six."

Nino's round face lit with a smile as warm as his wife's. "I don't mean today. We've been waiting for you much longer than that."

Before Rav could question the comment—every bit as cryptic as any of Maeva's—Nino released him and waved a hand toward a long table filled with food and bowls of punch. "I must go help my wife with the final preparations for tomorrow. As for you, Rav Temauri"—he slapped Rav on the back—"go meet everyone. And please, make yourself at home. Because, for the next seven days, that is exactly where you are."

Rav made his way around the room, introducing himself to the other members of the tour—two African-American sisters in their seventies—Sojourner and Septima—from South Carolina who were friendly with everyone else but decidedly frosty toward each other. A guy in his early twenties with tattoos all over his arms, Xaviar, who lived in Toronto, apparently, although he looked Latino and his words, though few and far between, held a hint of Spanish. And the gentleman Nino had been talking to when Rav entered the room, Gregory from Sydney, Australia.

The final member of the group—the one Rav was the most drawn to but had the hardest time getting a bead on—was a woman about his age, also from Canada, who had freckles scattered across a nose that was pink from the tropical sun and strawberry-blonde hair that brushed across her shoulders whenever she turned her head.

She so closely resembled the fictional Anne from Prince Edward Island that he nearly laughed when she told him her name was Annie. The warning look she shot him stopped him. Obviously, she'd received that reaction before and didn't appreciate it.

For some reason, the tingling in his arms and legs had started up again the moment he'd laid eyes on her. They hadn't gotten much further than introductions, though, when Gregory from Australia wandered over to join them.

"Excuse me. I think I'll go get a drink." Annie's green eyes had met Rav's briefly before she nodded and turned away.

Rav chatted with Gregory for a few minutes, hoping she would return. She didn't. Rav attributed the disappointment he felt over that—way out of proportion, given their brief interaction—to the fact that he continued to struggle to get his bearings as the evening wore on. He wasn't the only one. All the tourists appeared to be walking around in a bit of a daze as though, like him, they were wondering how they had ended up here and what lay in store.

As Septima joined him and Gregory and began regaling them with stories of her and her sister's travels, Rav's gaze drifted often to Annie. She talked to Xaviar—who looked even more confused than Rav felt—for a minute or two before encountering Sojourner at the food table. The two of them meandered past the platters and bowls, adding appetizers to their plates and chatting as they walked.

At one point, Annie threw back her head and laughed. The sound caught at Rav's chest, and he couldn't tear his gaze away. Then she glanced over and caught him watching her, and the amusement faded from her face.

Heat crawled up his neck as he returned his attention to Septima and Gregory. For the next little while, as Rav made several unsuccessful attempts to extricate himself from the conversation—and from Septima's grip on his arm—Annie wandered around the room, studying the pictures hanging on the walls and fingering the ornaments on the trees.

When Rav was finally able to make his excuses and head over to the food table, Annie was gone. He surreptitiously glanced around the room as he filled a small bowl with *poe*, a starchy pudding made from taro root and flavored with bananas, papayas, and vanilla. Although his mother hadn't cooked a lot of homemade meals, especially after the accident, she did make *poe* often when he and his brothers were growing up. The sight and smell of it stirred up mixed emotions in Rav, and he set the bowl on the table and scanned the expansive space again.

"She went up to bed, honey." Sojourner reached past him for a bowl.

"Who?" Rav feigned innocence.

Sojourner tilted her head. "The one you've been watching all evening."

Ah. He thought he'd been more discreet than that. Rav contemplated protesting, but Sojourner's voice, her southern accent as thick and sweet as the dessert, held enough kindness woven through the amusement that he left it alone.

This was a seven-day tour. He'd have plenty of time to get to know Annie—and everyone else—starting with breakfast the next day.

December Twentieth

Annie didn't show up to breakfast. Their first meal together was buffet style, with tour group members coming and going. Although he searched the room when he walked in, Rav didn't see Annie. He filled a plate and settled across from Gregory at one of the four tables in the dining room. Sojourner and Septima joined them a few minutes later, but Xaviar sat by himself at another table, ate quickly, and then disappeared up the stairs where their rooms were located.

Even after finding his belongings—one small suitcase and a carry-on bag—waiting for him the night before outside the small, comfortable upstairs bedroom Nino had shown him to, and the email confirming that a full refund for the rest of his stay at the Blue Heron would be issued to his credit card in two to three business days, Rav struggled to comprehend that what was happening was real.

Given the craziness of the past twenty-four hours, it was entirely possible that he had imagined Annie. She wasn't in the office area when they all gathered there in preparation for heading out on their first excursion. If she actually had been there the night before, was she still planning to be part of the tour?

If not, Rav should have tried harder to speak to her the night before. He couldn't remember ever having such a strong reaction to meeting a woman. Had he lost the opportunity to get to know her better? He frowned. It wasn't love he was searching for. Was it?

Neither he nor his brothers dated much. By high school, the color of his skin seemed to become less of a liability and more of an asset. Other than everyone assuming he'd be great at soccer, which he wasn't, guys were friendlier and girls more interested in him than they had been in the past.

After everything that had happened to his family, though, Rav was guarded, hesitant to let anyone get close. Alain had a girlfriend now, but as great as Carly was and as good a fit as the two of them were for each other, Alain didn't strike Rav as being truly happy.

So, despite his initial reaction to the redhead with the compelling laugh, a relationship with a woman likely wasn't the ultimate answer for Rav either. Which meant he needed to focus, work on fixing whatever was wrong with himself before he attempted to involve anyone else in his life.

Despite the self-admonishment, when Annie slipped into the office and pressed her back to the wall just as Nino strolled to the front of the group and turned to face everyone, the tingling started up again, and Rav had to force himself to look away from her so he could concentrate on their host.

"Attention, everyone." Nino clapped his hands. "I trust you all slept well and enjoyed a good breakfast."

Everyone nodded, and Nino continued. "Today we begin our week-long Christmas exploration of the beautiful island of Tahiti. To kick off our quest, we'll be taking the ferry from Papeete to the island of Moorea. There we'll be doing a little kayaking, so we can enjoy an up-close-and-personal encounter with the incredible creatures beneath the sea."

Kayaking. Rav pursed his lips. He could live with that. His hometown of Pemberton sat in a valley ringed by mountains with the beautiful Lillooet River running through it. Rav had kayaked numerous times on the river with his buddies and always enjoyed it.

He shoved back the twinge of homesickness that thought sparked and focused on Maeva, who stood next to her husband. She tugged a piece of paper from the pocket of her bright-pink capris. "At the start of each day of the tour, you will be paired with someone else in the group. Stick together for the day and watch out for each other, okay?"

Glancing down at the paper, she read out their names in groups of two. Although Rav had been hoping to be assigned to Annie, Maeva and Nino had matched him with Gregory from Australia. Gregory, who was standing next to Rav, elbowed him in the arm. "All right with you, mate?"

Rav nodded. "Sure." This guy looked as though he had lived some life. Could be an interesting day.

When he climbed aboard the small bus that waited for them outside the back door, the driver, a short man with a round belly and a smile that stretched from one side of his face to the other, held out his hand. "Welcome aboard. I am Oro."

Rav shifted his bag with a change of clothes and a couple of bottles of water in it from his right hand to his left so he could shake hands with the man. "Good to meet you. I'm—"

"Rav Temauri. Yes. We had nearly given up on you."

Rav narrowed his eyes. Given up on him? What did that mean? Not wanting to hold up the line, Rav didn't hang around to ask. Maybe he'd get another chance this week.

He found an empty seat and slid onto the bench. Gregory dropped down next to him, and Rav shifted a little to give him more space.

Annie walked by their seat, clutching her bag to her chest. She glanced briefly at Rav before continuing on toward the back of the bus to join her partner for the day, Sojourner. Rav didn't look behind him to see where she ended up, only turned to contemplate his seat mate as the engine roared to life and the driver pulled out onto the street.

"So, Gregory, what brought you to Tahiti?" This close up, he realized the man wasn't as old as he'd first thought, maybe early sixties, like Nino and Maeva. Gregory's face was a little weathered, as though he spent a lot of time in the sun, which could explain why he had appeared older at first glance.

"My wife is with her sister. I was alone for Christmas, so I decided I needed an adventure."

His accent was strong, but not so strong Rav couldn't understand him. He would have to pay attention when his partner-for-the-day spoke, though. He attempted to pinpoint what it was he caught in the man's voice when he spoke about his wife. Love, for sure. What would that be like, to be in a lifelong relationship with someone you adored? Would he ever experience that? He rested the back of his head against the window. "What's your wife's name?"

"Sharon. I call her my Rose of Sharon."

Rav's forehead wrinkled. "Rose of Sharon?"

"Yeah. You know, from the Bible."

"Oh. No. I haven't heard that. I guess I haven't been reading the Bible often enough lately. Or ever, really. Not since—" Rav pressed his lips together. Had he actually been about to bring up the accident with a total stranger? He didn't talk about that with anyone.

As bizarre as this whole situation still felt, something about the atmosphere Maeva and Nino had created made it easy to open up and share with each other. Too easy. The tingling in Rav's arms and legs started up again, but colder this time. He rubbed his arms absentmindedly. Would Gregory push him on what he'd been about to say?

He didn't, only offered Rav a rueful grin. "I haven't read it much myself lately."

Rav took a shot at changing the subject. "It's a nice term of endearment, though. Your wife must love that."

With both hands, Gregory gripped the bag he'd rested on his knees. "She docs."

Before Rav could question him further, the bus slowed, and the driver pulled into the port area where they would board the ferry. The red-and-white boat waited at the dock, and in twenty minutes they had set off. Annie and Sojourner disappeared inside, where there was a small cafeteria and lots of seating.

As tempted as Rav was to follow, he and Gregory found a spot along one side of the upper deck. According to Nino, this was the high-speed ferry for passengers, no vehicles, which meant the trip should only take about twenty-five minutes. Rav set his bag at his feet and rested his forearms on the railing. "Have you ever been to Tahiti?"

"No." Gregory kept his gaze on the far horizon. "I've never done much traveling, although I've always meant to give it a burl, you know?"

Rav didn't know exactly, since he'd never heard the word *burl*. From context, he guessed it meant try it. He'd go with that, anyway. "And you finally did."

"Yeah. I'm giving it a fair go. You?"

"I've never traveled either. My parents are from here, so I thought this might be a good place to start."

"Makes sense. She sure is a beaut."

"Yes. She is." Rav contemplated the teal-blue water they were skimming over. "Did you know before you came you'd be part of this tour?"

For the first time since they'd left port, Gregory swung his attention from the horizon to Rav. "Absolutely not. I didn't really plan anything much. Guess I thought I'd be a bludger, lazing about the beach. Then, a couple nights in, I was feeling homesick and went to a pub." He lifted one hand in the air. "What is that, do you think? We head off on a trip thinking a new place will be fun and exciting, then we immediately search out something that makes us feel like we're home."

Rav didn't really get that, since the last thing he'd want to search out was anything that reminded him of his home. Then he remembered the sensation that had filled him when he walked into The Back Door Christmas Tour Company. As though he'd come home, only nothing like the one he'd known growing up. A real home. That sensation had brushed lightly over him like a warm, tropical breeze. So yeah, maybe, on some level, they *were* all seeking something like that. "I get what you're saying."

Gregory studied him a moment. "You do, don't you? Anyway, I'd a really bottled the trip if I hadn't sat down on a stool and started talking to the bartender. End of the night, he handed me a card and told me to call the number."

"And you did."

Gregory shrugged. "It all seemed a bit strange, so I wasn't going to. For some reason, maybe with Christmas coming, the idea wouldn't let go of me. Next day, I punched in the number. What's happened since," he waved a hand toward Nino and Maeva, standing with their backs to them on the other side of the ferry, "well, I'm gobsmacked."

Rav laughed. Although he felt more in need of a translator than he had since arriving in Tahiti, even with the cabbie, he could get the gist of what his new *mate* was saying. "Me too."

"I don't know what's happening, that's deadset. But something tells me she'll be right."

She'll be right. Rav liked that. The spinning in his head that had started up while he was still on the phone with Maeva's sister eased a bit, and he drew in a deep breath laden with the scent of the wind and the sea. "I'm inclined to agree with you."

"Generally a good idea, mate."

Rav chuckled. Although this was the rainy season in Tahiti, the sun peeked out beneath low-hanging clouds. The temperature was around sixty-eight degrees Fahrenheit. Cool enough, especially out here on the water and with a strong breeze whipping around them. Tane was glad for the navy windbreaker he'd pulled on as he was leaving his room.

Although he was used to the river and to mountains, having grown up in the shadow of them, he never tired of the sight of tree-covered peaks and sparkling water, and he reveled in both as they skimmed across the waves.

When their destination—the port of Vaiare—appeared in the distance, Rav decided to duck inside to use the facilities before they disembarked. He didn't see Annie when he glanced into the cafeteria, but Sojourner sat at a table, a paper cup in front of her. Likely Annie sat opposite her, out of sight behind a low wall.

When he emerged from the men's bathroom a few minutes later, Annie was coming out of the women's at the same time. Although

Rav had told himself it didn't matter if he saw her or not, his pulse rate did ratchet up. Which was crazy. He knew nothing about the woman beyond her name. He smiled. "Hey, Annie."

Green eyes peered out beneath the wide brim of a white hat. "Hey. It's ..."

Apparently, she knew even less than that about him, which stung a bit. Maybe more than a bit.

He was about to supply his name when she added, "... Rav, right?"

At least it had come to her. Eventually. "That's right. How was the trip over?"

"Good. We've just had a cup of tea. Are you guys—"

The ferry jolted as it bumped against the dock, and Annie stumbled a little to one side. Rav grasped her elbows lightly to steady her. "You okay?"

A pink flush crossed her cheeks. "I'm good, thanks."

Rav let her go. "What were you saying?"

Annie smoothed the front of her green T-shirt—the exact shade of her eyes. "Oh. I just wondered if things were going well with you and Gregory."

His name she remembered. Rav shook it off. "They are, actually. I'm not convinced we speak the same language, but he seems like a great guy."

She laughed—the mesmerizing laugh that had caught his attention the night before. The crazy idea that he could happily spend the rest of his life trying to make her laugh flitted through his mind, but Rav shut it down fast.

The ferry jolted again, but Annie pressed a hand to the wall. "I've kind of been thinking the same thing about Sojourner. I mean, she's been telling me about some of her favorite foods, and I have no idea what Frogmore Stew is or boiled peanuts or a pig pickin', and I'm pretty sure I don't want to."

Rav grinned. "The pig-pickin' sounds like it could be okay, but I'm with you on the others. Have you asked her if she's ever tried poutine or a beavertail?"

Annie snapped her fingers and pointed at him. "Good idea. I haven't had much of a chance to get a word in edgewise, but I'm definitely asking her that at some point today."

Sojourner must enjoy talking as much as her sister. Was that what was causing tension between the two of them?

Now that he'd heard Gregory's story, Rav was dying to ask Annie how she happened to end up on the tour. Before he could, the loudspeaker crackled and a voice announced that they would be able to leave the ferry shortly.

Annie pushed away from the wall. "Well, I better get back to my partner. If I hold her up, I'm worried she'll say 'Bless your heart' to me in the same tone she used with the man behind the counter who spilled her tea and a woman who cut in line ahead of her. Pretty sure it wasn't a compliment."

Rav chuckled. "Ah. The southern blessing. Could be good or bad, depending on context and tone of voice. Not sure I'd want to be on the receiving end of the kind she offered either of those people. I should get back to Gregory, anyway. See you on shore."

She nodded before disappearing through the doors to the cafeteria. Rav watched her longer than he should have, given that his partner would be waiting on deck, wondering where he'd gotten to. Was there an Australian version of *bless your heart?* Still grinning, he made his way up the stairs to the deck.

Rav dipped one end of his paddle and then the other into the clear, brilliant-blue water of the lagoon. The kayaks were see-through, constructed of the same material as airplane windows, according to Nino, which was very cool and allowed them to peer below the water as they glided across the surface.

Colorful coral rocks dotted the sandy ocean floor, fish of vibrant colors and endless patterns swimming between them. Huge stingrays, gray bodies rippling, drifted beneath the bottom of the vessel.

Clouds still hung low, but it hadn't rained. Occasional rays of sun broke through, warming Rav and showering sparkles onto the waves. He'd just begun to relax into the beauty and serenity when a scream behind them shattered the calm. Several people called out his and Gregory's names. Rav whirled around. The paddle struck the side of the kayak, and he nearly lost his grip on it but managed to grab it before it flipped into the ocean.

He and Gregory were the farthest from shore, and the other three kayaks in their group were retreating quickly, heading for the beach. It took Rav about two seconds to figure out why. Between them and the closest kayak, three fins protruded from the water. No, four. With the other paddlers now in shallow water, the sharks had apparently decided to turn their attention on his and Gregory's kayak, as the fins were heading in their direction. In seconds, the first dark shadow had glided beneath the clear bottom of their craft.

Rav swallowed. He was no expert, but that looked like it could be a blacktip, which he only knew because on the plane he'd read a few articles about water activities in and around Tahiti and come across one that described a blacktip attacking a kiteboarder. The guy hadn't died, but he did sustain serious injuries. He hadn't been in a kayak, though. Would the sharks attempt to tip over their boat?

The tingling along his arms and legs started up, cold and biting, and a heavy weight formed in his stomach. He might not be sure about much in his life right now, but Rav was sure about one thing. He was not ready to die.

Another shark swam underneath them, the fin grazing the bottom of the boat. Rav tore his gaze away from the sight to check on Gregory. Like him, his partner had rested his paddle on his knees and was staring at a shark swimming past the kayak on his left. He uttered a word Rav hadn't heard before but didn't have to be Australian to understand, given the context. If their situation wasn't so dire, he might have laughed.

Gregory shot him a look. "Sorry."

"Don't be. I was thinking pretty much the same thing in my head."

"I can deal with snakes and crocodiles. No idea about sharks. Any suggestions?"

"I read an article that said shark attacks on kayaks are rare." The words were barely out of Rav's mouth before one of the sharks bumped the side of the boat. Both he and Gregory gripped the sides, managing to hold onto their paddles in the process. Which was good, since they were the only weapons either of them had and their only hope of getting to shore.

Still gripping the sides, Gregory stared at the fin sliding by a foot from his knuckles. "So, we're just lucky, you're saying?"

"Apparently."

"We get out of this, I'll be buying myself a scratchie then."

Was that a lottery ticket? Rav loosened his grip on the boat slightly. The circumstances were bad, but he'd far rather be in them with someone who'd crack a joke in the face of danger than lose it completely.

What would Tane do? The question that had guided almost every decision Rav had made in his life flashed through his mind now. *Stay cool. Assess the danger. Calmly leave the situation if possible.*

"I think we should attempt to slowly paddle to shore."

Another shark bumped into the boat, and he tightened his grip again. While it might be the best plan they had, Rav had no idea whether the sharks would allow them to simply row away.

"I could jump in."

Rav's head jerked up, and he gaped at his partner. Was that another joke that lost something in the cultural divide between them? "What?"

The pale-blue eyes that locked on his were deadly serious. "I could go into the water. Distract them so you could get back to shore."

"No way." The sharks were circling them now, but they'd moved a few feet out from the kayak. Cautiously, Rav let go of the sides and straightened, tightening his fingers around the paddle. "Your wife would never forgive me if I let anything happen to you. We're partners. We stick together."

Gregory nodded and let go of the kayak. Rav turned around to face forward. Just before he lowered the end of the paddle into the water, he glanced over his shoulder. "Oh, that article said to avoid splashing as much as possible, as that attracts them, so once we're turned around, let's each use one end of our paddles and stay on opposite sides."

"Got it."

Careful not to touch any of the sharks, Rav slid the end of the paddle into the water and drew it alongside the vessel. Gregory paddled on the same side and the craft gradually turned toward shore. When they were facing the beach, drops of water hit Rav's back as Gregory swung his paddle to the other side.

The sharks continued to circle as the men began the painstaking voyage back. Rav drew in one slow, deep breath after another to keep panic at bay. An image of the church he and the cabbie had driven by materialized in his mind. Rav had thought about God occasionally over the years, wondered if he might be real. If so, this would be as good a time as any for him to show himself. Would Tane pray at a time like—

Enough. Rav was an adult. It was time for him to start making decisions by himself. Figure out his own life without wondering what his brother would think. The memory of the crumpled letter in his pocket started to wander into his brain, but Rav slammed the door to keep it out. He needed to focus.

A fin cut through the water, close enough to Rav's paddle that he had to lift it out of the way. Whether or not Tane would pray, Rav was going for it. *God, if you're there, would you help us out? Please? Like you did with that guy and the whale? He didn't die, right? If you could do that for me and Gregory, that would be great. Thanks.*

Had he done it right? The same sensation he'd felt staring at that cross did ripple through his chest, but he didn't have time to think about what it could mean. Rav lowered the paddle. For now, he needed to concentrate on getting to shore.

Although they stuck close, none of the sharks bumped the boat again. Halfway back, Rav looked up to see another kayak coming toward them. Nino sat on the front seat, but Rav couldn't tell who was in the back. Likely, he should suggest they turn around and save themselves, but the idea of more of them out here, fending off their predators, was too great a comfort.

By the time Nino reached them, the bottom of the ocean was only three or four feet below them. Nino turned his paddle sideways to slow the kayak as they drew alongside Rav and Gregory. Annie sat in the back. She lifted her paddle from the water as Nino gripped the side of Rav's boat. "You guys okay?"

"So far," Rav said. "We'll be better when we're on dry land, though."

Nino offered him a tight smile as he pushed away and began turning around. "Let's get you there then."

They paddled silently for a couple of minutes. Although they passed over rocks and coral, no fish were in sight. Not surprising, since they were surrounded by … Rav glanced around. Actually, they weren't. Whether because of the reinforcements or the shallowness of the water, the sharks had fallen back.

In seconds, both boats bumped against sand. Rav and Nino climbed out and splashed through the water as they tugged the kayaks up onto the beach. They were immediately swarmed by the rest of the tour group, everyone asking if they were all right. Even Xaviar punched Rav lightly in the arm and said, "Glad you're okay, man."

Septima, her hands clasped in front of her chest, said, "I was fixin' to row back out to you too, honey, but Sojourner suggested my efforts might be better put to praying for the two of you."

Rav managed a smile. "Your sister is very wise."

"She'd be the first to say so."

When Sojourner frowned, Septima slid a hand through the crook of her sister's elbow. "And she would be right."

That seemed to ease a little of the tension radiating between them, and Sojourner smiled. Septima hooked her free hand around Annie's elbow, and the three of them wandered off across the sand.

"I was planning to go with Nino, but she insisted she needed to be the one. She's a brave girl."

Rav tore his gaze from the retreating women to glance down at Maeva, standing in front of him, her eyes a swirling mixture of concern and relief. "Yes, she is."

Maeva stepped closer and wrapped her arms around his waist. "I was so worried. I prayed and prayed the two of you would get back safe."

Rav hadn't been sure how to respond to her physical affection when they'd first met. Now he simply settled in and hugged her, Maeva's maternal touch conveying more affection than any words could. When she let him go, he cleared his throat. "I prayed too."

"And the good Lord answered."

"Apparently." Between them, they had sent up a lot of frantic prayers. Could that truly be why they stood ankle deep in white sand and hadn't been torn to pieces? In case, Rav shot a glance at a patch of blue between gauzy clouds. *Thanks.*

When he looked down at her again, Maeva's deep brown eyes probed his before she smiled. "Are you hungry?"

Rav laughed. She was a mother, all right. "I could eat something." He was ravenous, suddenly, which surprised him. After the close call they'd had, he wouldn't have been surprised if he hadn't been able to eat for a while. The reception he and Gregory had gotten at the beach, though, from this group that had, even after knowing each other for such a short period of time, inexplicably bonded, had leached the horror from his bones and eased the cold tingling across his flesh.

Rav held out a hand to Nino, standing nearby. "Thank you for coming out there after us."

Nino grasped his hand and pulled him into a hug, slapping Rav on the back a few times before letting him go. "Of course. You are in my care this week, Rav, all of you. Nothing will happen to any of you. Not if I have any say in it."

His throat was still thick from Maeva's hug, and Nino's words, his *care*, didn't help. Rav only nodded. He still had no real idea what was going on, how he had gotten into this situation, but it no longer mattered.

He slung his arm around Gregory's shoulders. "You all right, buddy?"

Gregory offered him a half-grin but didn't meet his eyes. "I'm thinking I'll be pulling out my Bible again as soon as I get home. And I could use a tallie, but yeah, sure."

"A tallie?"

"You know, a beer?" Gregory held out his hands, his right palm hovering a good foot above his left.

A *big* beer, then. "Ah. Got it." Rav wasn't a drinker—too afraid he would lose the rigid control he kept on himself and his circumstances—but after what had just happened, if there'd been one available, he might have made an exception. Except ... He contemplated the people wandering around the beach—Annie, Xaviar, and Nino pulling pieces of driftwood into a circle and

Maeva, Septima, and Sojourner tugging plastic containers out of cooler bags.

Maybe he didn't need anything more than this moment on the beach to feel, for the first time in a long time, that he was part of something bigger than himself.

On the ferry ride home, he and Gregory returned to the upper deck. Both of them rested their arms on the railing and gazed out at the whitecaps, the swooping seagulls, the tinges of pink and orange stretching across the sky beyond the mountains.

After a few minutes of silence, Rav nudged Gregory in the elbow. "Thank you for what you did this afternoon, offering to go into the water for me. It was heroic."

Gregory frowned. "There was nothing heroic about it. That was all cowardice, believe me."

Rav turned to face him, leaning a hip against the rail. "What are you talking about? You were willing to die for me."

Gregory continued to stare out across the water. "As much as I wanted you to live, that wasn't why I offered."

"Then why?"

His partner didn't answer for so long, Rav wondered if he would. Maybe what had happened today had created a false sense of closeness in Rav's mind and Gregory had no interest in baring his soul to Rav.

Then Gregory pushed himself up, wrapping his fingers around the railing. "I didn't lie when I told you my wife was with her sister." He let go and turned to look at Rav. "Because her sister died five years ago."

Jolts of shock slithered through Rav. "Oh."

Gregory exhaled. "A few weeks before Christmas last year, Sharon was alone at home, eating lunch, and she choked on something. When I got home from work, hours later, I found her on the kitchen floor." He rubbed the side of his hand over his forehead. "A loss like that, so sudden, no warning. It messes with a person, ya know?"

In a way, Rav did know. One night in his childhood had changed his life forever. It wasn't the same as losing the person who was like the other half of you, though, so maybe he had no right to comment.

Gregory didn't seem to need him to. He lowered his hand and met Rav's gaze. "We were married thirty-five years and then she was gone, and I was alone."

"Oh man. I'm really sorry, Gregory." The sorrow billowing through him caught Rav by surprise. Scared him a little. He'd spent his life guarding his heart, keeping everyone except his brothers at bay. Tane's letter had reminded him how much even letting those few people in could hurt. So how had Rav so quickly let his walls down with this group of strangers?

"Thanks." Gregory waved a hand weakly through the air. "The thing is, I've been feeling completely stonkered ever since. Deep in this hole I had no idea how to pull myself out of. That's why I took this trip. It was an attempt to somehow claw my way out of the dark. I hadn't sunk far enough to think about offing myself. But today, staring down at those sharks, it occurred to me there might be an easy way out. Then you told me we were partners, and we were sticking together, and I realized that maybe I'm not as alone as I'd been feeling. Soon as that came to me, the thought of ending it all disappeared as quickly as it had come."

Gregory offered him a wry grin. "Not to mention I'd have to face Sharon after, and she'd a got me up good for pullin' a stunt like that. So, it's me who should be thanking you for saving my life today—and keeping me from a good tongue-lashing—not the other way around."

Huh. Was this what Rav had been searching for? Being part of a community that watched out for each other? Would that fill the emptiness inside? "I get what you're saying. When we arrived back at the beach today, and everyone was so happy to see us, I felt like that too. Like I wasn't alone."

"Good feeling, isn't it?"

"It is. Very good." Although something still seemed to be missing. He rubbed a palm over his chest.

Gregory turned back to the water. "You think it's chance, all of us getting together?"

Rav turned back, too, and propped his elbows on the railing, clasping his hands together. Gazing up at a patch of clear sky between drifting clouds, the first stars twinkling against a backdrop of indigo, he said, "You know what? I'm beginning to believe it's not."

December Twenty-First

Rav kept a close eye on Sojourner, his partner for the day, as they picked their way along the uneven stone walkway leading to the Arahurahu Morae, one of the open-air temples in Tahiti.

Septima and Sojourner were very mobile, and neither appeared to need or want any help on these excursions. Still, they were in their seventies, and if either went down, it could cause a serious disruption to their holiday. And it would cast a shadow over the entire group. Rav definitely didn't want that to happen on his watch.

That morning, they'd taken the bus along the Circle Road, following the east coast of the island. Their first stop was this sacred site in the valley of Tefa'aiti, ringed by trees and mountains. A light drizzle fell from the sky, and Rav lifted the hood of his windbreaker with one hand while struggling to keep his black umbrella over Sojourner as she forged ahead.

They passed a reddish structure that looked a bit like one of the many totem poles scattered around his home province of British

Columbia, except shorter and with only two beings, clearly a male and a female, stacked one on top of the other. Some kind of gods?

As they approached the raised stone altar, they walked by another idol-looking statue. This one, a woman with a stern face, was huge and dark and carved of stone. Rav repressed a shudder.

The temple area was well kept up with a large, raised, rectangular area comprised of loose, moss-covered stones. A massive wall made of the same stones had been erected at the far end.

A thick silence hung over the place. To some, it might seem peaceful and holy. These sites had long been held sacred by Polynesians, Rav's people. Shouldn't he feel something here? Even if he wasn't yet convinced God was real or cared about him, this place felt as empty as he had been inside for so long.

He'd wondered that morning when Nino told them they were going to a temple if maybe he would find answers here. Instead, he experienced only a slight foreboding, a heaviness that weighed him down more and more the longer they stayed. Human sacrifices had been part of the sacred rituals and ceremonies carried out on this site. Was that the reason for the darkness that hovered over the place?

When Maeva announced that it was time to go, Rav was relieved. The rain had tapered off, and he closed the umbrella and followed Sojourner along the pathway through the trees back to the bus.

Before they climbed aboard, he shrugged out of his windbreaker and shook off the drops of moisture. If only he could as effortlessly shake off the uneasiness clinging to him like the moss clung to those temple stones.

Everyone was quiet as they pulled out of the lot. Even Sojourner, who had chatted non-stop on the drive from Papeete, appeared deep in thought as she gazed out the window at the palm trees, thatched-roof huts, and ocean flashing by.

They stopped at a small restaurant that advertised *poisson cru*, the national dish of Tahiti, as its specialty. Rav's *maman* had made the dish a few times, and he'd always enjoyed it, so he was game to try it here. Several others did as well, although when the server described it as raw tuna marinated in coconut milk and lime juice, Annie looked so repulsed that Rav couldn't help but laugh. She and Sojourner and Septima had sandwiches instead, something Gregory informed them was called a *cut lunch*, which made sense.

Rav made a quick trip to the men's room before they got back on the bus. When he came out, Annie, who was spending the day with Xaviar, was about to head into the ladies' room.

"We really need to stop meeting like this," she quipped.

Rav grinned, although he didn't mind these meet-ups, since they were the only times the two of them had had a moment alone since the tour began. "What did you think of the temple?"

Her smile faded. "I didn't like it. There was something dark about that place."

"I felt that too. I thought that maybe, since my ancestors are Polynesian, I might be drawn to the sacredness, but it turned out I couldn't get out of there fast enough."

Annie propped a shoulder against the wall as if she had all day to talk to him. "Is that why you're here in Tahiti, trying to connect with your roots?"

"I don't really know why I'm here, to be honest. I made the spontaneous decision to come after getting some disappointing news. I'm looking for something, but I'm not sure what."

"I get that."

She sounded so dejected that Rav almost reached out, but he had no idea how a gesture like that, even if only intended to comfort, might be received. "Why—"

"Two-minute warning," Nino called from the dining area.

Annie pushed away from the wall. "I better ..." She pointed to the washroom.

"Of course." Rav nodded. "We'll finish this conversation next time we meet outside the restrooms."

She laughed at that, which meant he'd accomplished his mission for the day. He was still smiling as he crossed the restaurant parking lot and boarded the bus.

The levity and conversation over the meal had dispelled the somberness that had trailed after them when they left the temple site. Everyone was much more animated on the short bus ride to their next destination—The Water Gardens of Vaipahi, in Taravao.

The gardens had been well named. Everywhere Rav looked he saw ponds and pools. The hum of a waterfall played a constant soundtrack in the background as they wandered along the rough dirt path. According to the sign at the entrance, the gardens contained over seventy-five different types of flowers and plants. The dampness in the air and lush shades of green—how was it possible there were so many?—dotted with red and yellow and orange gave the place a rainforest feel, heightened by the drops that had begun to sift down from gray skies again.

He and Sojourner paused at a bridge to gaze at the Vaipahu Falls. Sojourner had been ducking out from under the umbrella all day, but Rav made another attempt to hold it over her now.

She wrapped her fingers around the shaft, gently tugging the umbrella from him and sliding it closed. "Don't you ever let yourself simply *feel* the rain, Rav?"

Had he? When he was a kid, maybe. When he and Tane and Alain had escaped the hell that was their home for a few glorious hours to tromp through puddles and wrestle each other in the wet grass and mud.

Not since then, though. Rav closed his eyes and tipped his head to allow the drops to splatter onto his face. He forced himself not to move, not to think, simply to—as Sojourner had suggested—*feel*. Feel the coolness of the drops. The slight tickle as they slid along his cheek and down his neck. A warm, light wind ruffling his hair.

Being still heightened his other senses too. He breathed in the scents of rain and gardenias and damp earth. The background sounds he hadn't paid much attention to separated now into the soft roar of the falls, the splashing as it dropped into the pool below, the rippling of water over rocks—all different yet blending together like parts of an orchestra.

Bird calls too. Rav could make out several different ones, accompanied by the humming of insects. The awareness that he was part of this too—of the beautiful, harmonious creation surrounding him—swelled within him like that orchestra reaching the crescendo of a spellbinding piece of music.

Rav opened his eyes. Next to him, Sojourner stood gripping the railing of the bridge, her face tilted to the sky, her eyes still closed, her short, gray curls plastered to her head. A look of complete serenity had settled over her features, flowing out from her as discernably as the tension often did when Septima was around.

Sojourner opened her eyes and contemplated him. "You look peaceful."

Did he? Was that the soft, rippling sensation he'd felt deep inside a few times lately? "I was just thinking the same about you."

"That isn't usually your life, is it?"

He thought about protesting, but her voice held as much kindness and compassion as it had the night she'd teased him about looking for Annie. Besides, she wasn't wrong. "No, I guess it isn't."

She rested slightly gnarled fingers on his hand. "Rough home life growing up?"

"You could say that." His stomach tightened. Would she press him for details? That would shatter the peaceful feeling fast.

Sojourner patted his hand before pulling her arm back. "I'll be praying that peace finds a place in the very core of you and settles right in."

"Thank you." His throat had thickened again, and he cleared it. "How did you know?"

"There's something in your eyes. Like you want to reach out but don't trust that the one you reach out to won't slap your hand away."

Wow. She'd nailed him. Rav never would have been able to put into words how he'd always felt deep inside, but Sojourner had captured it exactly.

She lifted her face to the heavens again. A longing to hold on to the peace he'd experienced earlier gripped him, and Rav did the same. For a few moments, he soaked in the cooling rain and the trilling of the birds. Then Sojourner spoke again, so low he had to lean in to catch it.

"I'm sorry, Rav. Sorry for all that slapping away. You didn't deserve it."

Was that true? Without realizing it, he'd accepted that he did deserve it. Was that why he felt such a compulsion to help his family, to never—until he'd jumped on a plane a few days ago—abdicate his responsibilities at home or work? Had he spent his entire life trying to earn approval from everyone so they wouldn't push him away?

Rav ran his fingers through his damp hair. Was that why Tane's letter hurt so much—it felt like another slapping away of Rav's hand? How could it not? Rav didn't reach out to anyone like he did to his oldest brother. Didn't care what anyone else thought of him as much as Tane.

While Tane would never intentionally hurt Rav or push him away, him choosing his job over his family—over Rav—again and again felt exactly the same.

Hmm. Maybe, if Rav could stop reaching, Sojourner's prayer would come true, and peace might actually settle inside him the way it had with her. Although ... he snuck a peek at his partner.

Sojourner didn't always seem to be at peace. Especially around her sister.

"Maybe I'll pray for peace for you too," he murmured, as much to warn God he might be approaching him again shortly as to return the favor to Sojourner.

One eye cracked open, and she peered up at him. "Thought you'd slip that one in, did ya, honey? Bless your heart."

For the life of him, Rav couldn't tell from the tone of her voice if he'd just received the good or bad kind of southern blessing. Then she reached over and gripped his hand tightly, and a drop of moisture slid down her cheek that he was pretty sure hadn't fallen from the sky, and he knew.

Gently, he grasped her fingers, closed his eyes, and lifted his face to simply let himself *feel* the cooling rain as it washed away the last remnants of darkness.

DECEMBER TWENTY-SECOND

They'd delayed leaving that morning until the rain that had driven down all night in sheets gradually tapered off. Their driver, Oro, held out a fist to him as Rav boarded the bus. "How goes the journey, *mon ami?*"

Did Rav wear across his chest, like that faded Coca-Cola logo on his cabbie's T-shirt, the fact that this trip was some kind of quest for him? Almost everyone he had encountered seemed to be aware of it. If they all knew so much about him, could one of them just give him the answers he sought instead of standing on the sidelines watching him flounder his way along on his own?

He thought about that as he slid onto the seat next to his designated partner for the day, Xaviar. As completely alone as he had felt after getting Tane's letter and while impulsively jumping on a plane, Rav didn't feel that way now. The days he'd spent with Gregory and Sojourner had shown him that they were all here for each other. Would he experience that with Xaviar?

The kid was staring out the side window, and Rav took the opportunity to study the arm Xaviar had rested on his tattered backpack. Rav hadn't noticed it before, but the scrolling lines running from the kid's wrist and disappearing under the sleeve of his black T-shirt were actually letters entwined with roses and thorns and leaves. Another language, though. Latin, maybe?

"Can I ask you a question?"

Still staring out the window, his partner shrugged. "You can ask."

"Will you answer?"

Xaviar's lips twitched slightly. "Depends on what you ask."

"What does it say on your arm?"

Xaviar glanced at it before returning his gaze to the sky and ocean on the other side of the glass. "*Perfer Et Obdura, Dolor Hic Tibi Proderit Olim.*"

Latin with the hint of a Spanish accent, as though he'd spoken the language as a child. And he'd clearly mastered English. How many languages did this kid speak? However many it was, Rav was beginning to suspect there was a lot more to him than met the eye. "What does it mean?"

"Curiosity is a poison, not only for those who drink it but for everyone around it."

"Really?"

His seatmate shot him a look. "No."

So, also fluent in sarcasm. Okay then. Had he been this mouthy with Annie yesterday? Rav squelched the protectiveness that threatened to rise. It wasn't his job or place to protect Annie. Although he didn't know her that well yet, he suspected she was more than capable of taking care of herself and wouldn't appreciate it if he suggested otherwise. Besides, when they'd spoken outside the washrooms the day before, she'd seemed perfectly fine, so spending time with Xaviar clearly hadn't bothered her. "What does it actually say?"

"I believe that's more than one question."

"Because you've yet to give me a straight answer."

Xaviar rolled his eyes. "Fine. It means *Be strong and endure. Someday this pain will be useful to you.*"

Hmm. Why would he get something like that permanently etched on his arm? Had he experienced that much pain he needed to remind himself to be strong and endure through it? Somehow Rav doubted the kid would answer that question if asked. Not after the crack about the perils of curiosity, which had clearly been meant as a roadblock to Rav's attempt to get to know him better. Maybe after they'd spent more time together, built up a bit of trust, Xaviar would be more inclined to open up. Although that could take a whole lot longer than they had in Tahiti.

They were heading west today on the island's main road, *Avenue du Général de Gaulle*, once again following the coastline. Their first stop, twenty minutes after leaving their accommodations, was Pointe Arohoho, where they disembarked and went looking for the trou du souffleur—or blowhole—at the edge of the ocean.

Xaviar stood silently next to Rav—shocker—as waves crashed beneath the rocks, sending a spray of white water shooting several feet into the air. His partner appeared unimpressed by the sight, although he didn't object when Rav stayed there watching for several minutes. Rav even closed his eyes at one point to experience the cool drops and allow his senses to take it all in like Sojourner had encouraged him to do in the gardens.

This place—the power and beauty of the jagged rocks and cascading water and the ocean spread out endlessly beyond it—moved Rav far more deeply than the sacred site they'd visited the day before. Why was that? Because it hadn't been created by human hands? Was he ready to accept that all this beauty around them was the work of an intelligent designer? A benevolent God who saw him and cared about what Rav was going through?

Maybe.

"What do you think?" Rav kept his gaze toward the horizon, hoping that might encourage Xaviar to speak.

"It's cool."

Rav glanced sideways at his partner. Xaviar's features were tight, controlled, as though he'd mastered the art of schooling them somewhere within the short range between boredom and contempt. He wasn't as adept at controlling his voice though, and Rav caught the hint of awe even in those two words.

"Ever seen anything like it?"

Xaviar snorted. "No."

Rav shifted his gaze back to the water. "Not much of a traveler, I take it."

"This is the first time I have left Toronto."

"Why Tahiti?"

"It was the farthest I could get with the money I had."

The kid's quiet words, spoken in a curt tone that suggested he was about done talking, ignited a firestorm of questions in Rav's mind. Xaviar had spent all his money on this trip? Did he have enough to get back home? If so, how would he live when he did? What had driven him to leave? And how had he ended up here, as part of The Back Door Christmas Tour Company?

He was about to push his luck and start asking when Nino's voice, calling them all to lunch, cut him off. Xaviar spun around and started for the beach beyond the blowhole. Rav trudged after him. Maybe he'd have the chance to press Xaviar further later, find out if he was going to be okay. Rav had no idea what he would do if he wasn't, but he was gripped suddenly with the driving need to find out.

Annie was helping Nino and Maeva unpack food from two large coolers when Rav reached the beach. She looked up as he approached, and her eyebrows drew together. Could she read the angst on his face? The reassuring smile he offered her didn't wipe the quizzical expression away. Likely because he wasn't at all reassured himself. The same protectiveness that had risen when he'd thought about how Xaviar might have treated Annie rose again, towards Xaviar this time. Which was ridiculous. The kid was tough. He certainly didn't need some strange man, who wasn't much older than he was, barging into his life and attempting to fix things for him.

Besides, hadn't Rav decided he needed a break from taking care of everyone?

Be strong and endure. Someday this pain will be useful to you.

The pieces of the puzzle that was Xaviar were starting to come together. The kid had obviously endured a lot. Did he have anyone in his life he could turn to?

Lost in thought, Rav didn't see Annie approach. Only when she stopped next to him, her hands full of paper plates and plastic cutlery and leaned close to whisper, "Everything okay?" did he manage to pull himself from his spiraling thoughts.

"I'm not sure." Rav kept his voice low too. "Trying to figure Xaviar out."

"Ah. I spent yesterday doing the same thing. He's hurting, for sure, but I suspect there's a pretty decent human being hiding behind all those walls."

Exactly what Rav had been thinking. "Here." He took the plates from her, and they crossed the beach—her bare feet sinking into the sand—to set the table for everyone. The beach he and Gregory had rowed to so frantically while attempting to get away from the sharks had been shimmering white, like many of the beaches Tahiti was known for.

The grains of sand on this one glimmered black in the sunlight that had broken through the low-hanging clouds. Rav had heard of beaches with black sand—lava that had hardened and shattered when it met the cold seawater and then been crushed to tiny pieces and smoothed by centuries of pounding waves. He'd never seen one for himself, though, and he sank onto a bench and leaned down to pick up a few grains to rub between his fingers. They left a streak of black on his skin, and he wiped his fingers across the side of his jeans. It made sense there would be lava sand in Tahiti, since the entire island was comprised of two dormant volcanoes.

Annie took the seat across from him. Xaviar settled at the far end of the next table over, clearly putting distance between himself and Rav. Would Rav be able to close that distance when they traveled to Teahupo'o near the northern tip of the island after lunch? If not, it would be a long afternoon.

Oro, Nino, and Gregory had settled on rocks near the edge of the water to eat, and Septima, Sojourner, and Maeva joined Xaviar at his table. Were they intentionally giving him and Annie space? Rav's neck warmed a little, but he couldn't bring himself to mind.

"Hey." He reached across the table to touch the side of his hand lightly to Annie's. "I haven't had a chance to thank you for coming out in the kayak to rescue Gregory and me from the sharks."

Annie shook her head. "I didn't do anything."

She didn't stiffen or pull away from his touch, which likely—hopefully—meant that the dejection he'd caught in her voice the day before, the empathy when he'd mentioned the disappointing news that had driven him to jump on a flight to Tahiti, wasn't the result of abuse or mistreatment from a man. If the two of them had a chance to talk—really talk—before the tour was over, would she be willing to share her story?

Was he willing to reveal his past to her? The thought didn't tighten his muscles as painfully as it usually did, so perhaps he was.

Rav pulled his arm back. "Are you kidding? You risked your life for people you barely know."

She pursed her lips as she studied him.

"What is it?"

Annie toyed with a piece of lettuce dangling from the sandwich on her plate. "It's just ... what you're saying is true, that we all hardly know each other, but somehow it feels not true. Do you get what I mean?"

The closeness he felt wasn't only in his mind, then. "I do get it. I've never experienced anything like this attachment I feel to people I've just met."

"Me neither."

With his fingers, Rav brushed a few crumbs off the end of the picnic table. "How did you end up in this group?"

Sadness drifted into her eyes, and Rav couldn't tear his gaze away. As much as he would love to make her laugh every day, he wanted equally to be able to banish that sadness.

Not his job, he reminded himself sternly.

Annie wiped her fingers on a paper napkin. "I came to Tahiti a few days ago to get away from ... stuff at home."

At home? Marriage problems? Did she have a husband? His chest tightening, Rav glanced at her fingers. No ring.

When he looked up again, she was gazing at him, a slight smile on her face, as though she knew what he'd been wondering. The warmth in his neck intensified.

"Issues with my dad, mostly," she clarified, the smile fading. "The decision was a bit reactionary, and, like you, I didn't give it a lot of thought. Naively, I assumed I would be able to find a hotel room somewhere after I arrived, but I dragged my suitcase to ten different places, and no one had space. At the last hotel I went to, the desk clerk took pity on me, likely because I looked ready to sit down and burst into tears. She told me she might know of a place and gave me a card with a number to call. I got through to Maeva and she invited me to come right over. As you might have noticed, I was hesitant at first, overwhelmed, even. I almost left that night, but I'm glad I didn't."

Not as glad as he was. Rav leaned closer. "This desk clerk, did she get really secretive when she was handing you the card?"

Annie's eyes widened. "She did, actually. She looked all around and then bent over the counter to speak quietly to me, like she didn't want anyone to overhear. How did you know that?"

"I had the same experience. Only I was calling around to tour companies, trying to book a spot for a day tour. The woman who answered the phone at the last place I called—Golden Island Tours, which is in the front of Nino and Maeva's building—asked if I was all alone for Christmas. When I said I was, she lowered her voice as though she was telling me some big secret and instructed me to come to the building the next evening and to be sure to use the back door. Gregory said a similar thing happened to him, only it was the bartender at a bar he went to after arriving on the island who gave him a card."

"Weird." Annie had picked up her plastic spoon and was tapping it on the table next to her plate. That spark of curiosity that had driven him to follow the instructions Maeva's sister had given him, despite the possibility he could be walking into danger, flared in her eyes. "Who are all these people, do you think, and how do they know who to send to The Back Door Christmas Tour Company?"

"Other than the woman I talked to, who is Maeva's sister, apparently, I have no idea." Rav tossed his cutlery and napkin onto his empty plate. "All I know for sure is I'm glad I ended up here."

Annie's smile sent a cloud sifting through his chest as warm and soft as the sand. "So am I."

At their next stop, Xaviar either couldn't or didn't try to hide his awe at the waves of Teahupo'o, near the northern tip of the island. Some of the best, most exhilarating and dangerous surfing took place here, the shallow coral reef, the swell, and the wind combining to create the highest and heaviest waves in the world. Rav only knew that because he'd watched the recent summer Olympics in France, including the surfing events that took place here at Teahupo'o. The waves ranged from six to nine feet but could get as high as twenty-three.

One swell after another rolled toward them, breaking and crashing before they reached the shore. The sight and sound of all that teal and white water rushing in was overwhelming. In the shadow of the phenomenon, Rav felt small and insignificant. Still, the wildness and sheer power ignited that same sense Rav had experienced at the edge of the blowhole earlier, the idea that nothing he was looking at could have come into being through sheer chance.

If some source of might and creativity far greater than any of the tiny humans clustered on the shore—or the brave souls attempting to surf those massive swells—was behind the creation of the wind and water, and that source cared anything for them, that had to mean they weren't actually small and insignificant. That their lives had meaning and purpose. Didn't it?

Rav struggled to wrap his mind around the possibility, around the meaning of that rippling sensation flowing through his chest again.

Next to him, Xaviar murmured, "Puchica."

Rav glanced at him. "Puchica?"

Xaviar blinked, as though he'd forgotten Rav was there. "Yeah. It means wow. Those barrels are amazing."

Rav contemplated a tunnel created as a wave crashed in over itself. "Do you surf?"

Xaviar shrugged, which appeared to be his default response to pretty much anything Rav said. "Nothing like this, but my friends and I did try it on Lake Ontario a few times before ..."

"Before what?"

Sullenness settled over Xaviar's face. Also his default look, although it had cleared, briefly, as he'd watched the swells. For a moment he didn't answer, only gazed out at the crashing waves. Then he lifted his chin. "Before I went to prison."

"Oh." Before today, the news that Xaviar had spent time behind bars wouldn't have shocked Rav. Were both he and Annie wrong to think Xaviar was a good guy behind all his defenses? For some reason, Rav didn't believe they were. "I'm sorry, man."

Xaviar's dark eyes narrowed. "Sorry? For what?"

"That you had to go through that."

His partner stared at him. "What makes you think I didn't deserve it?"

"I'm not sure, exactly, but something does. Worst case, you were young and stupid, but I suspect there is more to it."

"Well," Xaviar ran the toe of his sneaker through the sand. "No one else has even considered that possibility, so ... thanks."

"Want to tell me about it?"

With a heavy exhalation of breath, Xaviar slid the worn pack from his shoulders, dropped it on the sand, and lowered himself to sit next to it.

Rav joined him.

The rest of the group had wandered off along the shore, leaving the two of them alone. For a moment, the crashing of waves was the only sound. Then the kid drew in a long breath. "Three years ago, I was in a car with another guy late at night. He was driving fast, and we got pulled over. The other guy panicked. While we were waiting for the cops to come to the window, he started babbling about drugs in the glove compartment and that he would be deported if the police found them. He begged me to say they were mine. He said I was only nineteen, and it was a first offense, so they'd let me off. I'd been born in Canada, and he hadn't been, so he pointed out that they wouldn't kick me out of the country. He said, if I did this for him, he'd stand by me, do everything he could to help.

The cops ordered us out of the car, and they searched it and found a bunch of stuff—TNT, Molly, Skag, Roxy. Dude was running a full pharmacy."

Xaviar bent his legs and wrapped his arms around his knees. "I said they were mine, not realizing that my phone, which I thought had been stolen a few months earlier, was in the glove compartment with the drugs. The other guy had taken it and used it to set up deals, so they didn't only have me on possession but possession with intent to traffic."

Rav's stomach twisted into knots. The old I swear the drugs aren't mine defense might have come off as a sad cliché, except that the kid's eyes didn't reflect guilt or regret. They held the deep pain of betrayal. "Did you tell the truth in court?"

Xaviar shook his head. "No. I'd given him my word. And I trusted what he told me. In the end, though, he didn't stand by me, never came to see me or say anything in my defense. And they didn't let me off easy. I did the full two years. Just got out a few months ago."

"Have you seen that guy since?"

Xaviar pulled his knees tighter to his chest. "Yeah. After I was released, I went home. He was there."

Those same bolts of shock that had slithered through Rav when Gregory told him his wife was dead shot through him again. "He was there because ..."

"He's my big brother."

"Oh man." Rav propped an elbow on his knee and rubbed his forehead hard with the tips of his fingers. "What did he say to you?"

"Nothing. Our father met me at the door. Told me to get out and not come back. That I was no longer part of the family. I looked past him at my brother, who was standing in the kitchen watching. He didn't say a word, so I turned around and left. That was six months ago, and I haven't seen any of them since."

Rav shifted around in the sand to face him. "That's messed up, Xaviar."

The kid shrugged. "They're scared. They don't want to be kicked out of Canada. I get that. And I shamed them. I get that too."

"But the drugs weren't yours."

"My parents don't know that. And they never will. Not unless my brother tells them one day."

Suddenly Rav understood what it was that had drawn him to Xaviar, what he had seen to make him think he wasn't a bad kid, only a hurting one. He'd seen himself. "Sojourner told me yesterday that there's something in my eyes. Like I want to reach out to others, but I'm afraid to in case I get my hand slapped away."

Xaviar nodded. "I can see that."

"I can see it in your eyes too. Sojourner told me she was sorry for all that slapping away, that I didn't deserve it. So, I'll say the same thing to you. You didn't deserve it, Xaviar. Any of it."

The kid started to shrug and then stopped, as if the gesture required too much effort. Or maybe he was just tired of pretending he didn't care. "Thanks."

Rav reached out and grasped Xaviar's forearm. "She told me that she would pray for me, that I would find peace. And while I'm sure her prayers carry a lot more weight than mine because I haven't prayed since I was a kid, I'm going to do the same for you."

DECEMBER TWENTY-THIRD

Rav tossed and turned all night, unable to get Xaviar's story out of his mind. He got why the kid had come to Tahiti. Like Rav, no doubt Xaviar had been hurting and alone and, not wanting to feel either during Christmas, had hopped a plane to get away from it all. The problem with the kind of hurt that shattered your heart was that those millions of tiny shards traveled with you wherever you went.

During dinner back at Maeva and Nino's, Annie had caught his eye and given him that questioning look again. Rav had only offered her a small smile and shaken his head slightly. Xaviar's story wasn't Rav's to share. Annie had nodded as though she understood, which Rav hoped she did. With every passing day, what she thought of him became more and more important.

He had hoped they might be paired together today as they headed to the Christmas market in Papeete, but when Maeva called out their names at breakfast, Rav was matched with Septima. The beaming smile she sent him across the table went a long way toward easing his disappointment.

Rav hadn't been sure if Xaviar would want to face him today. Maybe he'd regret sharing as much as he had. Instead, when Xaviar walked past him in the dining hall that morning, he'd said, "Morning, Rav," which was the first time he'd said Rav's name. Xaviar had then taken a seat at the far end of the table and chatted—chatted!—with Annie. When he got up to get more coffee, Annie had sought out Rav's eyes, such a look of wonder on her face as she lifted a hand in his direction, palm up, that Rav had laughed.

The sullenness was gone from Xaviar's face. Maybe sometimes all it took to start the healing was for one person to believe in you. To believe you. If so, Rav was more than willing to be that person for the kid.

When they trooped out the back door, Nino, dressed in navy cargo shorts and an orange shirt covered in yellow and red parrots, waited for them at the foot of the bus stairs. They gathered around him, and he held up a fistful of paper slips. "You have an assignment today as you browse and shop in the market. We're going to do a small gift exchange on Christmas Eve, so, as you board, I'll give each of you the name of another person in the group. Be on the lookout for something you think that person will appreciate. It doesn't have to be big or expensive but try to find something meaningful. Got it?"

They all nodded or murmured their assent. All but Xaviar. Rav caught the look of panic that flashed across the kid's features before he brought them under control, although no one else appeared to. Did he not like shopping? Was he worried he wouldn't be able to find the right thing?

It was the farthest I could go with the money I had. Ah. Of course Xaviar wouldn't have much money, since he'd been out of jail only a few months, his family had cut him off, and it likely wasn't the easiest thing to find work when you had a record.

Heat flowed through Rav. Xaviar's older brother, the one who should have been looking out for him, hadn't only stolen two years and likely any last vestiges of innocence from him. The ramifications of his selfishness and treachery would echo throughout Xaviar's life until the day he died. Rav didn't beat back the protectiveness this time but allowed it to zap through every cell in his body. As discreetly as he could, he tugged the wallet from his back pocket, pulled out a hundred-dollar bill, and returned the wallet to his pocket.

Xaviar stood at the back of the group, and Rav edged around everyone to come up next to him. The morning was clear but cool, and Xaviar wore a black hoodie. Rav slipped the bill into the hoodie pocket before slapping him on the back. "Enjoy the market, okay?"

Xaviar nodded. "You too." He was with Sojourner today, which eased Rav's concern. Whatever her difficulties with her sister, that woman was filled to the brim with compassion for others. And he knew from personal experience that a few words from her, a look, a brief touch, could ease a lot of pain. Even the deep-down kind that felt inextricably entwined around your heart and every other organ in your body.

Rav glanced at the sky, bright blue and cloudless for the first time that week, and decided this was as good a time as any to keep a promise. Could you make sure that happens for Xaviar today? Give him that peace Sojourner said she was praying for me to feel?

When he approached the bus doors, Nino's warm eyes met Rav's briefly as he handed him a slip of paper. "Keep using that gift, my friend," he murmured.

Gift? What gift? No time to ask, so Rav only nodded as he accepted the piece of paper and glanced at it. Sticking it in his front pocket with the crumpled letter he still stuffed there every day, he climbed the stairs. He beat Oro to holding out his fist, and the weathered face of the older Tahitian man broke out in a huge smile as he bumped Rav's knuckles. "Making your way along, aren't you, buddy?"

Rav wasn't sure how to answer that either. Before he could decide, Oro was peering past him to greet Gregory. Was the driver suggesting Rav was making his way along that journey he'd mentioned before? How could he tell?

Xaviar had headed straight to the back. Not wanting to make Septima walk that far, Rav swung onto a seat a third of the way from the front. His heart rate picked up when Annie took the seat in front of him and turned sideways to peer over the top. "What did you do to Xaviar?" she whispered. "He's like a different person today, almost ... happy."

Rav grinned. "I didn't do much. Only listened. I think you loosened him up for me the day before."

"Like the tight lid on a jar."

"Exactly."

She rewarded him with that laugh again, straightening around as Gregory lowered himself next to her. Septima made her way along the aisle, gripping the top of each seat as she passed by until she reached Rav.

Once they were settled, Oro pulled onto the street, and they began the short drive to the Christmas market. Rav had turned sideways to speak with Septima, so he caught the movement when Xaviar's head jerked up. When Rav glanced back, the kid was staring at him. Rav nodded and offered him a slight smile before shifting his attention to his partner again.

When they got off at the market, Xaviar grabbed Rav's elbow, pulled him around to the far side of a pillar, and held out the hundred-dollar bill. "I can't take your money."

"You didn't take it," Rav said calmly. "I gave it to you."

"Why?"

"You looked a little concerned when Nino mentioned buying a gift, so I thought you might need it."

"Why do you care?"

"I wanted to make sure you had enough to—"

"No." The kid shook his head. "I mean, why do you care about me?"

Rav contemplated him a moment before lifting his shoulders. "I don't have a little brother."

"Oh." The tension slowly seeped from Xaviar's body. "Well, as it happens, I have an opening for an older brother in my life."

"Then I've got your back, kid. So, stick the money in your pocket and say thank you."

"Oh, I see how it is." Xaviar grinned wryly. "A bossy older brother." He shoved the bill into his hoodie pocket. "Fine. But I'm going to repay you."

"I'd rather you didn't, but if it makes you feel better, then all right."

"It will."

"Out of curiosity, what would you do to earn money if you could choose any job?"

Xaviar didn't hesitate. "Build and fix car engines. Expensive sports cars, especially. Maybe even for racing. I have a lot of ideas ..." A hint of the sullenness Rav hadn't seen for a couple of days crossed the kid's face. "It's a stupid dream. I'll likely end up flipping burgers or something."

Before Rav could respond, Xaviar glanced past him. "Sojourner's waiting for me. I better go."

Although his heart hurt at the defeat and hopelessness in Xaviar's eyes, this wasn't the time or place to get into it, so Rav only nodded. "All right."

Xaviar brushed past him before turning back. "Rav?"

"Yeah?"

"Thank you."

"You're welcome."

Xaviar joined Sojourner, and the two of them disappeared into the crowds of shoppers.

Rav stared after him for a moment. A little brother. Someone else to take care of. Somehow the idea didn't bother him like it might have a few days ago. As much as Tane's absence hurt, Rav never doubted that his brother loved him. He never even doubted that, if he truly needed him, Tane would come, no matter what he was involved in at work. Tane had always had Rav's back. So, Rav hadn't lied to Xaviar. No matter what it took, he planned to have that kid's back too.

Rav scanned the area near the entrance to the market, searching for Septima. She stood with Annie and Gregory, watching a man and a woman at a booth filled with flowers demonstrating how to weave them together to form a lei.

Rav wandered over to stand next to his partner. The man on the other side of the counter hung a finished lei up on a nail. Then he plucked a large white flower with a yellow center from a bucket and held it out to Annie. "A beautiful flower for a beautiful woman," he announced, the words as heavily accented as the cabbie's who'd driven Rav to Maeva and Nino's place.

Annie, pink tinging her cheeks, accepted it from him. "Thank you. What kind is it?" She held it to her nose to breathe it in. Even from a few feet away, Rav caught the sweet scent that reminded him a little of his mother's jasmine soap.

"That is the Tiare flower," the man answered. "Tahiti is famous for this flower. If you wish, you can stick it in your hair." He touched his head behind his ear to indicate where.

"Choose which side carefully." The woman, flowers woven in her hair and hanging around her neck, came up beside him and smiled at Annie. "If you wear it on the right, it means you are single. The left side, near the heart, tells everyone you are taken."

Rav's eyebrows rose slightly. This could be interesting. After all, just because she'd come to Tahiti alone at Christmas and she wasn't wearing a ring didn't mean Annie was available. She might be dating someone or married but having relationship problems that had driven her to temporarily remove her ring. Although Rav had absolutely no claim on her, he didn't like the thought that she might be involved with someone else. At all.

Annie shot a sideways glance in his direction so brief Rav wasn't even sure it was for him. Either way, the flush had deepened on her cheeks when she looked at the man. "I'll just carry it like this," she mumbled, lifting the flower a little into the air. "Thank you. Merci beaucoup."

Without looking in Rav's direction again, Annie spun toward Gregory. "Shall we?"

He nodded, and the two of them strolled off. It took everything Rav had, but he managed not to watch them, only held out his arm to Septima. "Ready to go, ma'am?"

Her eyes gleamed as she slid a hand through his arm. "Fo' sho, honey."

Rav stuck close to her as she stopped at every booth, fingering colorful blouses and bags and setting a wide-brimmed hat on Rav's head before stepping back and taking a picture with the camera she carried in her purse. Rav hadn't realized anyone still used a camera. Was it even possible to get film developed these days?

He played along, posing for her wearing a couple of leis or holding up a tropical shirt whenever she lifted the camera and pointed it in his direction. Even, much to her delight, wrapping a long grass skirt around his waist at one point. When he wasn't doing that, he was keeping an eye out for a present for Annie, whose name was on the slip of paper in his front pocket.

He and Septima stopped for a few minutes to listen to a group of five men—all wearing floral shirts and leis and straw hats and sitting on overturned buckets—as they sang and played Christmas music on various stringed instruments.

When the two of them finally strolled off along an aisle between booths, the upbeat, joyful music accompanied them. Rav tapped his fingers on his thighs. "How did you and Sojourner end up on this tour?"

Septima lifted a papaya to her nose and breathed it in. "It was the funniest thing. The day after we arrived on the island, we went for a walk and stopped at a tea shop. We were both pretty tired and, admittedly, snapping at each other. The man and woman who owned the shop came over, but instead of asking us to be quiet, they joined us. They were lovely, and so interested in our lives that we ended up chatting for a couple of hours.

"When we were about to leave, the woman glanced at her husband. He nodded, and she took a card from her pocket and handed it to Sojourner. 'We believe this could be exactly what the two of you need,' she said. Then they left, disappearing into the back before we could ask any questions. Sojourner and I talked about it and decided that if people that kind and caring were vouching for this company, maybe they were right, and it was what we needed. We called Maeva, and before we knew it, we were checking out of our hotel and heading over." She handed Rav a small bag of mangoes. "Hold these, would you?"

Like the man and woman in the tea shop had done to her and her sister, she spun around and walked away from him, clearly shutting the door on the conversation. Rav sighed and traipsed after her, clutching the bag.

Tinsel and streamers had been strung up everywhere, the sight of the decorations jarring with the men and women in shorts and T-shirts, the pineapple, papaya and mangos, and the freshly caught fish.

After a couple of hours, Septima's steps slowed, and she rubbed her forehead with her fingers. Was she getting tired? "Here." Rav pressed a hand to her back and guided her to a small table in a quiet corner. "You sit here, and I'll get us lunch. Are you in the mood for something in particular?"

"Anything but that raw fish in coconut milk y'all were eating the other day will do just fine."

"Got it." Rav left her there and strode to a booth where he ordered two bottles of water and two servings of pua'a roti from a young woman with long, dark hair in a ponytail and a floral wreath on her head. Hopefully Septima would enjoy the crispy, glazed roast pork, one of Rav's favorite dishes. For dessert, he picked up fresh fruit and a small bag of firi firi, the Tahitian donuts fresh and hot from the fryer. That should give them enough of a sugar hit to keep them going until it was time to board the bus later that afternoon.

Which reminded him the clock was ticking and he really needed to find a gift for Annie. As soon as they finished eating, he'd focus on that. When he set the food in front of Septima, she leaned over it, drew in a long, deep breath, and let out a blissful sigh. "Bless you, Rav." She patted his hand as he sat down next to her. "You're an exceptionally good man. Do you know that?"

He shifted on the hard plastic seat. Would an exceptionally good man resent having to take care of his mother? Would he be selfish enough to be disappointed in his brother for failing to come home because he was out somewhere saving the world? "I assure you I'm not."

Her hand stilled on his. "Well, I assure you, far more emphatically, that you are, even if you can't see it. Everyone else can, I promise you. And I mean everyone."

She raised her eyebrows and lowered her chin, her look so pointed Rav might have laughed if so many thoughts weren't crowding into his mind. Was it possible no one else thought he was a terrible person? Did everyone in the group think he was interested in Annie? And wait, was Septima saying she thought Annie might be interested in him too? He cleared his throat. Focus. "Do you know what brought me to Tahiti?"

Interest sparked in her eyes. She set the fork down on the cardboard tray that held her pork and folded her hands on the table. Giving him her full attention. "No. But I'd love to."

"I hadn't seen my oldest brother in a few months and couldn't wait for him to come home for the holidays. Then he wrote to say he wasn't coming. I was so upset when I got his letter that without even really thinking about how it would affect them, I dumped the care of my mother on my other brother, Alain, and flew halfway around the world to get away from my life. So, I'm not a good person. I'm a bad, selfish one."

Septima reached for his hand and wrapped her fingers around it the way her sister had. "First of all, being heartbroken when someone you love hurts you doesn't make you bad. It makes you sad. And listen to yourself. Sounds like you have dedicated your life to taking care of your mother and probably others. Which doesn't surprise me, since I've watched you take care of all of us this week. That's who you are, Rav."

Huh. Was Septima right about all that? Like Sojourner, she'd seen a lot of life and those brown eyes of hers—of both of theirs—held a lot of wisdom along with that compassion and kindness. So maybe. "I never really saw myself that way."

"Well, you should. Because all of us see you that way. We think you are finer than frog hair. And I mean all of us." She offered him that pointed look again.

This time he did laugh. At the frog hair thing as much as the look. "If there's something you'd like to say, Septima, go ahead and say it."

She squeezed his fingers. "I only want to say one thing, and it's this. There's a beautiful girl here who looks at you every chance she gets when she thinks you aren't lookin' at her. A real peach who shares your big heart and your desire to help those around her. She's searching for something too—or someone, rather. Sojourner and I are praying you will both find him and offer your hearts up to him so that, when the time is right, you'll be ready and able to fully open your hearts to each other."

Rav was pretty sure Septima had just said a lot more than one thing. Either way, her words resonated with him. He was searching. And he was beginning to see that it might not be a something but a someone he was searching for. Maybe she was right about Annie too. Rav was certainly open to that idea if Annie was. Depending on which ear she'd stick that Tiare flower behind, of course. "I'll think about everything you said, Septima. I promise."

"Good. Then we quely theirs on this."

When he stared at her blankly, she smiled. "In Carolina, that means we agree, honey. And don't you feel bad about giving yourself the time and space to figure all this out. Your mom and brother will be okay, I'm sure. We all need to take a break sometimes for our mental, physical, and spiritual health."

Rav offered her a sheepish grin. "They are okay. I called Alain yesterday, and he said they were fine and to take all the time I needed to figure stuff out. Our mother is quite capable of taking care of herself. It's just that she's been through a lot, and she's lonely, so I want to be there for her."

"You see?" Septima let go of his hand and reached for her fork. "Family. You take care of each other, right? I reckon it was hard for your oldest brother not to be able to come home for Christmas."

"That's probably true." Rav hadn't taken time to see the situation from Tane's point of view. How alone did he feel right now, wherever he was, thinking of the rest of them together for Christmas? An ache spread through Rav's chest, and he rubbed his palm over it.

"I'm quite sure it's true." Septima nabbed a bite of pork with her fork. "I'm an ace bo about these things, you know."

"An ace bo?"

"An expert. Although Sojourner might say differently."

All right. She'd opened the door again. Rav was walking right on through this time. "Speaking of Sojourner ..."

Septima set her fork down again. "I handed that one to you, didn't I?"

"Yes, ma'am. And since you did, I have to ask. What happened between the two of you? You're both so amazing, I can't imagine what either of you might have done to upset the other."

She reached for a napkin and wiped a little grease from her chin before setting it on the table, her movements slow and deliberate. "All right. I'll tell you." She folded the napkin without looking at it, as though she didn't realize she was doing it. "Sojourner was our mother's favorite. Mama was always giving her the biggest piece of pie and letting her stay up late or get away with not doing her chores. Five years ago, Mama died. Our daddy was already gone, so she left everything to Sojourner—her house and all her money, which was quite a substantial sum."

"I can see how that would be hurtful for you. How did Sojourner feel about it?"

Septima blinked. Had she done the same thing Rav had—failed to consider the situation from her sibling's point of view? Rav unscrewed the red cap from his bottle of water and took a sip.

"You know, I guess I was so resentful, I never really thought to ask her."

"Was she mean to you when you were younger?" Rav couldn't imagine that about Sojourner, but then, people likely had never imagined what went on behind the closed doors of his home either. He set the bottle down with a thud.

"No, I can't honestly say she was, no more than any other girl might have been to a pesky younger sister. Which is why, to this day, we've stayed friends, even done a lot of traveling together. There has always been this shadow hanging between us, though, keeping us from getting as close as we should be. The specter of Mama and her favoritism."

Septima's eyes had taken on a distant, faraway look, as though she'd gone back in time in her mind. Rav ran his finger over the label on the water bottle—over the large red letters that spelled O'Tahiti—as he waited.

A good two minutes passed before Septima spoke. "Come to think of it, if I look back and really try to think of how Sojourner responded to the way Mama treated us growing up, I'd have to say she was ... uncomfortable." Septima pressed her fingers to her cheek. "After Mama died, Sojourner offered to split the inheritance with me, but I was too proud and stubborn to accept. And she's always tried to pay for my trips too, including this one, although that only ever made me madder." She lowered her fingers and met his gaze. "The specter between us wasn't Mama, was it? It was me. Me and my foolish pride and hurt feelings."

Seeing as how she appeared to be figuring it out on her own, Rav didn't answer.

Septima propped an elbow on the table and covered her eyes with her hand. Another minute of silence passed before she straightened. "All right, honey. I hear you."

Rav nearly smiled. "I didn't say anything."

"You said a lot by not saying anything. Come to think of it, the only other person I've ever shared this with, your Annie, said the same thing with her silence."

"She's not my Annie."

Septima waved that away. "What I'm saying is, you spill your woes out to good people and you're the one hard done by? They talk. Offer words of comfort. Tell you they're sorry for what you've gone through. You lay your grievances out before them and they say nothin'? Well, you can't argue with that kind of talk. You just gotta take it and then go make things right."

"From what I've seen of Sojourner, I'm guessing she will be very open to hearing what you have to say."

Septima reached over and patted his hand again. "I believe you and I quely theirs on that, honey."

December Twenty-Fourth

Rav had been paired with Annie for the day. Finally.

The two of them wandered side by side through the capital city of Papeete. They stopped and watched a Christmas parade pass by, the floats lively and colorful. Cheerful Christmas music blared, people playing banjos and other stringed instruments Rav didn't know the names of, including one that looked like a stick coming out of an overturned wash bucket.

Occasionally they caught a glimpse of other members of their group. Xaviar and Gregory strolled along the sidewalk, eating some kind of street food as they glanced into shop windows. Gregory said something to Xaviar, and they both laughed, which made Rav inexplicably happy. For both of them.

When they saw Septima and Sojourner, the two of them were walking arm in arm, heads bent so close together they didn't notice Rav and Annie. Clearly, Septima had wasted no time in going to talk to her sister. As Rav had suspected, Sojourner appeared to have wholeheartedly accepted her apology.

By unspoken agreement, he and Annie kept things light. They laughed a lot, Rav memorizing what had become his favorite sound in the world to replay over and over in his mind once he couldn't see her every day. That thought he worked hard to keep at bay so that, if these moments were to be his last with her, he could simply enjoy them.

Nino had told them that morning that they had been paired up today with the person whose name they had, so they could exchange gifts whenever the time felt right. So far Annie hadn't mentioned it, so Rav kept the small package he had to give her in his pocket until she brought up the idea.

He felt like a sixteen-year-old kid again, desperately wanting to reach for her hand but not at all sure how she would respond. Although he hadn't dated a lot, he'd gone out with enough women to know this was different—infinitely more precious than anything he'd experienced—and he didn't want to do anything to put it at risk.

As shadows lengthened and then dusk fell over the streets, the city came alive for the *Fête de la Lumière* or Festival of Lights. They had pre-dinner appetizers at a Polynesian bistro, sharing a large charcuterie plate with smoked duck breast bruschetta, Pork rillettes, green papayas marinated in spices, and bits of coconut and cheese as they watched the last tendrils of red and orange stretching across the sky.

Annie carried an actual camera in her bag too, one that appeared to be much fancier than Septima's little point-and-shoot. She took pictures of the food and the sunset, taking time to make adjustments for every shot.

Rav was glad, since it gave him the opportunity to study her, something he didn't think he would ever grow tired of.

After a few minutes, she returned the camera to its case—reverently, he noted—and picked up her fork. "Sorry."

"Don't be." Rav reached for a piece of coconut. "Are you a photographer?"

Her cheeks flushed, which he loved almost as much as her laugh. "I don't know if I can call myself that yet."

"But you'd like to be."

"More than anything. I've won a couple of awards and had my photos published in a few magazines and online."

"What's your big dream?"

She hesitated. "A gallery showing."

When he raised his eyebrows, she bit her lip. The glow in her emerald eyes drew him so strongly he had to clutch his fork and knife to keep from reaching for her. "All right. Big, big dream?" Annie paused before saying, "My own gallery." She pressed both hands to her cheeks. "I've only ever said that out loud once before."

Rav set down the knife and fork. "Then thank you for sharing it with me." He reached over and touched his fingers to her lightly freckled arm before pulling back. "That means a lot."

She lowered her hands to the table. "Thanks for not laughing."

"Laughing? Why would I laugh at such a beautiful dream?"

"It's just that, the other time I mentioned? It was to my dad. And that was his response."

His chest tightened at the hurt in her voice. "Do you want to talk about that?"

Annie shook her head, her strawberry-blonde curls brushing her back. "Not now. I just want to enjoy this amazing food and sunset. And the company." That last bit she said so quietly that he almost missed it.

"Me too. All of the above." Rav speared a piece of duck with his fork. "I'd love to see some of your photographs."

"If you give me your email address, I'll send you a few links."

He would far rather look at them *with* her, but the promise was something, at least. A way for them to keep in touch. Rav set down his cutlery and tugged the wallet from his back pocket. "Here." He handed her one of his cards and returned the wallet to his pocket.

"Rav Temauri, MBA, CA." She ran a finger over the words as she read. After a moment, she looked up. "You're a numbers guy."

"Yeah, specializing in small business start-ups, so when you're ready to look into that gallery, let me know. I might be able to help." He tried to sound casual, but he suspected he wasn't doing a great job of hiding the depth of emotion flowing through him as he *casually* discussed ways their paths might cross in the future.

Given the intensity in her eyes when they met his, he was right. "I will. Thanks."

They lingered there until well after darkness had fallen over the city and then walked around a little longer beneath the sparkling lights strung up everywhere. They were to meet the rest of the group on the beach for a popular Tahitian event—the Christmas Eve midnight picnic. Although Rav was looking forward to it, he wasn't quite willing to share Annie with everyone else yet. She didn't say anything about heading to the water either. Was it possible she felt the same way?

Midnight wasn't far off by the time they did meander down to the ocean. The beach was surrounded by coconut palms decorated with lights and ornaments made from shells. Different than the evergreen Christmas trees Rav was used to, but equally beautiful. In the distance, he could make out a long row of overwater bungalows glowing like jewels hovering above the ocean. Rav had never been in one—a bit out of his price range—but he guessed they would be amazing, especially here in Tahiti where they had been invented.

The smell of roasting pork from the suckling pigs slowly cooking over open fires hung thick in the air, and Rav drew in a deep breath. They joined the rest of the tour group and ate at two picnic tables, laughing and talking as though they had known each other for years. It had been the same every evening when they gathered for board games or charades in the large common room where they had first met and where they ate all their meals—as though an invisible thread wove around and among them, drawing them closer with every interaction.

When they finished their picnic, Septima and Sojourner announced they were heading back to their rooms, and Nino and Maeva offered to accompany them.

Gregory, Xaviar, and Annie were deep into a conversation. Restless, Rav wandered down to the shore. He pulled off his shoes and socks and stopped at the edge of the water, the waves rolling gently onto the sand and lapping at his toes. He still had Annie's gift in the pocket of his jeans. And tomorrow was the last official day of the tour. What would happen with the two of them after that? Sure, maybe they'd exchange emails occasionally, but would he ever see her again?

Rav stooped to grab a pebble and toss it out into the surf. It skipped a couple of times before disappearing beneath the surface. Would he ever see any of them again? His chest ached at the thought that he might not. Rav hadn't lied to Xaviar when he told him that already he thought of him as a little brother. The crazy, unfathomable truth of it was that they had all become like a big family—Maeva and Nino the mom and dad, Gregory a fun uncle, Septima and Sojourner wise old great-aunts, and Rav, Annie, and Xaviar the siblings. Except that Rav most definitely did not think of Annie as a sister.

So where did that leave them?

It left *him* feeling torn. As much as he had loved spending the holidays with these people, it felt strange, not being with his real family on Christmas Eve. Was Tane with Beck and Johnny or all alone? What would Alain and his mother be doing right now? Rav might have felt the need to get away, but suddenly he couldn't wait to get back to them. Making sure his mother was okay, spending time with her, wasn't a chore or a burden; it was a privilege. So maybe Septima had been right, and taking care of others was who he was. His gift, even. His eyes widened. Was that what Nino meant when he told Rav to keep using his gift?

A rock skipped across the water three, four times. Rav glanced to his right. Annie stood a few feet away, way too cute in denim shorts and a bright yellow T-shirt, water splashing over her bare feet.

Rav swallowed as he waded through the surf and stopped in front of her. "Impressive."

"Thanks." She offered him an impish grin and tilted her head. She'd tucked a white Tiare flower into her hair. Behind her right ear.

Rav's heart rate ratcheted up even more than it usually did when she was in the vicinity. In the glow of a nearly full moon, her green eyes grew as intense as they had been at dinner as she gazed at him. For a moment, neither moved. Then she lifted a thumb to point over her shoulder. "Want to sit?"

Rav turned to look. She'd spread a small blanket over the sand at the base of a coconut palm. A nearby tiki torch cast an orange glow over the strands of lights and white shells looped around the branches, falling over the blanket in a circle of flickering light and warmth. "Sure."

He followed her and, once she'd sat on the blanket, lowered himself next to her. The remaining *family members* in the group were likely watching, but Rav couldn't bring himself to care. Although he should likely think about setting a good example for his little brother.

"What's that smile about?" Annie was watching him, her red hair gleaming in the torchlight.

"I was thinking about how this group feels like a big family."

"Yeah. It's been nice, being part of something like that this week."

At the wistfulness in her voice, Rav leaned back on his elbows. "Given what you said at the restaurant, I take it you're not close to your family?"

She sighed. "I was. To my mom. But she died a year and a half ago."

He winced. "I'm sorry, Annie."

"Thanks." She tucked a red curl behind her left ear. "She was my best friend, and I'm an only child, so it hit me hard." She leaned against the trunk of the tree and gazed out over the water, moonlight glittering on the rolling waves. "For months, I was pretty much lost in this black hole. I kept reaching out to my dad, hoping the two of us could help each other through it, but he just wasn't there for me. I realized why when, eight months after my mom's passing, he told me he was getting married again, to a woman from his work."

Rav frowned. "That had to hurt, him moving on so fast."

"It did. Especially since I overheard some of their co-workers at the wedding talking about how the two of them had been having an affair for at least two years." She picked up a pile of sand and then tipped her hand, letting it slide slowly over her bare knees. "Suddenly, the big fight my mom and dad had the night she died made sense. They didn't argue a lot, so when I heard them yelling, I went and stood near my bedroom door, curious about what was happening. They were in the living room, and I couldn't make out what they were saying until my mother came into the front hallway. She yelled something about him knowing where he could go if he wanted sympathy because he wasn't getting it from her. Then she stormed out of the house, got in her car, and drove off."

Rav couldn't stand the pain in her voice, the way the hand she'd rested on the blanket inches from his trembled. Not without doing something to try and comfort her. He sat up and reached over to wrap his fingers around hers. "What happened?"

Annie didn't pull away, only drew in a shuddering breath. "The police showed up at our door an hour later. She'd lost control of the vehicle and slammed into a tree."

When her voice broke, he slid his other arm around her. Annie rested her head on his shoulder, their fingers still entwined. "My father's affair with that woman literally killed my mother. So yeah, it hurt when he turned around and married her. And it hurt when she told my dad she didn't want me spending Christmas with them because I looked too much like my mom and she couldn't stand to be around me. It even hurt when he said he'd pay for me to go away somewhere for the holidays. Although I'm thankful now that I took him up on the offer."

Rav rested his cheek against her soft curls. Everyone had a story of pain and betrayal, didn't they? As much as he would love to take away her sorrow, shield her from ever being hurt again, he couldn't. Nothing and no one could help with hurt that went that soul deep. Except maybe ...

He shot a look at the sky, stars twinkling against a backdrop of navy as far out over the ocean as he could see. *Could you help Annie?*

And Rav and Gregory and Xaviar and me and Maman and Tane and Alain? Ease our pain a little?

For the first time that he could recall, Rav's desperate pleas to God weren't met with nothing. Instead, that rippling sensation—as warm and comforting as the flames Nino stoked up in the fireplace every night—flowed through him again. The tightness in his muscles eased a little, and he nodded at the sky.

Then he whispered into Annie's hair, "I shouldn't say this, but I don't like that woman one bit. And I'm not your dad's number one fan either. Although I'm also extremely glad you took him up on his offer."

Remarkably, Annie laughed. Then she swiped away with her palm a tear that had started down one cheek. "I didn't mean to get into any of that tonight. There's something about you, Rav. You make it easy for people to bare their souls to you. I'll bet you've heard a lot of hard stories this week."

"I guess I have."

She rested her free hand on his chest. "Knowing you, all of them have hurt your heart, haven't they?"

He couldn't argue with that. "I suppose." Could she feel that heart thudding wildly beneath her fingers?

She tipped her head to look up at him. "Do you want to tell me your story?"

"Yes." He ran his thumb over the back of her hand. "I want to tell you all my stories. And I want to hear all of yours. Someday soon."

"But we only have tomorrow."

"That's true." He lifted her fingers to his mouth and kissed them. "If that's all you want."

She straightened and shifted to face him. "It's not."

"No?"

"Definitely not. I mean, I even did the whole flower-on-the-right-side thing." She flapped her hand toward the Tiare blossom that had slipped loose to dangle over her ear. "Which, by the way, is your present. So, Merry Christmas."

Rav laughed and let go of her so he could tug the blossom free. "I did notice that." He switched the flower to his other hand so he could gently tuck it behind her left ear. "Although I think I'd prefer you wear it on this side."

She smiled. "I think I would prefer that too. Besides, it's only a ten-hour drive between Pemberton and Calgary. Not that I looked into it or anything."

He grinned. "Of course not. And I definitely didn't look into it either, but it's more like nine hours and forty-six minutes. Less if someone was in a hurry to get there, which I would be."

"I would be too."

Rav dug into the front pocket of his jeans and tugged out a small package. "Merry Christmas, Annie."

Her eyes lit up and she clapped her hands a couple of times before reaching for it. Rav made a mental note to give her presents often in the future, warmth spreading through him at the thought that he might have the opportunity.

Annie pulled something wrapped in white tissue paper from the bag. Seconds later, she had freed the bracelet he'd found at the market—six small pearls on a tan leather strap.

Rav touched the line of pearls Tahiti was famous for. "One Tahitian black pearl for each of us. To remember this week and this group of people."

Her eyes shone in the moonlight when they met his. "I love it." She held out the bracelet and her left wrist. "Would you put it on?"

"Sure." Rav fastened it, his fingers brushing across her skin. "There's something else in there too."

She reached into the bag and tugged out a folded paper napkin. "What ...?"

He nodded at it. "Read it."

Annie unfolded the napkin and scanned it. After a moment, she looked up, her green eyes wide. "Is this a business plan?"

"Extremely rough, since I scribbled it out on the counter of the men's room, but yes." He brushed a bit of sand off her knees before cupping his hands over them. "It's doable, Annie. It'll take time and a lot of work, but it's doable."

She folded the napkin and pressed it to her chest. "Until this moment, I didn't believe that." Swiping the fingers of her free hand beneath her eye, she set the napkin on top of the paper bag and clambered to her feet. "Hold on."

Rav watched as she walked around to the other side of the tree, reached down, and then emerged carrying a rectangular package wrapped in brown paper.

She settled in front of him, cross-legged, and held it out. "I do have an actual gift for you."

"I was pretty happy with your other one."

Annie grinned and tapped the present. "Still. I wanted you to have this too."

Rav unwrapped the cardboard box and removed the lid. His throat tightened as he lifted out the picture frame to study the photographs she'd slid into the openings—one of him with each member of the group. Candid shots of Septima using that camera of hers to take a picture of him wearing a grass skirt. Gregory and him leaning on the railing of the ferry staring out over the ocean as they headed to Moorea. He and Sojourner standing side by side at the bridge overlooking the waterfall, their eyes closed and their faces tipped to the rain, and one of him and Xaviar gazing at the massive swells of Teahupo'o, a look of wonder on both their faces.

"Umm, I think we're going to need to get that gallery going sooner than later," Rav breathed, running a finger over each picture before looking up at her.

Annie's smile was tentative. "Really?"

"Yes. Absolutely. These are incredible." Rav glanced down at them again. A gift of memories he would cherish forever. His finger stilled on the last box, which remained empty. "There's no picture of you and me." When he lifted his head, she was holding her phone in one hand, her cheeks flushed in the light of the torch.

"I thought we could try to capture our first kiss."

"Oh." If he'd thought his heart had been thudding wildly before, she had to be able to hear it now. "I'm definitely game to try."

"Me too. Except ..."

"Except what?"

"I have a confession to make first."

"Okay." Rav drew out the word. Was she uncertain about them? If so, it might be better to hold off on the kissing, as much as it would pain him to tell her so.

"Do you remember the day on the ferry when we ran into each other outside the washrooms?"

"Vividly." Like every other moment they had spent in each other's presence.

"You know how I pretended not to remember your name?"

Pretended? "Um, yes. It hurt because I'd been so drawn to you from the moment I first saw you. Your name had been running through my head constantly, so when you forgot mine, I figured you didn't feel the same way."

"I'm sorry. It was stupid. I did feel the same way. In fact, when I told you I was overwhelmed and almost went home, that had a lot to do with how strongly I reacted to meeting you. After what my dad did to my mom, I was scared to get involved with anyone, and I knew right away you were someone I could become very involved with. So, when I saw you the next day, I pretended I hadn't been that affected by you, trying to put a bit of distance between us, I think."

"What changed your mind?"

"You. Even that brief conversation on the ferry made me feel as though I would be safe with you. That you weren't the type of man to hurt a woman the way my dad did."

"I'd rather cut off my own arm and toss it to those sharks than hurt you. Ever."

"I could sense that, which meant I was a goner from that moment on."

"Me too."

When she smiled, Rav shifted closer and took her face in his hands, reveling in the feel of her warm skin beneath his fingers. "So you know, if the first shot doesn't work out, I'm willing to keep at it as long as it takes to get a keeper."

Annie laughed. "That's very good of you."

He lifted his shoulders. "I'm a giver."

Her eyes grew intense again. "I know you are."

Leaning in, Rav pressed his mouth gently to hers. When he closed his eyes, letting himself *feel*, as Sojourner had encouraged him to do, the entire world narrowed down to Annie's soft lips beneath his, the waves crashing onto the shore, the aromas of coconut and Tiare flower drifting on the air.

Rav was able to form only one coherent thought before fully giving in to the sensations. Hopefully Annie would be able to capture this moment. Because it was perfect.

There was no chance he was falling asleep. As his time with The Back Door Christmas Tour Company rapidly drew to a close,

Rav's thoughts were consumed with moments from the past week. His life-altering time on the beach with Annie was foremost on his mind. Other memories crowded in, though, of the day he'd spent with each member of the group. Even now he struggled to comprehend that what had happened was real and not an elaborate dream he would wake up from at some point.

Maybe reading would help settle his raging thoughts. Rav tossed back the covers and made his way down to the common room, where shelves of books lined one wall. When he walked in, Nino was alone, sitting on a chair in front of the fire, his fingers resting on a hardcover book he'd set on the arm. He looked over and smiled warmly. "Rav. Join me." He pointed to the chair facing him.

When Rav was settled, Nino nudged his foot with his slipper. "Couldn't sleep?"

"No. Too much on my mind."

"Care to share?"

Rav blew out a breath. "It's been quite a week. I'm trying to wrap my mind around everything that's happened."

Nino contemplated him a moment before propping his elbows on the arm of the chair and clasping his hands in front of him. "Why did you come to Tahiti?"

The question caught Rav off guard, and he blinked. "I was looking for something, I think."

"Do you know what?"

"I'm not sure. I was feeling very alone and ... empty. I hoped that I might experience a connection to something here, in my homeland."

"And?"

Rav curled his fingers around the ends of the chair. How could he answer that? "I mean, in some ways the trip has wildly exceeded my expectations. I *have* felt part of something here, with you and the others in the group. I've connected with everyone, and they all feel like family now."

"Or maybe something more?" Nino's brown eyes twinkled.

Rav's neck warmed. "Yeah, I guess I've found that too, with Annie. We're going to keep seeing each other, find out where that might lead."

"I'm confident it will lead somewhere very special. Maeva and I wish you both every happiness."

"Thank you."

Nino tapped the tips of his fingers together. "It's gone then, that emptiness you felt inside?"

Rav mulled that over. Was it? As happy as he had been this week, as deeply as he had bonded with everyone, especially Annie and Xaviar, he had to admit that, no, the emptiness was not gone. He frowned. Why wasn't it gone? "It's not, actually. Not fully. Something's still missing, only I'm not sure what."

"If we find ourselves with a desire that nothing in the world can satisfy, the most probable explanation is that we were made for another world."

Something about those words resonated way down in Rav's chest, as though something long buried was being unearthed. "Another world?"

"Yes. The writer C.S. Lewis once said that. The point being that we are all living in a broken, fallen world filled with pain and disconnection and darkness. But somewhere inside us we long for more. We inherently know that we were created for something more than this. *Someone* more than only ourselves."

"God."

"Exactly. From the moment we are born, we all have that emptiness within us, and, as Blaise Pascal suggested, that 'infinite abyss can be filled only with an infinite and immutable object.' The Bible puts it this way, that God has set eternity in every human heart."

"You're saying that this emptiness I feel, this hole, can only be filled by God."

"It doesn't matter what I say. What does the whisper tell you?"

His forehead wrinkled. "The whisper?"

"Yes. There's a story in the Bible about this man, Elijah, who expected to find God in a mighty wind or an earthquake or a fire. But after all those things had passed by him, God came to him as a whisper."

Ah. Before he had come to Tahiti, Rav might not have been able to grasp that. After everything he had experienced this week, though, he understood what Nino was saying. Yes, he had sensed the power and creativity of God in all he had seen and felt. But God had spoken to him in a whisper that had rippled through him over and over, like soft waves unfurling onto the sand. "I get what you're saying. I did sense that this week."

"Well, listen to that, Rav. You and Annie and Xaviar. Pray. Read the Bible. And listen. That whisper will guide you all home."

"I will." He tightened his grip on the ends of the chair. "Can I ask you something?"

"Anything."

"How did we end up here?"

"This particular group, you mean?"

"Yes. Somehow it doesn't feel random."

"It's not." Nino lowered his hands to the chair and crossed one slippered foot over the other. "The Back Door Christmas Tour Company only offers one tour a year, this one. The other fifty-one weeks, a team of us are on our knees, praying that God will bring the people he wants here. Besides Maeva and me, there are six people on the team, and each of them prays specifically that the right person will come to them at the right time. For nine years now, that has happened for each of them, and the six people who were meant to be on the tour showed up at the door.

"This year, Vaheana was beginning to wonder if she might have missed her person, since the tour was about to begin. Then you called her, and she knew."

So, you're the one. Vaheana's statement made sense now. As did Maeva and Nino and even Oro's cryptic comments. If what Nino was saying was true, not one of the people in this group had ended up here by chance, as Rav and Gregory had suspected. God himself had brought them here. Rav was going to have to spend some time pondering that truth and what it might mean for him and for Annie and Xaviar and the rest of them.

The clock above the mantel chimed two times. Rav glanced at Nino's book. "Were you having trouble sleeping too?"

"No. I just didn't want to go up until I knew Xaviar was all right."

Rav raised his eyebrows. "Xaviar?"

"Yes. Like you, he is working through many things. He's outside, so I am waiting for him to come in."

"Do you think it would be okay if I went out and talked to him?"

Nino nodded. "I believe that you, more than anyone, have earned that right."

Rav stood. As he passed Nino's chair, he stopped and clasped the older man's shoulder. "Thank you, Nino. For everything."

"It has been our joy, son."

Son. Rav couldn't remember anyone ever calling him that. Although it wasn't what he was ultimately seeking, hearing it from Nino did fill a little of that gaping chasm in his chest. His throat too tight to speak, Rav only nodded and headed for the exit. A white trash can next to the door snagged his attention. He hesitated a moment, then reached into the front pocket of his jeans, tugged out the tattered letter from Tane, then crumpled it into a ball and dropped it into the can.

When he stepped outside, he could make out Xaviar standing at the back of the lot in the glow of the strings of light in the trees around him. His back was to Rav as he gripped the railing in both hands and stared out at the water.

Although Rav didn't make any effort to mask his footsteps as he approached, Xaviar didn't move as Rav came up to stand next to him at the railing. "You doing okay, kid?"

For a moment, Xaviar didn't answer. Then he expelled a breath. "I got thinking about how, after tomorrow, I'll be flying home, only I have no home to go to. No job. Nothing. A week ago, I might have been all right with that. But now, stupidly, I went and got attached to all of you." He let out a humorless laugh. "Maybe I'll stay here. I've been very popular this week, you know. Apparently, the Polynesians invented tattoos, and they're extremely meaningful to them. A lot of people have approached me to examine mine more closely and tell me how much they love them."

"Interesting. Still, I'm not sure that's reason enough to stay."

"Maybe not." Xaviar turned and slumped against the railing. "I know we've been playing at this family thing …"

Rav's hand flew up. "Whoa, whoa, whoa. I haven't been playing. I wouldn't do that to you. I do think of you as a little brother."

"Really?" Xaviar's tone was sarcastic, but the attempt was undermined by the flicker of hope in his eyes.

"Yes, really."

"But you hardly know me."

Rav contemplated him a moment. "You know, I mentioned something to Annie this week about how everyone here barely knows each other. She said that, although that was technically true, it didn't feel true. And I know what she means."

Xaviar nodded. "I guess I do too."

Rav ran a hand over his head. "Look. I have no idea what you think of God. I didn't know what I thought of him either when I arrived here. But so much has happened this week, so many experiences and so much beauty. And, as much as or more than anything else, the inexplicably powerful connections that have formed between us all. I can't come up with any explanation other than that a divine being who actually cares about each of us and what happens to us has brought us together."

Xaviar clasped his hands behind his neck. "Before I went to prison, I would have laughed at that idea. But some people came in every week and sang for us and said stuff like what you just said. They were really nice, too, treated us with respect, unlike the other prisoners and most of the guards. So, I started to think there might be something to it. After everything that's happened this week, I think I do believe that what you said is true. It's something I want to find out more about anyway."

Rav nodded. "Me too. Maybe we could do that together."

Xaviar's eyes narrowed. "How? We'll be thousands of kilometers apart."

"We don't have to be."

"What do you mean?"

Rav shifted his weight from one foot to the other, not sure how Xaviar would react to what he was about to say. "I don't know if you have anything still tying you to Toronto ..."

Xaviar shook his head. "I don't."

"Then what would you think about coming to British Columbia with me?"

The kid gaped at him for a few seconds before saying, "I mean, I have always wanted to go to BC. My ticket is for Toronto, though."

Rav waved a hand through the air. "We can work that out with the airline. Don't worry."

"What would I do? Where would I live?"

"For now, until you get on your feet, you could stay at my mother's place. She's alone in the house now and there are three extra bedrooms. My apartment's only a few minutes away."

"I can't impose on your mother like that. And what about your dad?"

Rav grimaced. "Actually, he's in prison and hopefully will be for the next few years at least, since he actually does deserve to be there."

"Oh." A shadow fell across Xaviar's features. "I'm sorry."

He understood then why Xaviar had reacted strongly when Rav had said those words to him. When they were real and genuine and carried on a river of sorrow, they were incredibly powerful. He swallowed. "Thanks. As for my mom, I ran the idea by her. She was delighted at the thought of having company."

"Even so, I don't know if I can. I wouldn't do it if I couldn't pay my own way, and believe it or not, very few people want to hire a drug dealer recently released from prison."

"My friend Brandon does."

"Brandon?"

"Yeah. He owns a garage in town. When I called him last night, he said he'd be happy to take you on. He's been thinking about getting into high-end sports cars, so he was thrilled to hear that's what you want to do."

"Really?" The sarcasm was gone from Xaviar's voice. "You just happen to know someone looking for an apprentice mechanic?"

Rav let out a short laugh. "It's a small town, and I've lived there my whole life. You could have named pretty much any occupation, and I likely would have been able to scrounge up someone willing to at least talk to you."

The kid still looked skeptical. "Did you tell Brandon …?"

"Everything? Yes. All he wanted to know by the time I finished was how soon you could start."

Xaviar unclasped his hands. "I almost didn't tell you the truth. I didn't think you would believe me."

"Well, I do."

The kid held out his right arm. Rav studied it in the light of the twinkling bulbs. More Latin twining through roses and vines. Xaviar ran his left index finger over the words. "Do you know what this one says?"

"No. What?"

"*Veritas vos liberabit.* The truth will set you free."

Rav clapped a hand on Xaviar's shoulder, which trembled slightly beneath his fingers. "And now it has."

Xaviar's dark eyes, glistening in the soft light, met his. "Are you sure, Rav?"

He tightened his grip. "I've never been more sure about anything—about anyone—in my life."

The kid drew in a slightly shuddering breath. "All right then. If you and your mom will have me, then I'll go with you." He tilted his head. "You know, I still haven't heard your story."

Rav let go of Xaviar and slid an arm around his shoulders to guide him toward the door. "Tell you what. I'll share it with you on the plane, when the two of us are on our way home."

December Twenty-Fifth

They went for one last walk as a group around the city, taking in the decorated palms and homes and wandering along the beach, waves crashing onto the shore, before returning to Maeva and Nino's. When they came into the office through the back door, several people were already there, clutching glasses of punch and chatting with each other.

Rav recognized only two of them, Oro the bus driver and, crazily enough, the cabbie who had brought Rav here. A broad smile crossed the man's face as he held out a hand. Rav's forehead wrinkled as he shook the hand of the cabbie, who wore a navy shirt with a Nike logo today and the same red beret he'd worn the day he drove Rav here. What was happening now?

A man and a woman a few years younger than Septima and Sojourner had been standing next to the punch bowl when they came into the office. The woman set her glass of punch down and flew at the sisters, wrapping her arms around both of them. The man approached more slowly, but with a huge smile on his face. The couple from the tea shop who had sent them here?

Annie's drawn-in breath when a woman in a floral blouse and black skirt came toward her suggested this must be the hotel desk clerk.

Xaviar lifted a hand in the direction of a middle-aged man in dress pants and shirt, whose eyes lit up as he strode over and slapped Xaviar's upper arm a few times. Rav hadn't heard that story yet. He suspected the kid hadn't made any plans beyond getting to the island. Likely he'd thought he could sleep outside, since it would be warm. Whether he'd have been able to eat was another matter. In any case, Rav was deeply grateful this man had found him and told him about the tour.

Maeva guided a woman who looked a lot like her—same brown eyes filled with light and warmth—over to him. "Rav, this is my sister, Vaheana."

Vaheana held out both hands. Rav didn't hesitate this time, only slid his hands into hers. "Vaheana. *Mauruuru*. Thank you." There was so much more he wanted to say to her. How grateful he was that she had been praying for him all year. That she had listened to that whisper when he called her and had sent him here to be part of the exact tour he'd needed without even realizing it. That she had promised to keep praying for him after he left. His throat had tightened, though, and the words wouldn't come, so he squeezed her fingers, hoping she would feel them. She seemed to, as the light flared brighter in her eyes as she smiled.

Nino gave them all a moment before clapping his hands. "All right, everyone. You'll have more time over dinner to talk to the members of our team—each of whom has been praying specifically for you over the past year and will continue to do so after you leave tomorrow."

Annie slipped her hand into his, and Rav smiled at her and squeezed her fingers. When he looked up, his eyes met Septima's. From across the room, she tilted her head and lowered her chin in the direction of his and Annie's clasped hands, her eyes gleaming and that pointed look on her face again. Rav returned the look, shooting a meaningful glance at the arm she had twined through Sojourner's. Such a beautiful smile creased her features that he couldn't have stopped the one that crossed his face if he'd tried.

Nino wrapped an arm around his wife and pulled her to his side. "All Maeva and I would like to say to you before we head into the dining room is that you are family now."

Maeva nodded. "Yes. If any of you ever finds yourself alone at Christmas, or you're simply missing this place and want to be here, you will always be welcome."

"That's right." Nino half turned toward the room where they had congregated that first night and held out his arm. "Come and meet the people from previous tours who have joined us this year—the rest of the family."

As the others passed through the doorway, Rav scanned the office—the gleaming wooden walls, the pictures hanging on hooks, the rug that looked like the ocean—and almost laughed. Had it seriously only been a week since he'd walked into this room with no idea where he was or what would happen to him?

His chest tightened as he followed Annie through the door. All the tables had been pushed together to form one long one that stretched maybe twenty feet across the width of the room. Other than a few empty seats for them, the chairs were filled with people all laughing and smiling and waving them over. Like family.

When Septima, Sojourner, and Xaviar reached them, several people stood and hugged them and pulled out chairs for them. Annie wandered over, too, but Rav paused a moment to take it all in. The flame that had flickered inside the night before flared again.

Could he put a name to it? He'd experienced tastes of it this week. It hadn't been at the Arahurahu Morae, but he'd felt it when he had seen the water shooting into the air through the blowhole at Pointe Arohoho and while viewing the beauty of the gardens at Vaipahi and the pounding swells at Teahupo'o. He'd sensed it when he and Gregory had reached the shore after escaping the sharks and been surrounded by the rest of the group and when Septima and Sojourner had grasped his fingers and looked at him with compassion and kindness. When hope had filled Xaviar's voice and when Rav had held Annie's face in his hands and seen their future in her emerald eyes. What was it?

It's been our joy.

Nino's words from the night before came to him. Was that what Rav had glimpsed this week while taking in the breathtaking views and spending time with the people around him? Joy? If so, he wanted more of it. More than hints and tastes and glimpses. He wanted to drink from the source of it as though standing at the foot of one of the many waterfalls in this country and opening his mouth to catch every drop of the water cascading over the rocks.

If everything Nino and Maeva had said was true about how each of them had ended up here, that source had to be God. Nothing and no one else could fill that emptiness inside him.

From her spot at the table, Annie's eyes, glowing with wonder and happiness, locked on his, and she patted the empty chair next to her. Rav smiled and took a step forward. A hand clasped his shoulder and he stopped.

Gregory leaned close and said, "Didn't I tell you, mate? I knew that she'd be right."

Rav grinned. "You did. And you were not wrong."

So no, Rav Temauri did not make impulsive decisions. Until the Christmas when he was twenty-six years old and made a wild, crazy, completely unplanned one. That decision changed his life forever. And not for a moment in the years that followed had he ever regretted it.

A NOTE FROM SARA

Dear Reader,

Home is a word fraught with emotion—happiness, grief, trauma, comfort, or fear. Our earthly homes exist in a broken, fallen world, making them the source, in varying degrees, of all those emotions and more. Only our eternal home promises true joy and love and peace forever. In that place we will enjoy perfect relationships with others and beauty beyond anything we can imagine here on this planet.

Through the grace and mercy of God, we can experience hints of those relationships, tastes of that home, and glimpses of the incomprehensible beauty that will surround us—all reminders that we were created for something more than this. That we were made for another world.

Dear ones, my hope and prayer for each of you is that you will experience those tastes and glimpses this holiday season—in deep friendships and relationships, in homes that are places of refuge from the world, and in breathtaking scenery that feeds the soul.

And every time you do, may you hear God whisper that one day all will be put right and there will be no more grief, trauma, or fear.

We will be his people and he will be our God, and his dwelling place will be among us forever.

May you be filled with joy this Christmas season as you celebrate the birth of the one who came to earth as a baby and who has promised to one day return and take all who believe in him home forever.

Sara

About Sara Davison

Sara Davison has a passion for writing stories that keep readers on the edge of their seats (and maybe swooning a little). Beyond that, she longs for readers to discover, as her characters always do, that whatever they are going through, they are never alone. God is always with them. A finalist for more than a dozen national writing awards, Davison is a Holt Medallion, Cascade, and two-time Carol Award winner for romantic suspense. She lives in Ontario with her husband, Michael, two 14-year-old cockapoo "puppies", and a cat. Like every good Canadian, she loves coffee, hockey, poutine, and apologizing for no particular reason.

Get to know her better (and sign up for her short, monthly newsletter) at www.saradavison.org

Titles By Sara Davison

THE MOSAIC COLLECTION: NOVELS
The Rose Tattoo Trilogy
Lost Down Deep
Written in Ink
Sharp Like Glass (2025)
two sparrows for a penny series
Every Star in the Sky
Every Flower of the Field
Every Bird That Falls
In the Shadows Series
The Color of Sky and Stone

THE MOSAIC COLLECTIONS: ANTHOLOGY STORIES
"Taste of Heaven" in *Hope is Born*
"Ten Bottles of Sand" in *Before Summer's End*
"Sixty Feet to Home" in *A Star Will Rise*
"I'd Like to Thank the Academy" in *Song of Grace*
"Star Light" in *The Heart of Christmas*
"Scarlet" in *All Things New*
"A Single Spark of Light" in *A Whisper of Peace*
"The Poppy" in *Dancing in the Rain*

"The Other Way" in *A Thrill in the Air*
"Five Things You Know About Me" in *Sounds Like a Plan*

The Night Guardians series
Vigilant

Guarded

Driven

Forged

Standalone
The Watcher

THANK YOU FOR READING

We hope you enjoyed *A Weary World Rejoices*, Mosaic's 2024 Christmas anthology. If you did, please consider leaving a short review on Amazon, Goodreads, or BookBub. Positive reviews and word-of-mouth recommendations are so valuable and appreciated, as they honor an author and help other readers to find quality Christian fiction to read.

Thank you so much!

www.ingramcontent.com/pod-product-compliance
Lightning Source LLC
Chambersburg PA
CBHW030646260626
47157CB00007B/2512